IDEAL

FICTION

Atlas Shrugged
The Fountainhead
Anthem
We the Living
The Early Ayn Rand
Night of January 16th
Three Plays

PHILOSOPHY

GENERAL

Objectivism: The Philosophy of Ayn Rand
by Dr. Leonard Peikoff

The Ayn Rand Lexicon
The Ayn Rand Reader
Philosophy: Who Needs It
The Voice of Reason
For the New Intellectual
The Cause of Hitler's Germany
by Dr. Leonard Peikoff
The Virtue of Selfishness
Ayn Rand Answers: The Best of Her Q & A

EPISTEMOLOGY

Introduction to Objectivist Epistemology

POLITICS/ECONOMICS

Capitalism: The Unknown Ideal
Return of the Primitive

ART, LITERATURE, AND LETTERS

The Romantic Manifesto
The Art of Fiction
The Art of Nonfiction
Journals of Ayn Rand
Letters of Ayn Rand

IDEAL

THE NOVEL AND THE PLAY

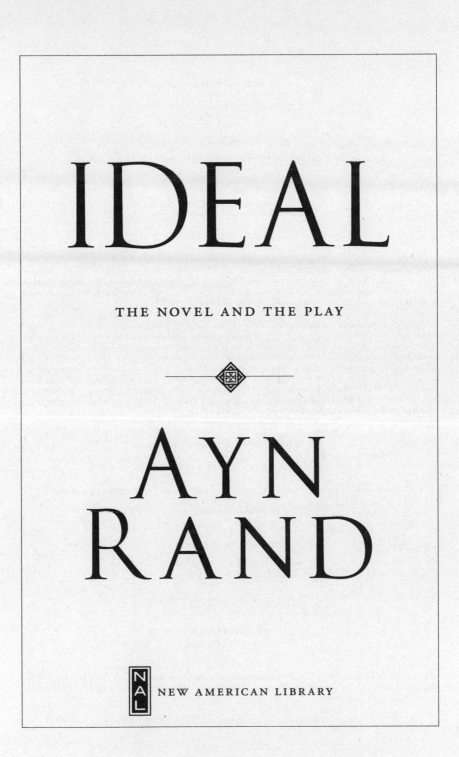

AYN
RAND

NEW AMERICAN LIBRARY

New American Library
Published by the Penguin Group
Penguin Group (USA) LLC, 375 Hudson Street,
New York, New York 10014

USA | Canada | UK | Ireland | Australia | New Zealand | India | South Africa | China
penguin.com
A Penguin Random House Company

First published by New American Library,
a division of Penguin Group (USA) LLC

First Printing, July 2015

REGISTERED TRADEMARK—MARCA REGISTRADA

NAL TRADE PAPERBACK ISBN: 978-0-451-47317-2

THE LIBRARY OF CONGRESS HAS CATALOGED THE HARDCOVER OF THIS EDITION AS FOLLOWS:
Rand, Ayn.
[Works. Selections]
Ideal: the novel and the play/Ayn Rand.
p. cm.
ISBN 978-0-451-47555-8 (hardback)
I. Title.
PS3535.A547A6 2015
813'.54—dc23   2015001507

Printed in the United States of America
1 3 5 7 9 10 8 6 4 2

Set in Adobe Garamond
Designed by Elke Sigal

CONTENTS

PART I
IDEAL: The Novel

PART II
IDEAL: The Play

PART I

IDEAL: The Novel

Introduction to *Ideal: The Novel*

In 1934, Ayn Rand wrote *Ideal* twice: first as a novel (fifty percent longer than *Anthem*), with which she was dissatisfied and edited only lightly; then, rewritten, as a polished stage play. Each version is the same in the four respects AR regarded as essential to literature (poetry apart): in each the same story conveying the same theme is enacted by (almost) the same characters; and despite large differences in editorial polish, each is written in AR's inimitable literary style. Although she chose not to publish the novel, she kept its typescript intact in her office.

Why did AR turn *Ideal* into a play? She never spoke to me about this but, to the best of my knowledge, the basic answer lies in the epistemological difference between the two literary forms. A novel uses concepts and only concepts to present its events, characters, and universe. A play (or a movie) uses concepts *and* percepts; the latter are the audience's observations of the physical actors, their movements, their speeches, et al. As an example, take novels made into movies, even if faithfully adapted. In the novel, the experience is complete simply through reading; now and then you may wish to see a character or event, but the desire is peripheral and transient. In the movie—while some form of dialogue, a conceptual element, is indispensable—seeing and continuing to see are required by the essence of the medium. You can be absorbed in a novel and wonder idly what a given scene would look like; but you do not watch the scene on-screen and wonder what it would read like.

Good novelists do work to give perceptual reality to their characters, but they do it within the limits of their form. Whatever their genius, they cannot give the reader an actual perceptual experience. Thus the crucial question in our context: What if a certain story by its nature requires such experience? What if its essential element(s) can be properly presented and grasped only by the use of perceptual means (in conjunction of course with the conceptual)?

The clearest example of such an element in *Ideal* is Kay Gonda's exalted beauty, spiritual *and* physical. This is the specific kind of beauty at the base of the play. It is the beauty not only of a heroine, but of an enchanting screen goddess—which is what makes it possible for her to be the embodiment for so many millions of their ideal. If this attribute of Kay's is not convincing, the story fails. And other things being equal, it seems that the perceptual in this context would win hands down over a purely conceptual treatment. A description of the actress Greta Garbo or the young Katharine Hepburn, however great the writer, could never fully convey (at least to me) the radiant perfection of their faces; yet, when looked at on-screen (if not as vividly as on the stage), they are taken in at a glance. (I choose these two examples, because they were AR's favorite female movie faces; Garbo was the inspiration for Kay.)

Here is another aspect of *Ideal* that may call for a perceptual element. The story in either version gives us a fairly rapid parade of characters—each stylized succinctly to represent a variant of the theme (the evil of betraying one's ideals), each presented in a single brief scene.

These characters are portrayed eloquently, but only with the sparing detail this type of stylization requires. Given this relative simplicity, not much about the characters is lost by AR's change of form, but an important value is gained. In regard to such an abbreviated parade, a description could not (I think) deliver the convincing impact of actual experience—i.e., could not make each one fully real. On the stage, by contrast, even a bit part can be real at once; we need merely look and we can see and hear him/her—face, body, posture, gait, dress, eye movement, tone of voice, etc.

Here is a third consideration. *Ideal* in either version has a story but not, in AR's definition, a plot (she was the first to make this point). Its beginning and end are logically connected, but the steps of Kay's quest as she moves from one traitor to the next are not presented as a logical progression moving step by necessary step to a climax. So perhaps AR came to think that, as a novel, the story might seem a bit slow, might be read as merely a static series of character sketches. By contrast, a play can more easily suggest movement in a story, even one without a plot, because it offers continual physical activity. By itself, of course, this last has no aesthetic value in any art form except the dance. But one can see that, in some cases, it might help to lessen the problem of a work being static.

None of the above is to be taken as disparaging the novel form. A novel's purely conceptual nature—its very *freedom* from the need to make its world perceptually available—allows it to create and make real, in each of its attributes, a complexity incomparably greater and more powerful than that possible to a play. If Kay Gonda is more real on the stage, Dagny Taggart is not; in fact, she is far more real to us in the pages of a book than she would be if we knew her only as an actress speaking lines. The reason is that a full grasp of her nature and force depends heavily not just on her dialogue and observable activity, but on the information we get from the novel's *non*-perceptual element. Three obvious examples: the novel gives us what goes on unspoken in her mind; what went on in her now unseen past; and countless revealing events physically impossible to put onstage or often even into a movie.

Even in regard to theoretically observable scenes, the novel does not merely describe what, if we were present, we would observe. On the contrary, the novel can impart unique information and achieve unique effects by taking hold of our perceptual faculty and *directing* it. The author directs us through the nature and scope of the details he selects for a given scene; he can go from an integrated abundance far more than the eye alone could cope with, down to a deliberate sparseness emphasizing merely one small aspect of a perceptual entity while ignoring all the rest as unimportant, a type of selectivity that a perceiver by himself could not perform (e.g., one architect is characterized in *The Fountainhead* mostly through his dandruff).

Then there is all the information and emotion we gather from the author's own use of evaluative words and connotations in narrative. And who knows how much more? To identify all the distinctive features possible to such a lengthy and comparatively unlimited art form as the novel is a task beyond my ability; I cannot even find a decent book about it. But I do want to add here a certain qualification: namely, many of a novel's attributes are possible to a limited extent in a play or movie—but the emphasis is on *limited*.

Every artistic form possesses certain unique potentialities and thereby lacks certain others. A play or movie made from a novel is almost always inferior to it because it cannot approach the complexity of the original work. By the same token, a relatively simple novel may be superior onstage, because of the power the story gets from the perceptual element. Novel and play, therefore, each within its own form, are equal—i.e., each fulfills AR's definition of art: "a recreation of reality according to an artist's metaphysical value judgments." It is the prerogative of the author to choose the genre of his work. AR, as we know, chose to put *Ideal* on the stage.

Although novel and play are equal in the above sense, a play's *script* by itself is not the equal of either. By itself, a script is not a work of art or a genre of literature. Novel and play alike, being complete, enable you fully to enter and experience the world they create. But the script by itself does not: it omits the essence in this context of literary art; it is written for perception (to be heard from a cast of actors seen on a stage), yet by itself it is detached from any such perception. To read dialogue by itself can certainly have value, but it is not the value of an artwork, merely of one of its attributes. This difference, I believe, is a major reason why novels are vastly more popular among readers than playscripts.

Like every playwright, AR chose the stage for *Ideal* on the premise that her play would be produced. In today's culture, however, there is no such production; most of us have and will continue to have no chance to see *Ideal* onstage, let alone to see it done properly—and even less chance to see a decent treatment if it were turned into a movie. The closest we can come to entering fully the world of *Ideal* is to read the novel. The comparison we face is a complete artwork with problems and a better artwork that is inaccessible to us.

But the novel has more than problems: it has many of the virtues uniquely possible to a conceptual treatment of the story. Although AR was dissatisfied with it, I do not think that by publishing it now I am contradicting her wishes. The reason is the nature of our culture now, plus the fact that so long a time has passed since her death. At this point, eight decades after the release of the play, no one can imagine that she considered this novel to be finished work, or fully worthy of her own standards of publication. In order to reaffirm her decision, we are *not* advertising this as "a new Ayn Rand novel." Indeed, my main purpose in writing this Introduction is to emphasize that and to suggest why, despite its many virtues, she rejected it—and then, in that context, to let you in on these virtues.

In praising the novel, I do not mean to minimize the changes AR made in recasting it, because in several respects the play is obviously more eloquent and dramatic. I have not tried to compare the two works page by page, so I cannot comment on all the changes (an impossible task). Novel and playscript are deliberately bound together in this volume, so the reader can discover and judge for himself their quality and difference.

Translating the novel into a play involved two essential tasks. One was the theatrical requirement to tell the story in briefer form—only through dialogue spoken in stageable scenes. The other was the writer's requirement to give the text a full editing. In regard to each of these, the changes are vast in number. In several passages, indeed, AR does not so much adapt or edit the novella as rewrite or even create from scratch.

There is, however, one change of substance, which goes beyond the above. In Chapter 3 of the novel, the central character is Jeremiah Sliney, an ignorant, dialect-speaking farmer. On her typescript, even before she started the play, AR slashed out the whole chapter, with ruthless lines signifying emphatic rejection. (I have seen her make such lines on my own manuscripts.) Dropping Sliney from the play, she instead took the name of a son-in-law of his, who had been an incidental character, and made him the scene's central character. In this reincarnation, Chuck Fink has an ideological identity: he is a member of the Communist Party.

I do not know AR's reason for this change, but I have some pretty good guesses. Sliney's ignorance and dialect make him less believable as a character in the play's context, i.e., less convincing as a conflicted idealist. For that role, an articulate urban intellectual is, I think, more believable. In addition, Fink brings to the story a new version of the evil it condemns: he is the man who betrays his ideal because of allegiance not to Babbitt or to God, but to Marx and the "social good." This is a much more philosophical approach to the causes of Kay Gonda's torture than Sliney's desire for money. And there is another reason that may be operative; AR may have thought that Sliney's betrayal of Kay could be taken as supporting a slogan she despised, namely: "Money is the root of all evil." Whatever her reason(s) for it, though, the change offers us a side benefit: Fink gave her the best opportunity in the play to satirize, and thus gives us, immersed in an often bleak context, a welcome chance to smile and sometimes even to laugh aloud.

Despite AR's deletion of Sliney, I have left him in the novel just as he was in its first draft. I do so not because of his scene's artistic value, but because it provides a small window into AR at work, a window that lets us see her power to create even in the earliest, unsatisfactory stage of a work, along with her absolutism in scrapping it if, like Rearden, she sees that it is not yet good enough. Of course, for the creator, the novel is not good enough, but for us, I think, its inadequacies do not diminish its value—both as art and as pleasure.

I first read the novel in 1982, the year AR died. I did not know about it until then, although I had long been familiar with the play. Sitting on a warehouse floor amid an overflow of her documents, I decided with a perfunctory interest to skim it a bit. To my surprise, I was drawn in and wholly absorbed, even at points in tears. When I finished, I felt a wrench, because I wanted to stay a little longer in Kay Gonda's world. This manuscript is so good, I felt, it's a shame it hasn't been made public. At last, thanks to Richard Ralston, its time has come.

During his lifetime, an author publishes his mature, accomplished works. But when he has gone, it is a common practice to bring out his unpublished material, including his juvenilia, his early, faltering attempts. This is especially common if he has become an immortal in his field whose every word, early or late, is avidly consumed by a large body of readers and a growing number of scholars. What you are about to read is one of AR's juvenilia written in her twenties when she was still ignorant of everything she would learn in the next fifty years. That's all this novel is, nothing more.

But how many mature writers, I wonder, can match the genius of AR or create her universe of logic and passion? Even in embryonic form, she is still there—and thus still here.

Leonard Peikoff
Aliso Viejo, California

A Note on the Manuscript of *Ideal*

I n 2004, while preparing recommendations about adding additional material to the revised edition of *The Early Ayn Rand*, I reviewed a manuscript of Ayn Rand's short novel *Ideal* in the collection of the Ayn Rand Archives. I gave it only a cursory look because the play of *Ideal* was written after the novel, and as that was the medium upon which Ayn Rand had finally settled, only the play had been included in the original collection.

In 2012, I (finally) decided that the novel deserved a closer look. I had heard wishful comments over many years from readers of Ayn Rand wondering if there might not be other novels somewhere in her papers. I decided that since there actually was such a novel, it should be reviewed carefully.

I read the 32,000-word typescript prepared in 1934 by the Rialto Service Bureau at 1501 Broadway in New York City. It immediately commanded my attention as unmistakably the work of Ayn Rand. I was also struck by the added dimension that the novel form provided. Two points in particular immediately stood out for me. The exposition made possible by the longer letters from Kay Gonda's fans as against their briefer versions in the play—which must be delivered as static speeches onstage or projected mechanically for reading by an audience—was often both clarifying and moving. The longer version of the letter from Johnnie Dawes, for example, provides a greater understanding of his character and action. Further, in the novel's first chapter, what amounts to an illuminating studio tour of Hollywood offices and personalities has no counterpart in the play. Both of these points greatly enrich the context for Kay Gonda's world and there are many other such enrichments.

Interesting in itself is how the novel demonstrates Ayn Rand's understanding of a crucial difference between writing for readers versus for listeners at a performance. More details and even more clarity, I think, are possible in a novel. But, of course, the dramatic impact of certain kinds of speech and the moral force they can convey are more effective onstage.

As Dr. Peikoff had probably not seen the novel for thirty years, it seemed like a good time to bring it to his attention. He was happy that I did so and asked me to quote in this Note what he said to me then: "Without you, Richard, where would Objectivism be?"

Richard E. Ralston
Publishing Manager
Ayn Rand Institute

1

Kay Gonda

"If it's murder—why don't we hear more about it? If it's not—why do we hear so much? When interviewed on the subject, Miss Frederica Sayers didn't say yes, and she didn't say no. She has refused to give out the slightest hint as to the manner of her brother's sudden death. Granton Sayers died in his Santa Barbara mansion two days ago, on the night of May 3rd. On the evening of May 3rd Granton Sayers had dinner with a famous—oh, very famous—screen star. That is all we know.

"Sorry we can't give you any lower lowdown—but we can suggest a few questions—if they have not occurred to you already. It would be interesting to know where that enchanting siren of the screen was on the night of May 3rd—after dinner. Or where she has been ever since. And if—as Miss Frederica Sayers maintains—there is nothing to whisper about, why are there such persistent rumors linking that certain famous name with the death of the great oil king of the West? All of which leaves Miss Frederica in the position of the West's oil queen and sole heiress to the Sayers millions—if any.

"Now, to change the subject. Many readers have called in inquiring as to the present whereabouts of Kay Gonda. This lovely lady of the screen has been absent from her Hollywood home for the last two days and the studio moguls refuse to reveal the why and the where. Some suspicious persons are whispering that the said moguls do not know it themselves."

The City Editor of the *Los Angeles Courier* sat down on the desk of Irving Ponts. Irving Ponts wore an eternal smile, wrote "This and That," star column of the *Los Angeles Courier,* and had a stomach which interfered with his comfort when he sat down. The City Editor transferred his pencil from the right corner of his mouth to the left, and asked:

"On the level, Irv, do you know where she is?"

"Search me," said Irving Ponts.

"Are they looking for her?"

"Ditto," said Irving Ponts.

"Have they filed charges against her in Santa Barbara?"

"Ditto."

"What did your police friends say?"

"That," said Irving Ponts, "wouldn't do you any good, because you couldn't print where they told me to go."

"You don't really think she did it, do you, Irv? Because why the hell would she do it?"

"No reason," said Irving Ponts. "Except, is there ever any reason for anything Kay Gonda does?"

The City Editor called Morrison Pickens.

Morrison Pickens looked as if in the sparse six feet of his body there were not a single bone, and only a miracle kept it upright, preventing it from flopping softly into a huddle. He had a cigarette which only a miracle kept hanging listlessly in the corner of his mouth. He had a coat thrown over his shoulders, which only a miracle kept from sliding down his back, and a cap with a visor that stood like a halo halfway up his skull.

"Take a little trip to the Farrow Film Studios," said the City Editor, "and see what you can see."

"Kay Gonda?" asked Morrison Pickens.

"Kay Gonda, if you can," said the City Editor. "If not, just try to pick up something about where she is at present."

Morrison Pickens struck a match on the sole of the City Editor's shoe, but changed his mind and threw the match into a wastebasket, picked up a pair of scissors, and cleaned his thumbnail thoughtfully.

"Uh-huh," said Morrison Pickens. "Shall I also try to find out who killed Rothstein[1] and whether there is any life after death?"

"Get there before lunch," said the City Editor. "See what they say and how they say it."

Morrison Pickens drove to the Farrow Film Studios. He drove down a crowded street of little shops, shrunken and dried in the sun, with dusty windowpanes ready to push one another out of the tight, grim row. Behind the panes he could see everything men needed, everything they lived for: stiff dresses with rhinestone butterflies, jars of strawberry jam and cans of tomatoes, floor mops and lawn mowers, cold cream and aspirin and a famous cure for gas in the stomach. Men

---

1 Arnold Rothstein, gangster who was allegedly behind the "fixing" of the 1919 World Series.

passed by, weary, hurried, indifferent, hair sticking to hot, wet fore-
heads. And it seemed as if the greatest of human miseries was not of
those who could not afford to enter the shops and buy, but of those who
could.

Over a little movie theater with a yellow brick front, a blank marquee, and a circle bearing a huge 15 CENTS in tarnished tinsel, stood the
cardboard figure of a woman. She stood erect, her shoulders thrown
back, and her short blond hair was like a bonfire snapped at the height
of a furious storm—a ferocious tangle of hair over a slim body. She had
pale, transparent eyes and a large mouth that looked like the mouth of
an idol of an animal that had been sacred. There was no name under the
figure, but the name was not necessary, for every passerby on every
street of the world knew the name and the wild blond hair and the
fragile body. It was Kay Gonda.

The figure was half naked under its scant garment, but no one noticed that. No one looked at it conventionally and no one snickered. She
stood, her head thrown back, her arms limp at her sides, palms up,
helpless and frail, surrendering herself and imploring something far
away, high over the blank marquee and over the roofs, as a flame held
straight for an insight in an unknown wind, as a last plea rising from
every roof, and every shop window, and every weary heart far under her
feet. And passing the theater, no one did, but everyone wanted dimly to
take off his hat.

Morrison Pickens had seen one of her pictures last evening. He had
sat for an hour and a half without moving, and if breathing had required attention, he would have forgotten to breathe. From the screen,
a huge white face had looked at him, a face with a mouth one wished
one could wish to kiss, and eyes that made one wonder—a wonder
which was pain—just what it was they were seeing. He felt as if there
was something—deep in his brain, behind everything he thought and

everything he was—which he did not know, but she knew, and he wished he did, and wondered whether he could ever know it, and should he, if he could, and why he wished it. He thought that she was just a woman and an actress, but he thought this only before he entered the theater and after he left it; while he looked at her on the screen, he thought differently; he thought that she was not a human being at all, not the kind of human being he'd seen around him all his life, but the kind no one ever knew—and should. When he looked at her, it made him feel guilty, but it also made him feel young—and clean—and very proud. When he looked at her, he understood why ancient peoples had made statues of gods in the image of man.

No one knew for certain who Kay Gonda was. There were people who said they remembered her when she was sixteen and working in a corset shop in Vienna. She wore a dress too short for her long, thin legs, with sleeves too short for her pale, thin arms. She moved behind the counter with a nervous swiftness that made people think that she belonged in a zoo, rather than in a little shop with starched white curtains and a smell of stale lard. No one called her beautiful. Men never approached her and landladies were eager to throw her out when she was behind in her rent. She spent long days fitting girdles to customers, her thin white fingers lacing strings tightly over heavy folds of flesh. The customers complained that her eyes made them uncomfortable.

There were also those who remembered her two years later when she worked as a maid in a disreputable hotel on a dark side street of Vienna. They remembered her walking down the stairs, holes glaring in the heels of her black cotton stockings, an old blouse gaping open at her throat. Men tried to speak to her, but she did not listen. Then, one night, she listened. He was a tall man with a hard mouth and eyes too observant ever to allow her to be happy; he was a famous film director who had not come to the hotel to see the maid. The woman who owned the place shrugged with indignation when she heard the maid laughing loudly, brutally, at the words the man whispered to her. But the great director denied vehemently the story of where he had discovered Kay Gonda, his greatest star.

In Hollywood she wore plain, dark dresses designed by a Frenchman whose salary could have financed an insurance concern. Her mansion was entered through a long gallery of white marble columns, and her butler served cocktails in tall, narrow glasses. She walked as if the carpets and the stairs and the sidewalks rolled softly, soundlessly, from under the suspicion of her foot's touch. Her hair never looked combed. She shrugged her shoulders with a gesture that was a convulsion, and little bluish shadows played between her shoulder blades when she wore long, backless evening gowns. Everyone envied her. No one said she was happy.

Morrison Pickens swung his long legs over the side of his open roadster and shuffled up the polished steps to the reception desk of the Farrow Film Studios. He said to the young man behind the desk, who had a face pink and stern as frozen strawberry custard:

"Pickens. Of the *Courier*. Want to see Mr. Farrow."

"Did you have an appointment?"

"Nope. That won't make any difference—*today*."

It didn't.

"Go right in, sir," said the young man eagerly, dropping the receiver on the answer of Mr. Farrow's secretary.

Mr. Farrow had three secretaries. The first one sat at a desk at a bronze railing, and she smiled icily, swinging the bronze gate open into an archway with a desk with three telephones and a secretary who rose to open a mahogany door into an office where a secretary rose to say:

"Go right in, Mr. Pickens."

Anthony Farrow sat at a desk lost in a vast, white ballroom. It had leaded windows the height of three floors. It had a white statue of a Madonna in a niche. It had a huge crystal globe of the world on a white marble pedestal. It had a white satin chaise longue which looked as if no one had ever approached it; no one had. It was Mr. Farrow's prize possession—and it was reported to have adorned, in days gone by, the boudoir of Empress Josephine.

Mr. Farrow had brownish-golden hair far at the back of his head and brownish-golden eyes. His suit matched the darkest thread of his hair, and his shirt—the lightest. He said: "Good morning, Mr. Pickens. Please sit down. I am delighted to see you," and extended an open box of cigars with a gesture worthy of the best close-up in a film of high society.

Mr. Pickens sat down and took a cigar.

"Of course," said Mr. Farrow, "you realize that it is nothing but a lot of preposterous nonsense."

"What is?" asked Morrison Pickens.

"The gossip to which I owe the honor of your visit. The gossip about Miss Gonda."

"Oh," said Morrison Pickens.

"My dear fellow, you must know how utterly ridiculous it is. I had hoped that your paper, a reputable paper like yours, would help us to prevent the spread of these totally unfounded rumors."

"That's easy, Mr. Farrow. It's up to you. The rumors being totally unfounded, you know, of course, where Miss Gonda happens to be, don't you?"

"Consider for a moment that wild story, Mr. Pickens. Granton Sayers—well, you know Granton Sayers. A fool, if I may be permitted to say so, a fool with the reputation of a genius—which is always the case with fools, isn't it? Fifty million dollars three years ago. Today— who knows? Perhaps fifty thousand. Perhaps fifty cents. But cut crystal swimming pools and a Greek temple in his garden. Ah, yes, and Kay Gonda. An expensive little plaything or artwork—according to how you want to look at it. Kay Gonda, that is, two years ago. Not today. Oh, no, not today. I know for certain that she had not seen Sayers for over a year previous to that dinner in Santa Barbara we've all heard about."

"So the romance was all over? Cold as ice?"

"Colder, Mr. Pickens."

"Sure of that?"

"Positive, Mr. Pickens."

"But perhaps there had been a quarrel between them, some quarrel which . . ."

"None, Mr. Pickens. Never. He had proposed to her three times to my knowledge. She could have had him, Greek temple and oil wells and all, any day she wished. Why would she want to kill him?"

"Why would she want to disappear?"

"Mr. Pickens, may I reverse the procedure of an interview with the press—and ask you a question?"

"Certainly, Mr. Farrow."

"Who in . . . who on earth started those rumors?"

"That," said Morrison Pickens, "is what I thought you could tell me, Mr. Farrow."

"It's preposterous, Mr. Pickens, worse than preposterous. It's vicious. Hints, whispers, questions. All over town. If I could see any point in it, I'd say someone was spreading it intentionally."

"Who would have a reason to do that?"

"That's just it, Mr. Pickens. No one. Miss Gonda hasn't got an enemy in the world."

"Has she a friend?"

"Why, of course, why— No," said Mr. Farrow suddenly, his voice earnest and puzzled by its own statement, "no, she hasn't." The way he looked at Morrison Pickens was real, simple helplessness. "Why did you ask that?"

"Why do you answer it like that?" asked Morrison Pickens.

"I . . . I don't know," said Mr. Farrow. "I'd never thought of it before. It just struck me suddenly that she hasn't really got a single friend in the world. Unless it's Mick Watts, who nobody could call a friend to anybody. Oh, well," he added, shrugging, "perhaps it's only natural. How can you think of friendship with a woman like that? She looks at you, but doesn't really see you at all. She sees something else. No one can guess what. She speaks to you—when she speaks, which isn't often—and you don't really know what she's thinking. Sometimes I'm sure that she doesn't think what we think at all, you and I. Things don't mean the same to her as to the rest of us. But what they mean and what she means—who can tell? And, actually, who cares?"

"About seventy million people or so, judging by your box office reports."

"Ah, yes. Which, perhaps, is all that matters. They worship her, millions of them. It's not admiration. It's not just fan enthusiasm. It's much more than that. It's worship. I don't know what she does to them all—but she does something."

"And how will her public react to—murder?"

"It's incredible, Mr. Pickens. It's fantastic. How can anyone believe it for a moment?"

"No one would believe it for a moment if Miss Gonda hadn't disappeared."

"But, Mr. Pickens, she hasn't disappeared."

"Where is she?"

"She always wants to be alone when she's getting ready for a new picture. She's at one of her beach homes, studying her new part."

"Where?"

"Really, Mr. Pickens, we can't have her disturbed."

"Supposing we were to try and find her. Would you stop us?"

"Certainly not, Mr. Pickens. Far be it from us to interfere with the press."

Morrison Pickens got up. He said:

"Fine, Mr. Farrow. We'll try."

Mr. Farrow got up. He said:

"Fine, Mr. Pickens. I wish you luck."

Morrison Pickens was at the door, when Mr. Farrow added:

"By the way, Mr. Pickens, if you are successful, could I ask you the favor of letting us know? You understand, we wouldn't want our great star disturbed, and . . ."

"I understand," said Morrison Pickens, walking out.

In the outer office of Mr. Sol Salzer, associate producer, a nervous male secretary fluttered up, insisting:

"But Mr. Salzer is busy. Mr. Salzer is very, very busy. Mr. Salzer is in story con—"

"Tell him it's the *Courier*," said Morrison Pickens. "Maybe he'll find a coupla minutes."

The secretary fluttered behind a tall, white door and hopped out swiftly, leaving the door open, twittering breathlessly:

"Go right in, Mr. Pickens, go right, right in."

Mr. Salzer was pacing up and down a spacious office with purple velvet curtains and pictures of flowers and Scotties in white frames. He said, "Sit down," without looking at Mr. Pickens, and continued his walk.

Morrison Pickens sat down.

Mr. Salzer's hands were clamped behind his back. He wore a steel-blue suit and a diamond stickpin. His curly black hair made a narrow peninsula in the middle of his white forehead. He crossed the office three times, then barked:

"It's a lotta baloney!"

"What?" asked Morrison Pickens.

"What you want to know. What you fellers waste your time making up and then fill your papers with on accounta having nothing better to print!"

"Are you talking about Miss Gonda?"

"I *am* talking about Miss Gonda! I'm talking about nothing else but! I should waste my time here with you if it wasn't for Miss Gonda! I wish we'd never signed her! A headache we should have ever since she came on the lot!"

"Oh, come, Mr. Salzer. You've supervised all her pictures. You must see something in her."

"Three million bucks cash per each picture. That's what I see! You go ahead and tell me a better reason."

"Well, let's talk about your next picture."

"So what about it? It's going to be the greatest, finest"—Mr. Salzer stopped to pound his desk with his fist—"most expensive picture you ever saw in your life! You can tell that to your paper!"

"Fine, I'm sure they'll be glad to know it. Also, they'll be glad to know its . . . starting date."

"Listen," said Mr. Salzer, stopping, "it's a lot of hooey! It's a lot of hooey what you're driving at! Because she hasn't disappeared!"

"I haven't said she has."

"Well, don't say it! Because we know where she is, only it's none of your business, see?"

"I wasn't going to say it. I was only going to ask whether Miss Gonda has signed her new contract with you people."

"Sure, she's signed. Of course. Certainly. She's just practically signed it almost."

"Then she hasn't?"

"She was going to sign it today. I mean, she *is* going to sign it today. She's agreed. It's all settled— Well, I'll tell you," Mr. Salzer said suddenly, with the despair of a person who must capture sympathy on film, anyone's sympathy. "What I'm afraid of is that it's all on accounta that contract. She's changed her mind again, maybe, and quit for good."

"Isn't that just a pose, Mr. Salzer? We've heard that after every picture."

"Yeah? You should laugh if you hadda crawl after her down on your knees like we done for two months. 'I'm through,' she says. 'Does it really mean anything? Is it really worth doing?' No! Fifteen thousand a week we offer her and she asks is it worth doing?"

"Then you think she's walked out on you this time? And you don't know where she's gone?"

"I don't like newspaper people," said Mr. Salzer, disgusted. "That's why I've never liked them. Here I'm telling you my troubles, all my confidential troubles—and you go starting on your old baloney again."

"That you don't know where she is."

"Aw, phooey! We know where she is. It's an aunt of hers, an old aunt from Europe, who's sick, and she's gone to visit her on a ranch out in the desert. See?"

"Yeah," said Morrison Pickens, rising, "I see."

He did not have to be announced to Claire Peemoller, star of Farrow Films, who wrote all the scripts for Kay Gonda's pictures. He just walked in. It was never necessary to announce the press to Claire Peemoller.

Claire Peemoller sat in the center of a long, low modernistic couch.

There was no spotlight lighting the place where she sat; it only seemed
as if there were. Her clothes had the trim, modernistic elegance of glass
furniture, suspension bridges, or transatlantic clipper planes. She looked
like the last word of a great civilization, hard, clean, wise, concerned
with nothing but the subtlest and deepest problems of life. It was only
Claire Peemoller's body, however, that sat on the couch; her soul was on
the walls of her office. The walls of her office were covered with enlarged
photographs of illustrations for her magazines. The photographs showed
gentle young girls and sturdy young men embracing, babies squinting
up at parents clutching hands in reconciliation over the crib, old ladies
whose faces could sweeten the blackest cup of coffee.

"Mr. Pickens," said Claire Peemoller, "I'm so glad to see you. It was
simply wonderful, but wonderful, of you to drop in. I have a great story
for you. I was thinking that the public has never really understood the
psychological influence of the little things in a writer's childhood that
shape her future career. It's the little things that count in life, you know.
For instance, one day when I was seven, I saw a butterfly with a broken
wing and it made me think of—"

"Kay Gonda?" asked Morrison Pickens.

"Oh," said Claire Peemoller, and her thin lips closed tight. Then she
opened them again to add, "So that's what you came about . . ."

"Well, surely, Miss Peemoller, you should have guessed that—
today."

"I did not," said Claire Peemoller. "I've never been under the impression that Miss Kay Gonda was the only subject of interest in the
world."

"I only wanted to ask you what you thought of all those rumors
about Miss Gonda."

"I haven't given it a thought. My time is really valuable."

"When did you see her last?"

"Two days ago."

"Not on May 3rd?"

"*Yes*, on May 3rd."

"Well, did you notice anything peculiar in her behavior then?"

"When has she behaved in any manner that wasn't peculiar?"

"Would you mind telling me about it?"

"I mind it very much indeed. And who wouldn't? I drove all the way down to her house, that afternoon, to discuss her next script. It's a lovely story, but lovely! I talked for hours. She sat there like a statue. Not a word out of her, not a sound. Down-to-earthiness, that's what she lacks. No finer feelings in her. But none! No sense of the great brotherhood of men under the skin. No—"

"Did she seem worried or unhappy?"

"Really, Mr. Pickens, I have more important things to do than to analyze Miss Gonda's moods. All I can tell you is that she wouldn't let me put in a little baby or a dog in the script. Dogs have much human appeal. You know, we're all brothers under the skin and—"

"Did she mention that she was going to Santa Barbara that night?"

"She doesn't mention things. She throws them at you in pails. She just simply got up in the middle of a sentence and left me flat. She said she had to dress, because she was having dinner in Santa Barbara. And then she added: 'I do not like missions of charity.'"

"What did she mean by that?"

"What does she mean by anything? 'Charity'—just imagine!—to have dinner with a multimillionaire. So then I just couldn't resist it, but couldn't! I said, 'Miss Gonda, do you really think you're so much better than everybody else?' And what do you suppose she answered? 'Yes,' she said, 'I do. I wish I didn't have to.' But actually!"

"Did she say anything else?"

"No. I'm the kind of person that simply does not understand conceit. So I did not care to continue the conversation. And I do not care to continue it now. I'm sorry, Mr. Pickens. But the subject bores me."

"Do you know where Miss Gonda is at present?"

"I haven't the faintest idea."

"But if anything's happened to her . . ."

"I'll ask them to put Sally Sweeney in the part. I've always wanted to write for Sally. She's such a sweet kid. And now you'll have to excuse me, Mr. Pickens. I'm very busy."

Bill McNitt sat in a filthy office that smelt like a poolroom: its walls were plastered with posters of the Gonda pictures he had directed. Bill McNitt took pride in being a genius and a he-man besides: if people wished to see him, they could well afford to sit among cigarette butts, next to a spittoon. He leaned back in his swivel chair, his feet on a desk, and smoked. His shirtsleeves were rolled high above his elbow, and he had big, hairy arms. He waved one huge hand with a golden snake ring on a stubby finger when Morrison Pickens entered.

"Spill it," said Bill McNitt.

"I," said Morrison Pickens, "have nothing to spill."

"Neither," said Bill McNitt, "have I. Now beat it."

"You don't seem to be busy," said Morrison Pickens, sitting down comfortably on a canvas stool.

"I'm not. And don't ask me why. Because it's the same reason that keeps you so busy."

"I presume you're referring to Miss Kay Gonda."

"You don't have to do any presuming. You know damn well. Only that won't do you any good around here, 'cause you can't pump anything out of me. I never wanted to direct her anyway. I'd much rather direct Joan Tudor. I'd much rather . . ."

"What's the matter, Bill? Had trouble with Gonda?"

"Listen. I'll tell you all I know. Then beat it, will you? Last week it was, I drove down to her beach house and there she was, out at sea, tearing through the rocks in a motorboat till I thought I'd have heart failure watching it. So she climbs up to the road, finally, wet all over. So I say to her: 'You'll get killed someday,' and she looks straight at me and she says: 'That won't make any difference to me,' she says, 'nor to anyone else anywhere.'"

"She said that?"

"She did. 'Listen,' I said, 'I don't give a hoot if you break your neck, but you'll get pneumonia in the middle of my next picture!' She looks at me in that queer way of hers and she says: 'Maybe there won't be any next picture.' And she walks straight back to the house and the flunky wouldn't let me in!"

"She really said that? Last week?"

"She did. Well, I should worry. That's all. Now beat it."

"Listen, I want to ask you—"

"Don't ask me where she is! Because I don't know it! See? And what's more, none of the big shots know it, either, only they won't say so! Why do you suppose I'm sitting here like fly food, drawing three grand a week? Do you think they wouldn't get the fire department to drag her back if they knew where to send for her?"

"You can make a guess."

"I don't make guesses. I don't know a thing about the woman. I don't want to know a thing about the woman. I'd never want to go near her if for some fool reason the yokels didn't part with their cash so readily for a peek at that bleached pan of hers!"

"Well, now, I couldn't quote that in the paper."

"I don't care what you quote. I don't care what you do as long as you get out of here and go to the—"

"The publicity department—first," said Morrison Pickens, rising.

———

In the publicity department, four different hands slapped Morrison Pickens' shoulder, and four faces looked at him, sweetly bland, as if they had never heard the name of Kay Gonda before, and it took an effort to remember it, and remembering it, they found they knew nothing but the name. Only one face, the fifth, bent closer to Morrison Pickens and whispered:

"We don't know a thing, pal. Not allowed to know. And wouldn't know if allowed. There's only one person who might help you. Might, but probably won't. Go see Mick Watts. I'm sure the bum knows something."

"Why? Is he sober, for a change?"

"No. He's drunker than usual."

Mick Watts was Kay Gonda's personal press agent. He had been fired from every studio in Hollywood, from every newspaper on both coasts, and from many others in between. But Kay Gonda had brought him to the Farrow lot. They paid him a large salary and did not object to him as they did not object to Kay Gonda's Great Dane on Anthony Farrow's Josephine chaise longue.

Mick Watts had platinum blond hair, the face of a thug, and the blue eyes of a baby. He sat in his office, his head buried in his arms on the desk. He raised his head when Morrison Pickens entered, and his blue eyes were crystal clear—but Pickens knew that they saw nothing, for two empty bottles lay conspicuously under his chair.

"Nice weather we're having, Mick," said Morrison Pickens.

Mick Watts nodded and said nothing.

"Nice, but hot," said Morrison Pickens. "Awful hot. Supposing you and me slip down to the commissary for something cool and liquid?"

"I don't know a thing," said Mick Watts. "Save your cash. Get out."

"What are you talking about, Mick?"

"I'm not talking about nothing—and that goes for everything."

In the typewriter on the desk, Morrison Pickens saw the sheet of a press release which Mick Watts had been composing. He read, incredulously:

"Kay Gonda does not cook her own meals or knit her own underwear. She does not play golf, adopt babies, or endow hospitals for homeless horses. She is not kind to her dear old mother—she *has* no dear old mother. She is not just like you and me. She never was like you and me. She's like nothing you rotters ever dreamt of."

Morrison Pickens shook his head reproachfully. Mick Watts did not seem to mind his reading it. Mick Watts sat there, looking at the wall, as if he had forgotten Pickens' existence.

"You could stand a drink, once in a while, couldn't you, Mick?" said Morrison Pickens. "You look thirsty to me."

"I don't know a thing about Kay Gonda," said Mick Watts. "Never heard of her. . . . Kay Gonda. It's a funny name, isn't it? What is it? I went to confession once, long ago—very long ago—and they talked about the redemption of all sins. It's a funny thing to yell 'Kay Gonda' and to think that all your sins are washed away. Just pay two bits in the balcony—and come out pure as snow."

"On second thought, Mick," said Morrison Pickens, "I won't offer you another drink. You'd better have something to eat."

"I'm not hungry. I stopped being hungry many years ago. But she is."

"Who?" asked Morrison Pickens.

"Kay Gonda," said Mick Watts.

"Any idea where she's having her next meal?"

"In heaven," said Mick Watts. "In a blue heaven with white lilies. Very white lilies. Only she'll never find it."

"I don't quite follow you, Mick. What was that again?"

"You don't understand? She doesn't, either. Only it's no use. It's no use trying to unravel, because if you try, you end up with nothing but more dirt on your hands than you care to wipe off. There are not enough towels in the world to wipe it off. Not enough towels. That's the trouble."

"I'll drop in some other time," said Morrison Pickens.

Mick Watts rose, and staggered, and picked up a bottle from under his chair, and took a long drink, and, straightening himself to his full height, raising the bottle, swaying, said solemnly:

"A great quest. The quest of the hopeless. Why are the hopeless ones always those to hope? Why do we want to see it, when we're luckier if we don't even suspect that it could ever be seen? Why does she? Why does she have to be hurt?"

"Good day," said Morrison Pickens.

The last place Morrison Pickens visited on the lot was the dressing room bungalow of Kay Gonda. Miss Terrence, her secretary, sat in the reception room as usual. Miss Terrence had not heard from Kay Gonda for two days, but she appeared at the bungalow promptly on the dot of nine and sat at her spotless glass desk till six. Miss Terrence wore a black dress with a blinding white collar. She wore square, rimless glasses and her nails were shell-pink.

Miss Terrence knew nothing about Miss Gonda's disappearance. She had not seen Miss Gonda since her trip to Santa Barbara, two days ago. She supposed, however, that Miss Gonda had been back at the studio, after that dinner, sometime during the night. For when she, Miss Terrence, had entered the bungalow on the following morning she had found that from among Miss Gonda's fan mail, six letters were missing.

2

George S. Perkins

"Dear Miss Gonda,

I am not a regular movie fan, but I've never missed a picture of yours. And I can't even say that I like your pictures. For instance, I enjoy the Willie Wookey comedies much more. Only there's something about you which I have to see. Sometimes I think that the day I stop wanting to see it, that day I'll know I'm not alive anymore. It's something I can't give a name to, something I had, but lost, but you're keeping it for me, for all of us. I had it long ago, when I was very young. You know how it is: when you're very young there's something ahead of you so big you're afraid of it, but you wait for it and you're so happy waiting. Then the years pass and it never comes. And then you find one day that you're not waiting anymore. It makes you sad, and that's silly, because you didn't even know what it was you were waiting for. I look at myself and I don't know. But when I look at you—I do.

And sometimes I think that if ever, by some miracle, anything like you came into my life, I'd drop it all and follow you, and gladly lay down my life for you, because, you see, I'm still a human being.

Very truly yours,
George S. Perkins
S. Hoover Street
Los Angeles, California"

On the afternoon of May 5th, George S. Perkins received a promotion. He was made Assistant Manager of the Daffodil Canning Company. The boss called him into his office to congratulate him. The boss said:

"If ever a man deserved a raise, you're it, G.S."

George S. Perkins straightened his knitted tie of green and blue stripes, blinked, cleared his throat and answered:

"I feel greatly honored and I shall do my best."

The boss said:

"Of course you will, old boy. Now, what about a little cough medicine for the occasion?"

George S. Perkins said:

"I don't mind if I do."

The boss filled two glasses that had red rims and funny black figures of drunks leaning against lampposts. George S. Perkins got up to take his glass, and the boss got up, and they clinked glasses across the desk.

"Here's looking at you," said the boss.

"Mud in your eye," said George S. Perkins.

They emptied the glasses and the boss said:

"Bet you're just itching to get home and tell the news to the little woman."

"Mrs. Perkins will be most grateful, same as myself," said George S. Perkins.

Outside the boss' office, the advertising manager—who was a wit—twisted the sparse blond hair into a curlicue in the middle of George S. Perkins' scalp, saying, "Always knew you had the stuff, old boy, old boy, old boy."

George S. Perkins sat down at his desk to finish the day's work. He had sat at the desk every working day of the last twenty years. He knew every grain in its old wood and the charred spot of a cigarette burn someone had left there carelessly a long time ago. He had not noticed how and when the bright broad varnish had disappeared and how the long, grayish bands had come to cross its wide expanse. He had not noticed how the little wrinkles had come in the skin between his fingers; but his hands were still the same, white and soft, with fingers too short for his body, and when he closed them into helpless little fists, soft creases, like bracelets, still crossed his wrists, like the wrists of a baby.

His face had not changed, and his office had not changed, everything in it familiar, inescapable, like the lines of his face. The legs of the filing cabinet had worn deep cuts in the carpet, and the sun had burnt the carpet to a soft gray, leaving a darker brown patch under the filing cabinet. He had sat there while somewhere at home a wedding had been waiting for him, while in a used car lot a dealer had been waiting with his first automobile, while in a hospital his wife had been awaiting a new life to enter their lives. He had stared hopefully, miserably, happily, wearily at the same spot on the wall by the watercolor, a gray spot that looked like a rabbit with a round snoot and one long ear.

On a shelf by the window stood tiers of bright cans with green and red and pink labels fading softly into one shade of dusty yellow: peaches and apple butter and mincemeat and salmon. They stood erect, immovable like stout bars. Sometimes he thought foolishly that the bars were rising across the windowpane. But he liked the can of salmon, because he had suggested to the artist the green tangle of parsley on the white plates by the juicy pink slice, and the artist had said, "Great idea, Mr. Perkins. Just the right touch. The appeal to elegance."

Beyond the window, a tangle of roofs and chimneys stretched to the far horizon. The sky was turning a muddy brown beyond the roofs, with a faint reddish hue, like dishwater after a dinner when beets had been served. But there were a few spots of pink scattered over the brown, a pink soft as petals of apple blossom in the spring. Many years ago, at that hour, George S. Perkins remembered watching the pink beyond the cornice of a tall old house and thinking dimly of what lay there, beyond the house, and farther, beyond the pink, in some strange countries where the sun was just rising, and of what could happen to him there, very far away, what would happen—someday. But he had not thought of that for many years, and a big black skyscraper had risen to hide the old house, and on the roof of the skyscraper there was an electric sign for Tornado Motor Oil, a tangled web of metal against the sunset.

George S. Perkins took two letters from his recent mail, one from a famous golf club with a return envelope enclosed for his initiation fee, the other from an expensive tailor. He made a ring with a red pencil around the tailor's address. He must also look up a good gym, he thought, would have to do something about that stomach of his; a bulge would spoil the classiest suit, not a big bulge, but still a bulge.

The light went on in the Tornado Motor Oil sign beyond the window, huge letters going on and off, thick drops outlined in yellow neon tubes, falling, in jerking spasms, from a long nozzle into a bucket. George S. Perkins got up and locked his desk, whistling a tune from a musical comedy he had seen in New York while on his honeymoon. The advertising manager said: "Well, well!"

George S. Perkins drove home, whistling "Over There." The evening was turning chilly, and a fire burnt on the imitation logs in the fireplace of his living room. The living room smelt of lavender and deep-fat frying. A lamp was lit on the mantelpiece; it had a standard of two huge dice cubes and a shade covered with old whiskey labels.

"You're late," said Mrs. Perkins.

Mrs. Perkins wore a dress of brown crepe de chine with a large rhinestone clip in front that always snapped open, showing a slip that had been pink. She wore dark gray, service-weight stockings and brown comfort shoes. Her face looked like a bird's, a bird that had wizened slowly, drying out in the sun, and her nails were clipped very short.

"Well, dovey," said George S. Perkins gaily, "I have a good excuse for being late."

"I have no doubt about that," said Mrs. Perkins, "but listen to me, George Perkins, you'll have to do something about Junior. That boy of yours got a D again in arithmetic. As I've always said, if a father don't take the proper interest in his children, what can you expect from a boy who—"

"Aw, honeybunch, we'll excuse the kid for once—just to celebrate."

"Celebrate what?"

"How would you like to be Mrs. Assistant Manager of the Daffodil Canning Company?"

"I would like it very much," said Mrs. Perkins. "Not that I have any hope of ever being."

"Well, dovey, you are. As of today."

"Oh," said Mrs. Perkins. "Mama! Come here!"

Mrs. Shly, Mr. Perkins' mother-in-law, wore an ample dress of printed silk with blue daisies and hummingbirds on a white background, a string of imitation seed pearls, and a net over her heavy, graying blond hair.

"Mama," said Mrs. Perkins, "Georgie's got a promotion."

"Well," said Mrs. Shly, "we've waited for it long enough."

"But you don't understand," said George S. Perkins, blinking helplessly, "I've been made Assistant Manager—" He looked for a response in their faces, found none, added lamely, "—of the Daffodil Canning Company."

"Well?" asked Mrs. Shly.

"Rosie," he said softly, looking at his wife, "it's twenty years that I've worked for it."

"That, my boy," said Mrs. Shly, "is nothing to brag about."

"Well, but I've made it. . . . It's a long time, twenty years. You get sort of tired. But now . . . Rosie, now we can take it easy . . . easy . . . light. . . ." His voice sounded eager and young for a moment. "You know, *light* . . ." and died again, and added apologetically, "Easy, I mean."

"What are you talking about?" asked Mrs. Perkins.

"Dovey, I've been sort of . . . planning . . . thinking on the way home. . . . I've been thinking of it for a long time, nights, you know . . . making plans. . . ."

"Indeed? But your wife's not let in on any of it?"

"Oh, I . . . It was just sort of like dreaming . . . and you might've thought I was . . . unhappy, and it isn't that at all, only you know how it is: you work and work all day, and everything goes nicely, and suddenly you feel like you can't stand another minute of it, for no reason at all. But then it passes. It always passes."

"I declare," said Mrs. Perkins, "I never heard the like of it."

"Well, I was just thinking . . ."

"You'll stop thinking this minute," said Mrs. Shly, "or the roast'll be all ruined."

At the dinner table, when the maid had served roasted leg of lamb with mint sauce, George S. Perkins said:

"Now, what I was thinking about, dovey . . ."

"First of all," said Mrs. Perkins, "we've got to have a new Frigidaire. The old one's a sight. No one uses iceboxes anymore. Now, Mrs. Tucker . . . Cora Mae, you don't butter a whole slice at once. Can't you eat like a lady? Now, Mrs. Tucker has a new one and it's a honey. Electric light inside and everything."

"Ours is only about two years old," said George S. Perkins. "It looks pretty good to me."

"That," said Mrs. Shly, "is because you're a very economical man, but the only thing you save on is your home and family."

"I was thinking," said George S. Perkins, "you know, honey, if we're very careful, we could take a vacation maybe—in a year or two—and go maybe to Europe, you know, Switzerland or Italy. It's where they have mountains, you know."

"Well?"

"Well, and lakes. And snow high up there. And sunsets."

"And what would we do?"

"Oh . . . well . . . just rest, I guess. And look around, sort of. You know, at the swans and the sailboats. Just the two of us."

"Uh-huh," said Mrs. Shly, "just the *two* of you."

"Yes," said Mrs. Perkins, "you were always a great one at making up ways of wasting good money, George Perkins. And my slaving and skimping and saving every little penny. Swans, indeed. Well, before you go thinking of any swans, you'd better get me a new Frigidaire, that's all I've got to say."

"Yes," said Mrs. Shly, "and we sure need a mayonnaise mixer. And a 'lectric serving machine. And it's about time to be thinking of a new car, too."

"Look," said George S. Perkins, "you don't understand. I don't want anything that we need."

"What's that?" asked Mrs. Perkins, and her mouth remained hanging open.

"Please, Rosie. Listen. You *must* understand . . . I want something I don't need at all."

"George Perkins! Have you been drinking?"

"Rosie, if we start that all over again—buying things—paying for things—the car and the house and the dentist's bills—more of it—all over again—and nothing else—never—and we pass up our last chance—"

"What's the matter with you? What's come over you all of a sudden?"

"Rosie, it isn't that I've been unhappy. And it isn't that I don't like what I got out of life. I like it fine. Only . . . well, it's like that old bathrobe of mine, Rosie. I'm glad I have it, it's pretty and warm and comfortable, and I like it, just the same as I like the rest of it. Just like that. And no more. There should be more."

"Well, I like that! The swell bathrobe I picked for your birthday. That's the thanks I get! Well, if you didn't like it, why didn't you exchange it?"

"Oh, Rosie, it isn't that! It's a swell bathrobe. Only, you know, a man can't live his whole life for a bathrobe. Or for things that man feels the same way about. Nice things, Rosie, only there should be more."

"What?"

"I don't know. That's just it. A man should know."

"He's touched in the head," said Mrs. Shly.

"Rosie, a man can't live just for things that do nothing to him—inside, I mean. There should be something that he's afraid of—afraid and happy. Like going to church—only not in a church. Something he can look up to. Something—high, Rosie . . . That's it, *high*."

"Well, if it's culture you want, didn't I subscribe to the Book-of-the-Month Club? Didn't I?"

"Oh, I know I can't explain it. There's just one thing I'm asking, Rosie, just one: let's take that vacation. Let's try. Maybe things would happen to us . . . strange things . . . the kind you dream about. I'll be an old man, if I give that up. I don't want to be old. Not yet, Rosie. Oh, Lord, not yet! Just leave me a few years, Rosie."

"Oh, I don't mind about your vacation. You can have your vacation—if we can afford it, after the important things are taken care of. You got to think of the important things first. Like a new Frigidaire, for instance. That old box of ours is a mess, all right. It never keeps anything fresh. Now, I had some apple butter and . . ."

"Ma-a," said Cora Mae, "Junior was stealing apple butter from the icebox. I seen him."

"I didn't!" yelled Junior, raising his pale face from his plate.

"You did, too!" screamed Cora Mae.

The third child, Henry Bernard Perkins, said nothing. He sat in his high chair, with his mush bowl, thoughtfully drooling on his oilcloth bib with a picture of Mother Goose.

"Now, for instance," said Mrs. Perkins, "supposing Junior ate the apple butter, I hate to think what it'll do to his stomach. I'll bet it was rancid. That icebox . . ."

"I thought it worked all right," said George S. Perkins.

"Oh, you did? That's because you never see what's under your nose. You don't care if the children eat wilted vegetables. But let me tell you, there's nothing worse'n wilted vegetables. Mrs. Tucker, she heard a lecture where the lady said that if you don't get enough stuff with vitamins what make bones the kids will get rickets. That's what they'll get."

"In my day," said Mrs. Shly, "parents sure did think of what they fed the young ones. Take the Chinese, for instance. They don't eat nothing but rice. That's why all the Chinks have rickets."

"Now, Mother," said George S. Perkins, "who ever told you that?"

"Well, I suppose I don't know what I'm talking about?" said Mrs. Shly. "I suppose the big businessman is the only one to tell us what's what?"

"But, Mother. I didn't mean . . . I only meant that . . ."

"Never mind, George Perkins. Never mind. I know very well what you meant."

"You leave Mama alone, George."

"But, Rosie, I didn't . . ."

"It's no use talking, Rosalie. When a man hasn't the decency to . . ."

"Mother, will you let Rosie and me . . ."

"I understand. I understand perfectly, George Perkins. An old mother, these days, is no good for anything but to shut up and wait for the graveyard!"

"Mother," said George S. Perkins bravely, "I wish you'd stop trying to . . . to make trouble."

"So?" said Mrs. Shly, smashing her napkin into the gravy. "So that's it? So I'm making trouble? So I'm a burden to you, ain't I? Well, I'm glad you came out with it, Mr. Perkins! And here I've been, poor fool that I am, slaving in this house like it was my own! Polishing the stove, only yesterday that was, till all my nails is broke! That's the gratitude I get! Well, I won't stand for it another minute! Not one minute!"

She rose, the soft creases of her neck trembling, and left the room, slamming the door.

"George!" said Mrs. Perkins, her eyes wide in consternation. "George, if you don't apologize, Mama will leave us!"

George S. Perkins looked up, blinking, the weariness of years whose count he had lost giving him a sudden, desperate courage.

"Well, let her go," he said.

Mrs. Perkins stood silent, hunched forward. Then she screamed:

"So it's come to that? So that's what it does to you, your big promotion? Coming home, picking a fight with everybody, throwing your wife's old mother out into the gutter! If you think I'm going to—"

"Listen," said George S. Perkins slowly, "I've stood about as much of her as I'm going to stand. She'd better go. It was coming to this, sooner or later."

Mrs. Perkins stood straight and the rhinestone clip snapped open on her chest.

"You listen to me, George Perkins." Her thin voice made dry, gulping sounds somewhere high in her throat. "If you don't apologize to Mama, if you don't apologize to her before tomorrow morning, I'll never speak to you again as long as I live!"

"All right by me," said George S. Perkins. He had heard the same promise many times.

Mrs. Perkins ran, sobbing, up the stairs to her bedroom.

George S. Perkins rose heavily and walked up the stairs, slowly, his head bent, looking down at the bulge of his stomach, the old stairway creaking under his steps. Cora Mae watched curiously to see where he would go. He did not turn to Mrs. Perkins' room; he shuffled slowly away, down the corridor, to his bedroom.

Junior stretched his hand across the table and stuffed hastily into his mouth the slice of lamb left on Mrs. Shly's plate. . . .

The clock in the living room struck ten.

All lights were out in the house, save a dim lamp in the window of George S. Perkins' bedroom. George S. Perkins sat on this bed, huddled in a faded bathrobe of purple flannel, and studied thoughtfully the toes of his old slippers.

The doorbell rang.

George S. Perkins started. That was strange; his window opened over the front porch and he had heard no steps in the street outside, nor across the lawn, nor on the hard cement of the porch.

The maid had gone for the night. He rose hesitantly and shuffled down the stairs, the steps creaking.

He crossed the dark living room and opened the door.

"Oh, my God!" said George S. Perkins.

A woman stood there, on the porch. She wore a plain, black suit buttoned high under her chin and a black hat with a brim like a man's, pulled low over one eye, and he saw a tight black glove glistening in the poor light, on a slender, incredible hand grasping a black bag. He saw blond hair spilled in the air under the hat's brim. He had never met that woman before, but he knew her face well, too well.

"Please keep quiet," she whispered, "and let me in."

His five fingers were spread wide apart over his mouth and he stuttered foolishly:

"You . . . you . . . you are . . ,"

"Kay Gonda," said the woman.

His hands dropped like weights to his side, pulling his arms down. He had to learn to speak again. He tried. He made a long sound and it came out like: "W-w-what—"

"Are you George Perkins?" she asked.

"Y-yes," he stuttered. "Yes, ma'am. George Perkins. George S. Perkins. Yes."

"I am in trouble. You heard about it?"

"Y-yes . . . Oh, my God! . . . Yes . . ."

"I have to hide. For the night. Can you let me stay here?"

"Here?"

"Yes. For one night."

It could not be his living room around them. It could not be his house. He could not have heard what he had heard.

"But you . . ." He gulped. "That is . . . how . . . I mean, *why* did you . . ."

"I read your letter. And I thought that no one would look for me here. And I thought you would want to help me."

"I . . ." He choked. "I . . ." The words, coming back, were burning his throat that had lost all habit of sound. "Miss Gonda, you'll excuse me, please, you know it's enough to make a fellow . . . I mean, if I don't seem to make . . . I mean, if you need help, you can stay here the rest of your life, and if anyone tries to . . . There's nothing I wouldn't do for you . . . if you need me . . . me . . . Miss Gonda!"

"Thank you," she said.

"Come this way," he whispered. "Keep quiet. . . this way."

He led her up the stairs, and she followed like a shadow, and he could not hear her steps behind his heavy, shuffling ones.

He closed the door of his room and pulled the blinds over the windows. He stood staring at the pale face, the long mouth, the eyes in the shadows of long lashes, the eyes that saw too much, the eyes that were like a sound, like many sounds, saying something he wanted to understand, always one sound short, the last one, the one that would let him know the meaning of what they were saying.

"You . . ." he stuttered. "You . . . You're Kay Gonda."

"Yes," she said.

She threw her bag down on his bed. She took off her hat and threw it on his dresser. She pulled off her gloves, and he looked, bewildered, at the long transparent fingers, at hands that looked like a vision of human hands.

"You mean . . . you mean they're really after you?"

"The police," she said. She added calmly: "For murder, you know."

"Listen, they can't get you. Not you. That don't make sense. If there's anything I can . . ."

He stopped, his hand at his mouth. Down the corridor, steps were approaching, heavy, hurried steps with mules flapping against bare heels.

"George!" Mrs. Perkins' voice called from behind the door.

"Yes, d-dovey?"

"Who was that who rang the bell?"

"No . . . no one, dovey. Someone had the wrong address."

They stood still, listening to the mules flapping away, down the corridor.

"That was my wife," he whispered. "We . . . we better keep quiet. She's all right. Only she . . . she wouldn't understand."

"It will be dangerous for you," she said, "if they find me here."

"I don't care . . . I don't care about that."

She smiled at him, the slow smile he had seen so many times at the bottomless distance of a screen. But now the face was there before him, and he could see a light shadow of red on the pale lips.

"Well," he blinked, spreading his hands helplessly, "well, you just make yourself at home. You can sleep right here. I'll . . . I'll go down to the living room and . . ."

"No," she said. "I don't want to sleep. Stay here. You and I, we have so much to talk about."

"Oh, yes. Sure . . . that is . . . about what, Miss Gonda?"

She sat down on the bed, without noticing it, as if she'd lived there all her life.

He sat on the edge of a chair, gathering his old bathrobe tightly, wishing dimly, painfully, that he had bought the new robe he had seen on sale at the Day Company.

Her wide, pale, wondering eyes were looking at him, as if she were waiting. He blinked and cleared his throat.

"Pretty cold night, this is," he muttered.

"Yes."

"That's California for you . . . the Golden West," he added. "Sunshine all day, but cold as the . . . but very cold at night."

"Sometimes."

He felt as if she had seized something somewhere very deep inside of him, seized it and twisted it in her strange, bluish fingers, and was pulling it, so that it hurt him, a pain he remembered having known very long ago, and now he knew he could feel it again, and it made him choke.

"Yes," he said, "it sure is cold at night."

She said: "Give me a cigarette."

He leaped to his feet, fumbled in his coat pocket, produced a package, held it out to her, the package trembling. He struck three matches before he could light one. She leaned back, a red dot trembling at the end of the cigarette.

"I . . . I smoke this kind," he muttered. "Easier on your throat, they are."

He had waited forty years for this. Forty years—to see a slender black figure sitting on the patchwork quilt of his bed. He had not believed it, but he had been waiting for it. He knew he had been waiting. What was it he wanted to say to her?

He said:

"Now, Joe Tucker—that's a friend of mine—Joe Tucker, he smokes cigars. But I never took to them, never did."

"You have many friends?" she asked.

"Yes, sure. Sure I have. Can't complain."

"You like them?"

"Sure. I like them fine."

"And they like you? They respect you and bow to you on the street?"

"Why . . . why, I guess so . . ."

"How old are you, George Perkins?"

"I'll be forty-five this coming June."

"It will be hard—won't it?—to lose your job and to find yourself in the street? In a dark, lonely street where you'll see your friends passing by and looking past you, as if you did not exist? Where you will want to scream out and tell them of the great things you know, but no one will hear and no one will answer?"

"Why . . . when . . . when would that happen?"

"When they find me here," she said calmly.

"Listen," he said. "Don't you worry about that. They won't find you here. Not that I'm afraid for myself."

"They hate me, George Perkins. And they hate all those who take my side."

"Why should they hate you?"

"I'm a murderess, George Perkins."

"Well, if you ask me, I don't believe it. I don't even want to ask you if you've done it. I just don't believe it."

"If you mean Granton Sayers . . . no, I don't want to speak about Granton Sayers. Forget that. But I am still a murderess. In so many ways. You see, I came here and, perhaps, I'll destroy your life— everything that has been your life for forty-five years."

"That's not much, Miss Gonda," he whispered.

"Do you always go to see my pictures?"

"Always."

"Are you happy when you come out of the theater?"

"Yes. Sure. . . . No. I guess I'm not. That's funny, I never thought of it that way. I . . . Miss Gonda," he said suddenly, "you won't laugh at me if I tell you something?"

"Of course not."

"Miss Gonda, I . . . I cry when I come home after every picture of yours. I just lock myself in the bathroom and I cry, every time. I don't know why. I know it's silly for a grown man like me . . . I've never told that to a soul, Miss Gonda."

"I know that."

"You . . . did?"

"I told you I'm a murderess. I kill so many things. I kill the things men live for. But they come to see me, because I make them see that they want those things killed. That they want to live for something greater. Or they think they do. And it's their whole pride—that they think and say they do."

"I—I'm afraid I don't quite get you, Miss Gonda."

"You'll understand someday."

"Look," he asked, "did you really do it?"

"What?"

"Did you kill Granton Sayers?"

She looked at him and did not answer.

"I . . . I was only wondering why you could have done it," he muttered.

"Because I couldn't stand it any longer. There are times when one can't stand it any longer."

"Yes," he said. "There are." And then his voice was steady and natural and sure of itself. "Look," he said, "I won't let the cops get you. Not if they had to tear the house down. Not if they came with gas bombs and such."

"Why?" she asked.

"I don't know . . . Only that . . ."

"Your letter, it said . . ."

"Oh," he faltered, "you know, I never thought you'd read the silly thing."

"It was not silly."

"Well, you must forgive me, Miss Gonda, but you know how it is with movie fans, and I bet you have plenty of them—fans, I mean, and letters."

"I like to think that I mean something to people."

"You must forgive me if I said anything fresh, you know, or personal."

"You said you were not happy."

"I . . . I didn't mean to complain, Miss Gonda, or . . . It was only . . . How can I explain? . . . I guess I've missed something along the way. I don't know what it is, but I know I've missed it, only I don't know why."

"Maybe it's because you wanted to miss it."

"No." His voice was firm. "No." He rose and stood looking straight at her. "You see, I'm not unhappy at all. In fact, I'm a very happy man—as happiness goes. Only there's something in me that knows of a life I've never lived, the kind of a life no one has ever lived, but should."

"You know it? Why don't you live it?"

"Who does? Who can? Who even gets a chance at the . . . the very best possible to him? We all bargain. We take the second best. That's all there is to be had. But the . . . the God in us, it knows the other . . . the very best . . . which never comes."

"And . . . if it came?"

"We'd grab it—because there is a God in us."

"And . . . you really want that? That God in you?"

"Look," he said fiercely, "I know this: let them come, the cops, let them come now and try to get you. Let them tear the house down. I built it—took me fifteen years to pay for it. Let them tear it down, brick by brick. Let them come, whoever it is that's after you . . ."

The door was flung open.

Mrs. Perkins stood on the threshold, her fist clutching her faded blue corduroy robe in a tight huddle in the middle of her stomach. A long nightgown of grayish-pink cotton hung to the tips of her pink mules with faded velvet bows. Her hair was combed tightly back to a thin knot, and a hairpin was sliding down her neck. She was trembling.

"George!" she gasped. "George!"

"Dovey, keep quiet. . . . Come in . . . Close the door!"

"I . . . I thought I heard voices." The hairpin disappeared between her shoulder blades.

"Rosie . . . this . . . Miss Gonda, may I present—my wife? Rosie, this is Miss Gonda, you, Miss Kay Gonda!"

"Indeed?" said Mrs. Perkins.

"Rosie . . . oh, for God's sake! Don't you understand? This is Miss Gonda, the movie star. She's . . . she's in trouble, you know, you've heard about it, the papers said . . ."

He turned desperately to his guest, waiting for support. But Kay Gonda did not move. She had risen, and she stood, her arms hanging limply at her sides, her huge eyes looking at them without blinking, without expression.

"All my life," said Mrs. Perkins, "I've known you were a rotter and a liar, George Perkins! But this beats it all! To have the nerve to bring that tramp right into your own home, into your bedroom!"

"Oh, shut up! Rosie! Listen! It's a great honor that Miss Gonda chose to . . . Listen! I—"

"You're drunk, that's what you are! And I won't listen to a single word out of you until this tramp is out of the house!"

"Rosie! Listen, calm yourself, for God's sake, listen, there's nothing to get excited about, only that Miss Gonda is wanted by the police and . . ."

"Oh!"

". . . and it's for murder . . ."

"Oh!"

". . . and she just has to stay here overnight. That's all."

Mrs. Perkins drew herself up and tightened her robe, and her night-gown stood out in a bump over her chest, a faded blue pattern of roses and butterflies trembling on the grayish pink.

"Listen to me, George Perkins," she said slowly. "I don't know what's happened to you. I don't know. I don't care. But I know this: either she goes out of this house this minute, or else I go."

"But, dovey, let me explain."

"I don't need no explanations. I'll pack my things, and I'll take the children, too. And I'll pray to God never to see you again."

Her voice was slow and calm. He knew she meant it, this time.

She waited. He did not answer.

"Tell her to get out," she hissed through her teeth.

"Rosie," he muttered, choking, "I can't."

"George," she whispered, "it's been fifteen years . . ."

"I know," he said, without looking at her.

"We've struggled together pretty hard, haven't we? Together, you and me."

"Rosie, it's just one night . . . if you know . . ."

"I don't want to know. I don't want to know why my husband should bring such a thing upon me. A fancy woman or a murderess, or both maybe. I've been a faithful wife to you, George. I've given you the best years of my life. I've borne your children."

"Yes, Rosie . . ."

He looked at her drawn face, at the wrinkles around her thin mouth, at the hand that still held the faded robe in a foolish knob on her stomach.

"It's not for me, George. Think of what'll happen to you. Shielding a murderess. Think of the children."

"Yes, Rosie . . ."

"And your job, too. And you just got that promotion. We were going to get new drapes for the living room. The green ones. You always wanted them."

"Yes, Rosie."

"They won't keep you down at the company, when they hear of this."

"No, Rosie."

He looked desperately for a word, for a glance from the woman in black. He wanted her to decide. But she did not move, as if the scene did not concern her at all.

"Think of the children, George."

He did not answer.

"We've been pretty happy together, haven't we, George? . . . Fifteen years . . ."

He thought of the dark night beyond the window, and beyond that night an endless world, unknown and menacing. He liked his room. Rosie had worked a year and a half, making the quilt for him. The woman had blond hair, a cold, golden blond, that one would never dare to touch. Rosie had knitted that tie, over on the dresser, in blue and green stripes, for his birthday. The woman had thin white hands that did not look human. In another year, Junior would be ready for high school; and he had always thought of that college where Junior would wear a black robe and a funny square cap. The woman had a smile that hurt him. Rosie cooked the best corn fritters, just as he liked them. The assistant treasurer had always envied him, had always wanted to be assistant manager, and now he had beat him to it. That golf club had the best links in town, and only the best of members, solid, respectable members; not with their fingerprints in the police files and pictures in all the papers as accessories after the fact of murder. The woman had spoken of a dark, lonely street where he would want to scream . . .

scream . . . scream. . . . . Rosie had been a good wife to him, hard-working, and patient, and faithful. He had twenty years to live yet, maybe thirty, no more. After all, life was over.

He turned to the woman in black.

"I'm sorry, Miss Gonda," he said, and his voice was efficient, like the voice of an assistant manager addressing a secretary, "but under the circumstances—"

"I understand," said Kay Gonda.

She walked to the dresser and put her hat on, pulling it down over one eye. She put on her gloves and picked up her bag from the bed.

They walked silently down the stairs, the three of them, and George S. Perkins opened the door. Kay Gonda turned to Mrs. Perkins.

"I'm sorry," she said. "I had the wrong address."

They stood and watched her walking away down the street, a slender black figure with golden hair that flashed once in the light of a lamppost.

Then George S. Perkins put his arm around his wife's waist.

"Is Mother asleep?" he asked.

"I don't know. Why?"

"I thought I'd go in and talk to her. Make up, sort of. She knows all about buying Frigidaires."

3

Jeremiah Sliney

"Dear Miss Gonda,

I think you are the greatest moving pichur star ever lived. I think yur moving pichurs is swell. I want to thank you from the bottom of my hart for the joy you giv us in our old age. There is plenty of other pichur stars onlie it aint the same thing. There aint none like you and never was. My wife and me just wait for evry pictur of yurs and we set thru all the shows and come back the nex day. It aint like if we just liked you. It is like goin to church goin to your picturs that's wat its like, onlie beter. I aint never understan it myself on akount of you act bad womin and such but what you mak me think of is a statoo of the Saint Mother of God what I see once onlie I dont no how that is. Yur what we'd like a doter of ours to hav bin onlie never had. We hav three children my wife and me, too girls of them onlie it aint the same. We are onlie old folks, Miss Gonda, an yur all we got. We want to thank you onlie I don't no how to say it on akount of I never rote no letter to a swell lady like you. And if ever we cood do sumthin to show how grateful we are to you we'd just die happie on akount of we aint got much longer to go.

Resspecfully yurs,
Jeremiah Sliney
Ventura Boulevard
Los Angeles, California"

On the evening of May 5th, Jeremiah Sliney celebrated his golden wedding anniversary.

The table was set in the middle of the living room. Mrs. Sliney had taken out the best set of silverware, and polished it all morning, and laid it out carefully under the light of a hanging brass oil lamp.

"Are we gonna have turkey?" she had asked that morning.

"Sure," Jeremiah Sliney had answered.

"It's the last one left, Pa. I was just thinkin' maybe if we took it to town we could get maybe—"

"Aw, Ma, there's only one golden anniversary in the whole of yer life."

She had sighed and shuffled into the backyard to catch the turkey.

The table was set for nine. The children had gathered to celebrate. After the lemon chiffon pie was served, Jeremiah Sliney winked naughtily and opened a gallon jug of his best hard cider.

"Well," he said, chuckling, "fur the occasion."

"You know very well," said Mrs. Eustace Hennessey, the oldest daughter, "that I never touch the stuff."

"I'll take Maudie's," said Mrs. Chuck Fink, the youngest.

"Now, now," said Chuck Fink, beaming, "everybody's gotta drink for the happy event. Can't hurt nobody! A little glass a day keeps the doctor away."

"I'm sure I won't let Melissa have any," said Mrs. Eustace Hennessey. "I don't know how some people do, but I bring my daughter up as a lady should be brung up."

Jeremiah Sliney filled eight glasses. Melissa Hennessey, the only grandchild old enough to be present, threw a dark glance at her mother, but said nothing. Melissa Hennessey spoke seldom. She was twenty, although her mother insisted that she was eighteen. She had faded brown hair in tight ringlets of an unsuccessful permanent wave around a face dotted with perpetual pimples. She wore a long green dress of dotted swiss with stylish ruffles, high and stiff on her shoulders, flat brown oxfords with fringed tongues, and a brand-new wristwatch on a leather band.

"Veter santee, as they say in society," said Mrs. Ulysses S. Grant Sliney haughtily, raising her glass.

"Aw, can the fancy stuff, Angelina," said Ulysses S. Grant Sliney gloomily. He had a long nose and a collar too wide for his thin neck, and he always looked gloomy.

Angelina Sliney shrugged. Her big celluloid earrings tinkled against her neck and the five celluloid bracelets tinkled against the knob of her wrist bone.

"A toast!" roared Chuck Fink. "Gotta have a toast."

"Aw, now," said Jeremiah Sliney, standing helplessly, hunched, embarrassed, spreading wide his two hands with a short stump in the place of his left forefinger. "Well, now, I never in my life . . . I wouldn't know how to . . . I . . ."

"I'll make it for you," said Chuck Fink, bouncing up. He was not very tall when he stood up; his vest was stretched over a round stomach; his smile was stretched over a round face with a short nose with wide nostrils.

"To the best little parents that ever breathed God's sunshine," said Chuck Fink, beaming. "Many happy returns to one happy family. Be it ever so humble, there's no place like the good old farm."

Mrs. Eustace Hennessey nudged her husband. Eustace Hennessey had gone to sleep, his long face nodding over his pie plate. He jerked, one hand fumbling for his glass, the other one for his mustache, twisting it mechanically up into a sharp, thin needle of a glossy, waxed black.

Then they all drank but Melissa.

Mrs. Jeremiah Sliney sat silently in the shadows at the head of the table, her little hands folded in her lap, her white lips smiling in a gentle, wordless blessing. She had the serene face of a wrinkled cherub and glossy white hair, well brushed, combed tightly to a yellow knob on the back of her head. She wore her best dress of patched purple taffeta and a little shawl of yellow lace held by her best pin of tarnished gold.

"Well," said Mrs. Eustace Hennessey, "the good old farm and all that is all very well, but I do think you oughta do something about that road, Pa. Honest, it's enough to shake a body's guts out to drive up here."

"Well," said Angelina Sliney, "you can stand a bit once in a while. God knows, you don't do it often."

"When I need telling to," said Mrs. Eustace Hennessey, "I'll choose the people to do the telling."

"Aw, now, Maudie," said Eustace Hennessey, yawning, "the road ain't so bad. You oughta see some of the roads a fellow's gotta travel in this here country."

Eustace Hennessey was a traveling salesman for a cosmetic concern.

"Some people," said Mrs. Chuck Fink, "sure do have to travel. And then again, some don't."

Chuck Fink owned his business, an all-night restaurant on South Main Street, Chuck's Place, with eight stools by the counter and an electric coffee boiler.

"Now, now, Flobelle," said Jeremiah Sliney, sensing danger, "we all do the best we can, as God permits."

When the table was cleared, and they all sat silently in a circle on stiff, worn chairs and stared at the windows where tall gray weeds rustled softly against the sills; when Jeremiah Sliney lit his pipe, and Eustace Hennessey lit his cigar, and Angelina Sliney lit a cigarette under the smoldering glances of her sisters-in-law, and Melissa disappeared mysteriously into the kitchen, Mrs. Jeremiah Sliney sighed sweetly and said timidly, her little hands opening and closing nervously:

"Now, about that mortgage . . . it's due day after tomorrow."

There was a dead silence.

"Funny how many people drive around these days," said Chuck Fink, looking at the distant headlights in the hills, "and at this time of the night. And in the hills, too."

"If we don't pay, they'll take the house. The mortgage people, I mean," said Mrs. Jeremiah Sliney.

"Hard times, these are," said Mrs. Eustace Hennessey. "We all have our troubles."

"If . . . It would be a shame to lose the old house like that," said Jeremiah Sliney and chuckled. His pale blue eyes blinked under a moist, whitish film. His gentle old face smiled hesitantly.

"We all have our cross to bear," sighed Mrs. Eustace Hennessey. "Times ain't what they used to be. Now, take us, for instance. There's Melissa's future to think about. A girl's gotta have a little something to offer to get herself a husband, these days. Men ain't so easily satisfied. It ain't like some folks what have their own business."

"Junior had the whooping cough," said Mrs. Chuck Fink hurriedly, "and the doctor's bills is something fierce. We'll never get outta debt. It ain't like some people that never knowed the blessing of parenthood."

She looked resentfully at Angelina Sliney. Angelina shrugged, her earrings tinkling.

"It's a good thing some people don't have no litter every nine months," said Ulysses S. Grant Sliney, gloomily. "A man's got a future to think about. How'm I ever gonna buy that meat counter of my own? Think I'm gonna sling hamburger for some other guy the rest of my life?"

"It's fifty years we've lived in this house," said Mrs. Jeremiah Sliney and sighed gently. "Oh my! What would ever become of us now?"

"With eggs the way they are," sighed Jeremiah Sliney, "and our last cow what we had to sell . . . we just don't have the money for the mortgage people at all." He chuckled. He always chuckled when he spoke, a hesitant little chuckle that sounded like a moan.

"Oh my!" sighed Mrs. Jeremiah Sliney. "It would be the . . . poorhouse for us."

"These are hard times," said Mrs. Eustace Hennessey.

There was a silence.

"Well," said Chuck Fink noisily, bouncing up, "here it is going on eleven and it's pretty near to twenty miles driving back home. Gotta be going, Flobelle. Time to hit the hay. Gotta get up early. It's the early bird that catches the good old nickels."

"Us, too," said Mrs. Eustace Hennessey, rising. "Melissa! Where's that girl gone to? Melissa!"

Melissa emerged from the kitchen, her face flushed red under the pimples.

There were many kisses and handshakes at the door.

"Now you run on to bed, Ma," said Mrs. Chuck Fink. "And don't you stay up late worrying."

"Well, so long, folks," said Chuck Fink, climbing into his car. "Cheer up and keep smiling. The darkest hour is just before the silver lining."

Mrs. Eustace Hennessey wondered why Melissa staggered uncertainly, getting into the car, as if she had trouble finding the door.

Mr. and Mrs. Jeremiah Sliney stood in the road and watched the three little red lights bumping away, low over the ground, in a soft cloud of dust.

Then they went back into the house, and Jeremiah Sliney locked the door.

"Oh my!" sighed Mrs. Sliney. "It's the poorhouse for us, Pa."

They had blown out the lights and pulled the blinds over the windows, and Mrs. Sliney in her limp flannel nightgown was ready to climb into bed, when she stopped suddenly, stretching her head forward, listening.

"Pa," she whispered, alarmed.

Jeremiah Sliney pulled the blanket from over his head.

"What is it?"

"Pa, d'you hear?"

"No. Hear what?"

"Sounds . . . sounds like someone was coming here."

"Nonsense, Ma. Some rabbit, most like . . ."

A hand knocked at the door.

"Lord in heaven!" whispered Mrs. Sliney.

Jeremiah Sliney fumbled for his slippers, threw an old coat over his shoulders, and shuffled resolutely to the door.

"Who's there?" he asked.

"Open the door, please," a low feminine voice whispered.

Jeremiah Sliney opened the door.

"What can I do for . . . Oh, Lord!" he finished, gasping, when he saw a pale face under a black hat, a face he recognized at once.

"I am Kay Gonda, Mr. Sliney," said the woman in black.

"Well, as I live and breathe!" said Jeremiah Sliney.

"Can you let me in?"

"Can I let you in? Can I let you in? Well, I'll be a— Come right in, ma'am, right, right in. . . . Ma! Oh, Ma! Come here! Oh Lord!"

He threw the door wide-open. She entered and closed it cautiously. Mrs. Sliney trudged in and froze on the threshold, her hands fluttering, her mouth wide-open.

"Ma!" gasped Jeremiah Sliney. "Ma, can you believe it? This here is Kay Gonda, the pichur star, herself!"

Mrs. Sliney nodded, her eyes wide, unable to utter a sound.

"I'm running away," said Kay Gonda. "Hiding. From the police. I have no place to go."

"Oh Lord! Oh Lord Almighty!"

"You heard about me, haven't you?"

"Have I heard? Why, who hasn't heard? Why, them papers said . . ."

"It was . . . murder!" whispered Mrs. Sliney, choking.

"May I stay here for the night?"

"Here?"

"Yes."

"Ye mean—right here?"

"Yes."

"Good God! Why . . . why, certainly, ma'am. Why, of course! Why, it's an honor ye're doing us and . . . and . . ."

"It's an honor, ma'am," said Mrs. Sliney, curtseying.

"Thank you," said Kay Gonda.

"Only," muttered Jeremiah Sliney, "only how did ye ever . . . I mean, how could ye . . . I mean, why would ye, of all places?"

"I had your letter. And no one would ever find me here."

"My . . . letter?"

"Yes. The letter you wrote me."

"Oh Lord, that? You got it?"

"Yes."

"And ye read it?"

"Yes."

"And ye . . . ye came here? To hide?"

"Yes."

"Well, will miracles ever cease! Why, make yerself to home, ma'am. Take your hat off. Sit down. Don't ye worry. No one will find ye here all right. And if any cops come nosing about, why, I have a shotgun, that's what I have! Make yerself to—"

"Wait a minute, Pa," said Mrs. Sliney, "that's not the way. Miss Gonda is tired, she is. She needs a room, a place to sleep, at this hour of the night."

"Ye come this way, ma'am . . . this way . . . the spare room. We have a nice spare room. No one'll bother ye."

Jeremiah Sliney opened a door, bowing. They let their guest enter and shuffled in hurriedly, breathlessly, after her. The room smelt of dried hay and pickles. Mrs. Sliney brushed quickly a cobweb off the windowsill.

"Here's a bed for ye," said Mrs. Sliney, hurriedly beating the pillow, pulling down a patched cotton blanket. "A nice soft bed for ye, ma'am. Just make yerself comfortable and sleep like a kitten."

"I'm sorry, ma'am, Miss Gonda. The place ain't so swell for a great lady like ye, but it's yours, same as this whole house. . . . My, I bet ye've seen some swell places out where the movie folk live!"

"It is very nice here, thank you."

"Just be careful of this chair, ma'am. It ain't very steady. . . . I bet it must make ye scared, don't it, when they work them cameras making pichurs?"

"I'll bring ye an extry blanket, ma'am. The nights are sorta chilly around here. . . . Oh my, what a pretty suit ye have, Miss Gonda! I reckon it cost all of twenty dollars, no less."

"I'll get ye some water in that pitcher, ma'am. And some nice clean towels . . . Dear me, ye look just like in them movies! I knew ye right at once!"

"Did it hurt ye, Miss Gonda, when that feller stuck you with that big knife, in the movie, last year that was?"

They fluttered nervously, eagerly about the room, without tearing their eyes from the strange visitor. Her slender shadow rose up the whitewashed wall, and her hair looked like a huge black flower on the ceiling with tangled petals flung wide.

"Thank you," she said, "I will be very comfortable here. . . . Please do not bother. I do not want to cause you so much trouble. Only, I will warn you, it's very dangerous, you know, keeping me here."

Jeremiah Sliney straightened his stooped shoulders proudly.

"Don't you worry about that, Miss Gonda. There ain't no cops in the world what can get you out of Jeremiah Sliney's house. Not while he's alive, they won't!"

Kay Gonda smiled and looked at them. Her eyes were round and clear and innocent like a frail little girl's, a very young girl in a dress too severe for her fragile body. She leaned against the dresser, and her hand looked like a piece of clouded crystal chiseled into old planks with bald patches of faded varnish.

"It is very kind of you," she said slowly. "But why do you want to take the chance? You do not know me."

"Ye . . . ye don't know, Miss Gonda," said Jeremiah Sliney, "what ye mean to us. We're old folks, Miss Gonda, poor old folks. We never had nothing like ye ever come to us. Cops, indeed! Ye don't think of cops in church, Miss Gonda, no more'n in this here room right now. And if . . .

oh gosh! Ye must forgive a driveling old fool like me! Just make yerself comfortable and don't ye worry about a thing. We'll be right here in the next room, if ye need anything. Good night, Miss Gonda."

There was no sound in the house, no light. Beyond the window, crickets chirped in the tall grass, a shrill, unceasing whistle, like the whining of a steady saw. A bird screamed somewhere in short, choked gasps and stopped, and screamed again. A moth beat dry, rustling wings against the window screen.

Kay Gonda lay on the bed, dressed, her hands under her head, her thin black pumps crossed on the faded old blanket. She did not move.

In the silence, she heard the bed creaking as someone turned over in the next room. She heard a heavy sigh. Then there was silence again.

Then she heard a voice, a soft muffled voice whispering hoarsely:

"Pa . . . You asleep, Pa-a?"

"No."

The woman sighed. Then she whispered:

"Pa, it's day after tomorrow . . . the mortgage is . . ."

"Yeah."

"It's seven hundred dollars, it is."

"Yeah."

The bed creaked as someone turned over.

"Pa-a . . ."

"Yeah?"

"They'll take the house."

"They sure will."

The bird screamed far away, in the silence.

"Pa-a, think she's asleep?"

"Must be."

"It's murder she's done, Pa. . . ."

"Yeah."

They were silent again.

"It's a rich feller what she's killed, Pa."

"The richest."

"Reckon his family, they'd like to know where she's at."

"What're ye talkin' about, woman?"

"Oh, I was just thinkin' . . ."

There was a silence.

"Pa, if they was told, his family, where she's at, it'ud be worth somethin' to them, wouldn't it?"

"Ye old . . . what're ye trying to—"

"Reckon they'd be glad to pay a reward. A thousand dollars, maybe."

"Huh?"

"A thousand dollars, maybe . . ."

"Ye old hag! Ye shut yer mouth before I choke ye!"

There was a long silence.

"Ma . . ."

"Yeah?"

"Think they'd . . . they'd hand over a . . . a thousand?"

"Sure they would. Them's folks with plenty of money."

"Aw, shut yer old face!"

A moth beat furiously against the window screen.

"It's the poorhouse for us, Pa. For the rest of our days."

"Yeah . . ."

"They pay more'n that for bank robbers and such, they do."

"Ye got no fear of God in ye, ye don't!"

"Fifty years, Pa. Fifty years in this house and now thrown out in the street in our old age. . . ."

"Yeah . . ."

"The children were born here, too . . . right in this room, Pa . . . all of them . . ."

"Yeah . . ."

"With a thousand, why, we'd have the house to the end of our days . . ."

He did not answer.

"And we could even build that new chicken coop we need so bad . . ."

There was a long silence.

"Ma . . ."

"Yeah?"

"How . . . how'd we go about it?"

"Why, easy. We just slip out while she's asleep. She won't hear a thing. We go to the sheriff's station. Come back with the cops. Easy."

"What if she hears?"

"She won't. Only we gotta hurry."

"The old truck rattles pretty bad starting."

"That's so."

"I'll tell ye what. We'll just push it out, the two of us, down to the road and down the road a ways, till we're far enough from the house. Ye just hold that board down that's loose in the back."

They dressed hurriedly, without a sound. There was only a faint creaking as the door opened and closed again. There was only a soft rumble down the driveway, a faint grating like a sigh lost in the grass.

They came back in a glistening car that skidded up to the door and stopped short, brakes screaming. Two blinding white headlights stretched far ahead, slashing the darkness. Two men in dark uniforms, their buttons sparkling, jumped out, and Jeremiah Sliney scrambled out after them, his coat hanging open at his bare throat.

When they entered the spare room, they found it empty. Only a strange, faint perfume still lingered in the air.

4

Dwight Langley

"Dear Miss Gonda,

You do not know me. Yet you are the only person whom I really know in the world. You have never heard my name. Yet all men will hear it, and they will hear it through you.

I am an unknown artist. But I know to what heights I shall rise, for I carry a banner that cannot fail—and that is you. I have painted nothing which was not you. I have never done a canvas on which you did not stand as a goddess.

I have never seen you in person. I do not need to. I can draw your face with my eyes closed. My spirit is but a mirror of yours. My art is but a radio set gathering the song which is you. I have no life but my art, and no art but you.

Some day, you shall hear of me again and not through a

letter of mine. Until then—this is only a first bow from your devoted priest—

Dwight Langley . . .

. . . Normandie Avenue

Los Angeles, California"

On the evening of May 5th, Dwight Langley received the first prize of the exposition for his last picture—*Pain*.

He stood leaning against the wall, shaking hands, nodding, smiling to an eager crowd that came streaming past him, pausing for a few minutes in a tight whirlpool around him; he stood like a rock in its path, a lonely, bewildered rock, cornered against the wall. Between handshakes, he brushed his forehead with the back of his hand, the cold back of his hand against his feverish eyelids. He smiled. He had no time to close his lips. His lips opened wide over even, white teeth in a tense sunburned face. His lids were half-closed over dark, haughty eyes.

There was a blue haze of fire around him. Beyond the tall windows, streetcars roared and a stream of white, round lights rolled, swirling, overflowing the street, rising in glittering sprays up the sides of the buildings; in twinkling signs, rising higher, to the roofs; still higher, to a few last specks of blue stars in the sky; and he thought that the huge white globes which seemed to float over him, under the ceiling, had been splattered into the room from the streets below, from the city aflame, closing in around him, greeting him.

A dull tide of feet rumbled against a marble floor. A huge fur of dark fox touched by a silver frost bobbed up and down through the tide. A long spray of bluish flowers bent from a black vase in a corner. A stifling mixture of delicate perfumes choked him, heavy as a fog over the lights.

On the walls, clear, resplendent, leaping out of the fog, the paintings stood like a row of trim combatants after a battle, proud in their defeat. One of them had won, the one that was his.

Dwight Langley nodded, and smiled, and said words he could not hear, and heard stealthy whispers in the crowd: "Kay Gonda, of course . . . Kay Gonda . . . Look closely at that smile . . . that mouth . . . Kay Gonda . . . Why, he . . . and she . . . Do you think? . . . Oh, no! Why, man, he's never met her. . . . I'll bet you. . . . He's never seen her, I tell you. . . . It's really Kay Gonda. . . Kay Gonda . . . Kay Gonda . . ."

Dwight Langley smiled. He answered questions he could not remember while he was answering them. He remembered the perfumes that choked him. He remembered the lights; and the hands that wrenched his; and the words, words he had prayed for, for such a long time, from old wrinkled heads who held his fate, and the fate of hundreds of others like him, and a newspaper woman with spectacles who insisted on knowing where he had been born.

Then someone had thrown an arm around his shoulders, and someone had shaken him, and someone had roared close to his ear: "Why, to celebrate, of course, Lanny, old pal!" and he was stumbling down endless stairs, he was riding in someone's open car, a cold wind tearing the hair on his hatless head.

They sat in a restaurant where people's chests were wedged into table edges, and table edges wedged into people's backs, and waiters glided sidewise, holding trays high. Dwight Langley did not know how many tables were occupied by their party or whether all the tables were occupied by their party. But he knew that many eyes were looking at him, and he heard echoes of his name rustling through the crowd, and he looked bored even though he would not miss one syllable. Glasses were sparkling and yellow, then empty, then sparkling and red, then empty again, then milky white with whipped cream running over the table, and someone across from him was bellowing loudly for ginger ale.

Dwight Langley leaned far across the table; a lock of black hair hung over his forehead and his white teeth glittered in his tanned face. He was saying:

"No, Dorothy, I won't pose for you."

A girl with straight, stubby hair that needed a cut was whining:

"Oh, hang it, Lanny, you're wasted as an artist, honest, you're wasted as just an artist, you ought to be a model, who ever heard of such a good-looking artist? You're ruining my career, if you don't pose for me, you are."

Someone broke a glass. Someone yelled insistently:

"What, no music? What, no music at all? No music of any kind? This is a hell of a joint!"

"Lanny, my pal, the yellow . . . the yellow of that woman's hair in that picture of yours . . . it's a new color . . . call it yellow since there's no other name . . . only it's not yellow . . . a new color, that's what you've done. . . . You could skin me alive before I could ever get anything like it."

"Don't try," said Dwight Langley.

Someone with a huge, red face stuffed a crumpled bill into a waiter's hand, muttering:

"Jush a mem'ry . . . Jush for a li'l mem'ry . . . You better remember that you had th' honor t' wait on the greatesht artisht of the twentiesh shnt'ry . . . th' greatesh damn artisht ever lived! . . ."

Then they were riding again, and one of the cars was held behind, and, driving on, they heard someone's loud argument with a traffic cop.

Then they were in someone's apartment, and a girl without stockings, in a very short skirt, and with protruding teeth, was shaking cocktails in a milk bottle. Someone turned on the radio and someone played Shubert's *Marche Militaire* on an upright piano out of tune. Dwight Langley sat on a broad daybed covered with faded cretonne, and most of the others sat on the floor. A couple tried to dance, stumbling over stretched legs.

Someone smelling of garlic was whispering confidentially:

"Well, Lanny, the troubles are over, eh? Pretty soon now it will be a Rolls-Royce at the door instead of the old wolf, eh?"

"Say, Lanny, do you know who that was who asked you to come have tea with him sometime? Do you? That was Mortimer Hendrickson himself!"

"No!"

"Yes. And if that guy says a fellow's made, he's made!"

"Did you ever," muttered the girl who needed a haircut, "did you ever see such long lashes as Lanny's on a man?"

Someone broke a bottle. Someone banged furiously at the bathroom door where someone else had been locked for a suspiciously long time. A woman with a long, black cigarette holder insisted on listening to a woman evangelist on the radio.

A landlady in a Chinese bathrobe came knocking at the door, ordering the noise stopped.

Someone was crying over a tall glass.

"You're a genius, Lanny, thash what you are, a genius, thash what you are, Lanny, and the world doesn't appreciate geniushesh . . ."

A young man with rouged lips played the *Moonlight Sonata* on the piano.

Dwight Langley lay stretched across the low bed. A slim girl with a blond, boyish bob and heavy breasts put her head on his shoulder, running her fingers through his hair.

Someone brought another gallon jug.

"Here's to Lanny!"

"To Lanny's future!"

"To Dwight Langley of California!"

"To the greatesht artisht that ever . . ."

Dwight Langley made a speech:

"The bitterest moment of an artist's life is the moment of his triumph. Not until the crowd surrounds him does he know how much alone he is. The artist is but a bugle calling to a battle no one wants to fight. The artist is but a cup offered to men, a cup filled with his own blood, but he can find no one thirsty. The world does not see and does not want to see that which he sees. Well, I'm not afraid. I laugh at them. I despise them. My contempt is my pride. My loneliness is my strength. I'm calling them to throw the doors of their lives open to the most sacred of all that is sacred, but those doors will remain closed forever . . . forever . . . What was I saying . . . Oh yes . . . forever . . ."

It was long past midnight when a car deposited Dwight Langley at the door of his studio on a quiet, palm-shaded street.

"No," he waved, staggering a little, at those who had brought him, "no, I don't want you to come up . . . I want t'be alone . . . alone . . ."

He walked swiftly across a neat lawn where a sign stood by the door: LADIES HATS MADE TO ORDER. HOMESTITCHING 5 CENTS A YD. A Spanish lantern hung over the open archway of the entrance. In a window at one side of the entrance two hats on wooden blocks stood dejectedly between voile curtains. In a window at the other side, a placard with a half-moon among stars announced: MADAME ZANDA PSYCHOLOGIST AND ASTROLOGIST. WHY WORRY? YOUR FUTURE FOR ONE DOLLAR.

He rose swiftly up the long, narrow, whitewashed Spanish stairway. A red carpet covered the stairs up to the second floor; the last flight, to the third, was bare, with the paint peeling off the creaking wooden steps, barely wide enough to let his slender body pass. He leaped two steps at once, light, exultant, his limbs swinging in the joy of movement, young, free, triumphant.

There was no light on his landing, but there was only one door—his—and he never locked it. He threw the door open.

Through tall windows, moonlight made broad blue bands across the room, across a jungle of paintings, and empty easels, and half-finished canvases leaning against chair legs. Through a broad skylight, a blue ray came to tear out of the darkness a charcoal sketch of Kay Gonda, a huge head thrown back, her neck curved, her breasts tense, naked.

Dwight Langley pressed the light button.

He stood still, frozen. A woman rose slowly and stood facing him at the other end of the room. Tall, erect, her shoulders thrown back, so slender that she seemed to sway in the draft from the door, and she stood, all black to the tips of her fingers, to the tips of her thin pumps, against a black velvet curtain, so that he saw only a face, at first, a luminous face of white light with shadows of blue light under its cheekbones.

He stood motionless, his eyebrows rising. She did not move; she did not say a word.

"Well?" he asked, at last, frowning.

She did not answer.

"What are you doing here?" he asked impatiently.

"May I stay here for the night?" she whispered.

"Here? What's the idea?"

"I'm in danger."

He smiled contemptuously, slipping his hands into his trouser pockets.

"Just who are you?" asked Dwight Langley.

The woman answered:

"I am Kay Gonda."

Dwight Langley crossed his arms and laughed.

"So? That's who you are? Not Helen of Troy? Not Madame Du Barry?"

Kay Gonda's eyes widened slowly, huge, unblinking; but she did not move.

"Come on," said Dwight Langley, "out with it. What's the gag?"

"Don't you know me?" she whispered.

He looked her over, his hands in his pockets, grinning scornfully.

"Well, you do look like Kay Gonda," he remarked. "So does her stand-in. So do dozens of extra girls in Hollywood. What is it you're after? I can't get you into pictures, my girl. I'm not even the kind to promise a screen test. Come on, who are you?"

"Kay Gonda."

"Prowling through the streets, entering strange houses?" He laughed bitterly. "There's only one Kay Gonda. I know her. But no one else does. I have dedicated my life to tell men of her. To awaken in their souls a hunger for her who is the unattainable. She can never enter our lives, nor our houses. Our fate is but to sing of her, and to pour our souls into a sacred, hopeless hymn, and to glory in our suffering and our longing. Only you can't understand. No one can. And now, out with it: what do you want?"

She crossed her hands behind her back, her shoulders hunched forward, but head raised, looking straight at him, in her eyes a plea that looked like a strange, quiet menace. She said slowly:

"I don't know. That's why I'm here."

"What's on your mind?"

"Nothing. Only that I'm so tired!"

"Of what?"

"Of searching. I've searched for such a long time!"

"For what?"

"I don't know. I thought maybe I could find it out—here."

"Come on, cut the joking! Who are you?"

She walked toward him. She stood, looking at him, her eyes pleading; she stood in the midst of paintings that were as dozens of mirrors tearing her body into dozens of splinters of reflections, throwing back at her her pale eyes, her white arms, her lips, her breasts, her bluish shoulders, mirrors playing with her body, coloring it in drapes of flaming scarlet, in tunics of luminous blue, while she stood, black and slender, only her hair alike all through the room, like dozens of pale golden stars scattered around them, filling the studio, rising from their feet to above their heads.

"Please let me stay here," she whispered, her lips glistening.

Dwight Langley stood erect, and his dark eyes were blazing.

"Listen," he said slowly, his voice tense as an electric current tearing through an overcharged wire, "I have but one life, like all people. Only their lives are broken into many words and values. Mine's all in one word, and that word is "Kay Gonda." That is all I bring to the world, all I have to tell it, all I have to teach. That is all my blood, all my religion. And you come to tell me that you are Kay Gonda, me, who would know her if anyone is ever to know her! Get out of here!"

"Please!" she whispered. "I need your help."

"Get out of here!"

"I took such a chance coming to you."

"Get out of here!"

"Don't you know how alone I am?"

"Get out!"

Her hands fell limply and her black bag swung at the tips of two lifeless fingers. She turned and walked to the door.

He stood, his throat heaving, his breath coming in gasps.

She walked out slowly, and he saw her hair in the darkness of the landing, and he heard her steps descending the stairs.

Dwight Langley slammed the door.

5

Claude Ignatius Hix

"Dear Miss Gonda,

Some may call this letter a sacrilege. Some may call it a betrayal of my sacred trust. And yet it is not. For when I write it, I do not feel as a sinner stooping to mundane matters. I feel as I do when I compose my sermons, and that is something which I fail to understand, which will pass the comprehension of any who might chance to read these humble lines.

A wide, wide world lies at your feet, Miss Gonda, a sad, sinful world to whom you are but the condensed symbol of all its flaming sins. To countless erring souls you are but the flower of evil, with all the power and all the dark beauty that evil has possessed since time immemorial. Yet when my sermons scourge those works of corruption which offer you to the world, I find no words in my soul against you.

For when I look at you, it seems to me sometimes—and the Lord forbid that any of my flock should ever hear this, for no understanding can I expect from their poor, blind hearts—it seems to me sometimes that we are working for the same cause, you and I. That is all I can say to you, for it is not in my power to explain it.

But when I lay my soul on the altar of the Eternal Spirit, when I call my brother man to the Truth of life, the sacred Truth and the sacred Joy that is beyond their sad little anguishes of the flesh, beyond their ephemeral little pleasures—it seems to me that in your heart there is that same eternal, transcendent, sublime Truth which my words struggle in vain to disclose to them. We are traveling different roads, Miss Gonda, you and I, but we are bound to the same destination.

Or are we? Perhaps, you may laugh in scorn, you great priestess of Mammon, at these words of a humble man of God who believes, in his folly, that *you* are that which he is trying to bring to this earth of ours. But I believe as I do, because, in my heart of hearts, I believe also that you will understand.

Your humble servant,

Claude Ignatius Hix

. . . Slosson Blvd.

Los Angeles, California"

On the evening of May 5th, Claude Ignatius Hix found only a dollar eighty-seven in his collection box.

He sighed and counted the worn nickels, the dull little coppers once more. He put them down carefully into a rusty tin box and locked it.

The Temple of Eternal Truth of the Spirit needed an organ so badly. Well, he would still get it. He would go without that reconditioned car he had been waiting to buy for such a long time; he could ride the trolleys a little longer, but he would get the organ.

He blew out the two tapers on the pulpit, tall, white, real tapers which he always lit for the services. He closed the windows. He took a broom from a corner and swept the floor carefully, between the long rows of narrow, backless, unpainted benches. The broom swished in the silence of the long, dim barn and the electric bulb in the middle of the ceiling threw his lonely shadow across the benches.

He stood at the open door and looked at the sky, which was clear with a bright moon; it would not rain tomorrow. He was glad. The roof of the Temple of Eternal Truth of the Spirit leaked badly between its unpainted beams.

Rain would spoil the long cotton bands nailed to the dark walls inside the Temple; bands with careful, even letters of red and blue, which he himself had painted for so many long, weary, painstaking hours.

BLESSED ARE THE MEEK: FOR THEY SHALL INHERIT THE EARTH.

BLESSED ARE THE POOR IN SPIRIT: FOR THEIRS IS THE KINGDOM OF HEAVEN.

HE THAT LOVETH HIS LIFE SHALL LOSE IT AND HE THAT HATETH HIS LIFE IN THIS WORLD SHALL KEEP IT UNTO LIFE ETERNAL.

Claude Ignatius Hix walked slowly up the aisle. His tall lean body was always carried erect, as if an old-fashioned photographer had clamped an iron vise to his back, to keep it faultlessly straight. His thick black hair was beginning to recede off his high forehead and white streaks were growing slowly on his temples. His head was carried high, and his long, thin face was stern, patient, serene in its haughty calm with its dark eyes, fiery and young among the first, dry little wrinkles. His clothes were always black and he carried his long, white fingers entwined on his chest, and his clothes made one think of somber, floating garments, even though his white collar was slightly wilted and his nails were not always clean.

He sat down on the steps of his old pulpit and his forehead fell wearily into the palm of his hand. He could no longer hide from himself the dim, growing anguish of his heart. The Temple of Eternal Truth of the Spirit did not fare so well anymore. His congregation was slipping away from him, slowly, steadily, like a thin trickle of sand from an old, leaking jug. Fewer faces were raised to his pulpit at each service, fewer hearts were there to receive the cherished, passionate words he had toiled so devotedly to prepare for them.

He knew well the reason. A rival had moved into his neighborhood, not six blocks away, and he had seen the old faces he knew so well in the new Church of the Cheery Corner, the Little Church with the Big Blue Dome, where the Reverend Essie Twomey "guided in glory." The Reverend Essie Twomey had chestnut curls worn down her neck and buds of Cecile Brunner roses in her curls. The Church of the Cheery Corner had shingled walls painted a thick, glossy white and a real dome of baby blue. Claude Ignatius Hix would not have minded it if his flock had found consolation and spiritual food outside of his Temple; but he did not believe in Sister Twomey's sincerity.

He had attended one of her sermons announced as "The Service Station of the Spirit" in big red letters over the door of her church. Sister Twomey had had a whole service station built behind her pulpit, with tall glass pumps labeled: PURITY, DEVOTION, PRAYER, and PRAYER WITH FAITH UNSURPASSED; and tall, slender young boys stood in attendance, dressed in white uniforms with gold wings on their shoulders, and white caps with gold visors and gold letters that said: Creed Oil Inc. She had preached a long sermon to the effect that when you travel the hard road of life, you must be sure that your tank is filled with the best gas of Faith, that your tires are full of the air of Kindness, that your radiator is cooled with the sweet water of Temperance, that your battery is charged with the power of Righteousness, and that you beware of treacherous Detours which lead to perdition. She had warned against blasphemous road hogs, and given long, vigorous samples of their blasphemy, as contrasted to the manner of a driver pure in heart. The congregation had laughed happily, and sighed thoughtfully, and dropped crackling bills into the collection box in the shape of a gasoline can.

Claude Ignatius Hix sat alone on his pulpit steps. Beyond his open door the night was dark and soft, and a lonely streetcar rattled somewhere in the silence.

This had been the evening when, for the first time in his life, he had not finished his sermon. It had been the best sermon he had ever written; he had squeezed, out of the depth of his soul, the most delicate, the most eloquent, words his faith could command. But when he had stood on the pulpit and looked down at the rows of gray, empty benches, at the white eyes of a blind old woman, the bowed neck of a lanky tramp who drew patterns with his toe in the dust of the floor, the nodding bald head of a beggar who had fallen asleep, the few stooped, frayed, weary, huddled bodies scattered through the room, his words had died on his lips. He had cut the sermon short, given his blessing, and watched them file out slowly, holding in his hand, guiltily, the tin cup with their humble donations.

He knew well why his Temple had been deserted that evening. The Reverend Essie Twomey was conducting one of her famous midnight services: "The Night Life of the Angels." It was a daring innovation that kept her humble parishioners up at a later hour than they had ever stayed before and it had proved to be Sister Twomey's greatest success. Claude Ignatius Hix had seen it: there was a bar built behind her pulpit, a glittering bar of tinsel and gold foil, with a bartender in flowing white robes, with a big white beard, vaguely reminiscent of Saint Peter, except for the fact that he had neglected to remove his pince-nez; there were angels in white garments, with white, powdered faces and lips painted a deep pink, sitting on tall stools, holding cocktails in the form of long paper scrolls with mixed quotations from the scriptures. The Reverend Essie Twomey, small and plump in a Grecian tunic of silver gauze, her white, round arms bare and loaded with calla lilies, talked for many hours, swaying, closing her eyes, moaning softly, chanting hoarsely, screaming triumphantly, her round cheeks stretched into a radiant smile.

He could not fight it. He had failed. He had nothing left but to move out of the neighborhood, to give up the poor souls for whom he had fought so desperately. He had failed.

He rose heavily from the pulpit steps and threw his shoulders back, and walked steadily down the aisle to the door. He pressed a button to light the electric cross on the wall, over his pulpit. That cross was his greatest pride, the most expensive fixture of his Temple, erected at the cost of many sacrifices, many privations through many long years. He lit it at night, when he went home, leaving the Temple door wide-open. Over the entrance was a sign, THIS DOOR NEVER CLOSES, and all night long in the depth of the dark, narrow barn a white cross of fire flamed on a blank wall.

Claude Ignatius Hix walked slowly across a desolate backyard to his home, a forlorn shack behind the Temple. The backyard was a dreary stretch of ruts and dried weeds, lighted red and blue by the thick spurts of steam billowing over a neon sign on a yellow brick laundry next door.

Halfway to his house, Claude Ignatius Hix stopped suddenly. He heard steps behind him, very light, hurried steps, and he turned to see the tall, dark shadow of a woman disappearing into the Temple.

He stood still, perplexed. He had never seen a visitor at such a late hour. And the stranger seemed well dressed; not the type of worshipper he had ever met in the neighborhood. He should not disturb her; but perhaps she needed advice in the secret sorrow that had sent her, long past midnight, to this lonely place of worship. He walked resolutely back to the Temple.

The woman stood under the cross. Her long black suit was severe as a man's; her golden hair rose like a halo over her face, the pale face of a saint. For the flash of a second, he thought suddenly, crazily, that a statue of the Madonna stood there, at his altar, in the rays of the cross.

He took a step forward. Then he stopped short. He knew her face, but he could not believe it. He passed his hand over his eyes. He gasped:

"You . . . you're not . . ."

"Yes," she answered. "I am."

"Not . . . Kay Gonda?"

"Yes," she said. "Kay Gonda."

"To what . . ." he stuttered, "to what do I owe this honor, the rare honor of . . ."

"To a murderer," she answered.

"You don't mean . . . you don't mean that it's true, those rumors . . . those vile rumors . . ."

"I'm hiding. From the police."

"But . . . how . . ."

"Do you remember a letter? A letter you wrote me?"

"Yes."

"That's why I'm here. May I stay?"

Claude Ignatius Hix walked slowly to the open door and locked it. Then he came back to her. He said:

"That door has not been closed for thirteen years. It will be closed tonight."

"Thank you."

"You are safe here. You are safe as in that kingdom beyond where no human arrow can reach you."

She sat down and took off her hat and shook her blond hair.

He stood looking down at her, his fingers entwined on his chest.

"My sister," he said, and his voice trembled, "my poor misguided sister, it's a heavy burden that you've taken upon your shoulders."

She looked up at him and in her clear, blue eyes was a sorrow no screen had ever shown to the world.

"Yes," she answered, "a heavy burden. And sometimes I do not know how much longer I want to carry it."

He smiled sadly. But in his heart it seemed to him that the long years of toil were light on his shoulders; in his heart was a great joy, such as he had never known. And he felt guilty.

He felt as if he were taking something to which he had no right, even though he could not name what it was nor how he was taking it. On the dark wall, the flaming cross looked at him with accusation, and the dozens of white bulbs were as dozens of eyes, fixed, stern, condemning.

Then he knew what it was that he had forgotten.

He turned away from her. His head was high and his fingers were tense and grim on his chest. He said softly, "You are safe here, sister. No one will follow you here. No one will reach you, but one person only."

"And who is that?"

"Yourself."

She looked up at him, her head bent to one shoulder, her eyes curious.

"Myself?"

"You may escape the judgment of the world. But the judgment of your conscience will follow you wherever you go."

She said softly:

"I do not understand you."

His eyes were blazing. He stood over her, grim, austere as a judge.

"You have committed a sin. A mortal sin. You have broken a Commandment. You have taken a human life. Will you carry that on your conscience to the end of your days?"

"But what can I do?"

"Great is the power of our Father. And great is His kindness. And forgiveness awaits the darkest of sinners who offers his penitence and confession from the depth of his soul."

"But if I confess, they will put me in jail."

"Ah, my sister, would you rather go free? What would you be profited if you shall gain the whole world and lose your own soul?"

"And of what account is a soul without a world to gain?"

"Ah, my child, pride is the greatest of our sins. Verily the greatest. Did not His Son say unto us: 'except ye be converted and become as little children, ye shalt not enter into the kingdom of heaven'?"

"But why should I want to enter it?"

"If you know of a life that is supreme joy and beauty—how can you help but want to enter it?"

"How can I help but want it here, *here*?"

"Ours is a dark, imperfect world, my child."

"Why is it not perfect? Because it can't be? Or because we don't want it to be?"

"Ah, my child, who among us doesn't want it? We all have that lost hope, that ray of light in the darkest one of us, that shining dream of something better than our lives, which it is not given us to reach."

"We all want it?"

"Yes, my child."

"And if it came, we would see it?"

"Yes."

"But would we want to see it?"

"Who among us would not give his life gladly for a glimpse of it? But ours is a world of tears and iniquity. And paltry are its best rewards. Yet eternal happiness awaits us there, beyond, and eternal beauty such as our poor spirits can never conceive. If only we renounce our sins and repent before Him. And you have sinned, my child. You have sinned heavily. But He is kind and merciful. Repent, repent with your whole heart, and He shall hear you!"

"Then you want me to be hanged?"

"My sister! My poor, lost, anguished sister! Do you not know that it is a greater sacrifice I am making than you are? Do you not know that I am wrenching my own heart out at the altar of our duty? That I would rather take you away and flee to the end of the world, and protect you with my last dying breath? Only it's a poor service I would be doing you. I would rather save your soul and see mine writhing in the worst of all mortal agonies!"

She rose and stood before him, fragile, helpless, and her eyes were wide, frightened and she whispered:

"What do you want me to do?"

"Take upon your shoulders, bravely and willingly, the cross of your punishment. Confess! Confess your crime to the world! You are a great woman. The world lays its homage at your feet. Humble yourself. Go out into the very crowd on the marketplace and shout to the hearing of all men that you have sinned! Do not be afraid of what punishment may await you. Accept it humbly and joyously."

"Now?"

"Right now!"

"But there is no crowd anywhere at this hour."

"At this hour . . . at this hour . . ." He knew suddenly the thought that had been growing dimly somewhere in his mind. "My sister, at this very hour, a large crowd is gathered in a temple of error, not six blocks away, a poor, eager crowd searching for salvation. That's where we'll go! I'll take you there. I'll bring you in to show those poor, blind souls what real faith can do. To them you will confess your crime. For their sake will you offer your great sacrifice, for your brother men!"

"My brother men?"

"Think of them, my child. You have a great duty to your brothers on earth, as you have to your Father in Heaven, for all are His children. Look at them! They suffer in sin and in sin do they perish. You have a great chance, verily a blessed chance, to show them the true light of the Spirit. Great is your fame and your name will be heard to the four corners of the earth. They will know of the woman I rescued, the great woman who heard the call of the Truth, and they will follow your example."

He was thinking of the broad white hall, dim with the breaths of thousands, thousands of eager eyes fixed hopefully on a gilded, tinsel altar. Right into the den of the enemy would he bring her, his greatest conquest, right before those faces that had turned from him, and let them all know what he could do, in his modest efforts for the glory of God. Kay Gonda! The great name, the magic name! Somewhere, beyond the tinsel bar, he could hear a flutter of white wings, of white wings and white newspaper sheets with letters of flame! "Minister Converts Kay Gonda! Evangelist saves the greatest murderess that ever . . ." They would come to him, rich and poor, from the farthest corners of the land; they would flock to him; they would . . . He felt himself reeling a little.

"Ah, my sister, they will repent even as you have repented. Your great crime will pave the way for a great miracle. Verily, great are the ways of our Lord and unfathomable is His wisdom!"

She put on her hat and tilted it lightly, carelessly, over one eye, as if she were ready for the signal of a camera. She tightened the metal clasp of her collar, lightly, with the tip of the straight finger, as if she had just finished a fitting in the studio wardrobe. She asked, and her voice surprised him in its light calm, "It's six blocks to that place, isn't it?"

"Why . . . yes."

"You do not want me to be seen walking in the street. Get a taxi."

He emptied the dollar eighty-seven from his tin box into his trembling hands. He ran, hatless, through dark streets, looking for a taxi. He found one, and leaped in, and rode back, his head throbbing.

The taxi stopped at the Temple and he made the driver blow his horn. No one answered. Then he saw that the door was wide-open. The Temple was empty. A white cross flamed over the pulpit, on a black wall.

6

Dietrich von Esterhazy

"Dear Miss Gonda,

There are not many things which I can boast of having never done, and writing to a film star being the last one left to me, I am taking advantage of it, to complete the record. I am sure this letter can be of no interest to you, among the thousands you get every day, but I want to add this drop to the ocean, if for no other reason than that I want to do it, and it is the last thing left to me which I can still want.

I will not tell you how much I have enjoyed your pictures, because I have not enjoyed them. I think they have been as tawdry as one can expect the world of today to welcome. I am afraid it is an ungracious admirer who greets you here. I hesitate on the word admirer, for admiration is a virtue long since buried, and that which bears its name today can only insult its object. I cannot speak of your great beauty, for beauty is a dangerous curse to a world prostrate in worship at the feet of more hideous ugliness than the past centuries could ever have dreamt possible. I cannot tell you that you are the greatest actress living, for greatness is the target at which all the greatest of this age are aimed, and their aim is precise, inexorable.

I have seen all of life there is to see, and I feel now as if I were leaving a third-rate show on a disreputable side street, staged by a manager of very poor taste, and played by awkward amateurs. I have drunk to the last drop that which some call, presumptuously, the "cup of life," and I found that it contained nothing but a thin, badly cooked soup without salt, which leaves one with a sickly taste in one's mouth and hungrier than when one started, but without any desire to eat further.

If I still find all this worth saying, if I am sitting here writing this letter to you, it is only because—in you—I have found one last exception, one last spark of that which life is not anymore. It is not your beauty, nor your fame, nor your great art. It is not in the women you have played—for you have never played that which I see in you, that which—with the last faith left to me—I believe you really are. It is something without name, something lost deep beyond your eyes, beyond the movements of your body, something to which one could wave banners, to which one could drink, for which one could go out into a last, sacred battle—if sacred battles were still possible in the world of today.

When I see you on the screen, I know suddenly what it

was that life has never given me, I know what I could have been, and I know—anxious, helpless, frightened—the fearful spark of what it means to be able to desire.

I have said that I am leaving the sideshow. It does not mean that I am dying. But if I do not bother to die, it is only because my life has all the emptiness of the grave and my death would have no change to offer me. It may happen, any day now, and nobody, not even the one writing these lines, will know the difference.

But before it happens, I want to raise what is left of my soul in a last salute to you, you who are that which the world could have been. *Morituri te salutamus.*

Dietrich von Esterhazy
Beverly-Sunset Hotel
Beverly Hills, California"

On the evening of May 5th, Dietrich von Esterhazy wrote out a check for one thousand and seventy-two dollars, while he had three hundred and sixteen dollars left in his bank account.

Lalo Jones shrugged her shoulders and whispered:

"I don't see why I have to stop, Rikki. If you let me stay a little longer, I'm sure I can win it back."

He said:

"I'm sorry. I'm a little tired. Do you mind if we go now?"

She threw her head up, her long pearl earrings swaying like moist pink raindrops against her shoulders, and rose impatiently.

The tight ring of black coats and white, naked backs closed again around the roulette table. The huge white lamp in a slanting shade, low over the table, made a yellow pool in the blue, smoke-filled dusk, a pool edged by glistening black heads with neat parts, and heads of soft, golden waves, and heads of silvery gray, and tiny pink ears sparkling with diamonds, all bending over a spot where chips clicked dryly and something whirred sharply, hissing in a sudden silence.

"What's the matter, Rikki?" Lalo Jones asked, putting a soft little hand on his black sleeve. "I must say you're not the best of company tonight."

"My dear, I am ever helpless in your charming presence," he answered indifferently.

"A drink, Rikki? Before we go? Just one?"

"As you wish."

Beyond a broad arch, glasses glittered in a row like thin, upturned silvery bells in a haze of smoke, over a dark bar. Soft music came from nowhere, a whirling tune that gasped, breaking on sharp, high notes.

Lalo Jones raised a glass to her lips slowly, as if she was tired. Her movements were always slow, weary with the most graceful lassitude. Her arms and shoulders were bare, round and sunburnt, soft with a fuzz one could not see, but guessed, like the fuzz of a peach which one wanted irresistibly to feel. She drew her shoulders into a soft, lazy huddle, leaning with one elbow on the bar, resting her chin on the back of a little dimpled hand with tapering, gracefully drooping fingers. She wore a simple ring with a huge pink pearl, round and dully lustrous like her shoulders.

"But we'll have to go to Agua Caliente, Rikki," she was saying, "and this time I'll put it all on Black Rajah. He's going to run and Marian says she knows for certain—she has it straight from Dicky—that it's a cinch. By the way, Madame Ailen is sure she can get that French perfume for me, the real thing, if you pay her a hundred or something to order it. . . . They make the most impossible martinis here. . . . By the way, Rikki, my chauffeur's wages were due yesterday. And, Rikki . . ."

Dietrich von Esterhazy was listening, and if he answered, neither he nor Lalo knew it. His empty glass stood at his elbow, but he did not order another, even though Lalo was sipping slowly her third one.

A glistening gentleman slapped his shoulder, and Lalo nodded to him lazily, and the gentleman roared confidentially at some joke he had just heard, and Lalo laughed, showing little sparkling teeth, and Dietrich von Esterhazy smiled, looking into space.

Then he threw a twenty-dollar bill to the bartender and turned away without waiting for the change. Behind his back the bartender was bowing eagerly, hurriedly.

"What I like about you, Rikki," Lalo whispered, clinging to his arm as they made their way to the cloakroom, "is the manner you have of knowing how to spend money."

Dietrich von Esterhazy smiled. When he smiled, his thin mouth drew into a longer line, without opening, and his lower lip stuck out slightly, and deep, ironic little wrinkles creased his pale, lean cheeks. He had golden blond hair, and silvery blue eyes, and a tall body, erect, precise, a body born for uniforms and evening clothes.

In the cloakroom, he held Lalo's wrap for her, and the white ermine cuddled in soft, lazy folds to her shoulders.

Then they were swaying in the deep cushions of his Duesenberg, and Lalo stretched out her little satin pumps, and put her dark, perfumed head on his shoulder.

"Sorry I lost that money," she whispered lazily. "It wasn't very much, though."

"Not at all, my dear. Glad you enjoyed the evening."

Dietrich von Esterhazy suddenly felt very tired; his hands fell limply between his knees, and he had no strength to lift them.

The car drew up smoothly at the door of a tall, trim building with a gilded, softly lit lobby beyond the glass entrance.

"What? Taking me home already?" Lalo asked, wrinkling her little nose. "Don't you want me to go with you? To wish you good night?"

"Not tonight. Do you mind?"

She shrugged, tightening the white ermine under her chin. She stepped out, throwing back over her shoulder:

"Well, phone me sometime. I'll answer—if I feel like it."

The door closed and the car tore forward. Dietrich von Esterhazy leaned back, his hands hanging between his knees.

When he stepped out at the door of the Beverly Sunset Hotel, he said to the chauffeur:

"I won't need you tomorrow, Johnson."

He had no intention of saying that; but when he had said it he knew why he had.

He crossed the long lobby swiftly, swinging his cane under his arm. Upstairs, in his suite, where soft light made circles on a soft carpet, and long drapes seemed to swallow all sounds from the city far below, he put on a dark satin lounging jacket, walked to a table where a crystal decanter and spotless glasses were waiting for him, took a glass, hesitated, and put it down again. He walked to the window, pulled the drapes aside, and stood motionless, looking at the lights twinkling over the silence of a sleeping city.

It had been so sudden and now all was so simple. He had not planned to write that check; a few hours ago, he had problems, a thick web of problems he was too weary to untangle; now he was free, free at one useless stroke he had not intended striking.

He had other debts: his hotel bill, Lalo's new Packard, his tailor's bill, the diamond bracelet he had given Hughette Dorsey, the bill for that last party he had given—and cocaine was expensive, the sable coat for Lona Weston. And although he had repeated it to himself for the last few months, he knew suddenly, for the first time, that he had nothing left.

He had felt it vaguely, uncertainly, for the last two years; but a fortune of several millions did not disappear without a few last convulsions; there had always been something to sell, to pawn, to borrow on; always someone to borrow from. This time, the fortune lay still, dead in the fearful silence of a few hundreds in some bank, of closed safe deposit boxes, and unpaid bills. Tomorrow, Count Dietrich von Esterhazy would be called upon to explain the matter of a bad check. He would not be there for the call. Count Dietrich von Esterhazy had but one night left to live.

The thought left him completely indifferent; that surprised him, but he was indifferent even to his own indifference. There, below, beyond those lights twinkling in dim windows, men were struggling in agonies such as no hell could hold, to hang on to that precious, worthless gift of life which he was giving up, lightly, wearily, as if tossing a tip to a waiter.

Fifteen years ago, arrogant and young, last descendant of a proud old name, he had been thrown out of Germany by the revolution, with many millions in his pocket and an infinite contempt in his heart. He had wandered all over the world, strewing away, in his footsteps, his fortune and his spirit, drop by drop, with each step. He knew it had been fifteen years when he looked at the calendar; when he looked into his soul it seemed like fifteen centuries.

He dimly remembered chandeliers reflected in a polished floor and high-heeled slippers on slender, glistening legs; a hard, golden tennis court and his body swift, light, in white trousers and a damp white shirt; a propeller roaring through space and a flat, endless earth swaying very far below; white gulls and a motor shrieking through salty sprays, his hands on a wheel, his blond hair under a blue sky; a little ball spinning dizzily through squares of black and red; white bedrooms and white shoulders leaning back, limp, exhausted. And not one moment was worth reliving. Not one foot of ground was worth retraveling, in an empty world to which a lonely, haughty aristocrat, drugging an anguished brain, could not be reconciled.

That was ended. He could still wear his trim evening clothes and beg lonely dollars from those who had them, a brazen nonchalance hiding an obsequious smile, pleading an equality that would exist no longer; he could carry a shining briefcase and talk glibly of bonds and interest, and bow like a well-trained valet. But Dietrich von Esterhazy had too much good taste.

He would do it in the morning. One bullet could end so much. He would go, weary and alone, without a great cause, without a last worthy gesture, end his life for the sake of a few moments of gambling by a woman he had never loved.

The telephone rang.

He lifted the receiver wearily.

"A lady wishes to see you, sir," a polite, expressionless voice informed him from the desk below.

"Who is she?" asked Dietrich von Esterhazy.

There was a silence. Then the voice answered:

"The lady declines to give her name, sir. But she will send it up to you."

Dietrich von Esterhazy let the receiver drop and yawned. He lit a cigarette and stuck it mechanically into the corner of his mouth. A hand knocked at his door. A stiff chest with two rows of polished buttons stood on the threshold, two straight fingers holding a sealed envelope.

Dietrich von Esterhazy tore the envelope open. The note contained but two words:

"Kay Gonda."

Dietrich von Esterhazy laughed.

"All right," he told the bellhop, "have the lady come up."

If it was a joke, he wanted to know whose joke and why. When a hand knocked at his door again, his thin lips smiled without opening, and he said:

"Come in."

Then the door opened and his smile disappeared. He did not move but for one hand that took his cigarette and descended slowly.

Dietrich von Esterhazy bowed calmly from the hips and said:

"Good evening, Miss Gonda."

She answered:

"Good evening."

"Please sit down." He moved a comfortable armchair. "I am greatly honored." He offered her a cigarette, but she shook her head.

She remained standing, looking at him from under the brim of her black hat.

"Are you sure you want me to stay?" she asked. "It may be dangerous. You have not asked me why I came."

"You came—and that is all I have to know. Unless you wish to tell me now."

"I want to tell you that I am hiding from the police."

"I guessed that."

"I'm in danger."

"I understand. You do not have to explain, if you would rather not discuss it."

"I'd rather not. But I must ask you to let me stay here for the night."

He bowed again, swiftly, precisely. He said:

"Miss Gonda, had we met two centuries ago, I would have laid my sword at your feet. Unfortunately, this age does not believe in swords.

But my life and my house are at your feet, gratefully, for the great honor of being selected to help you."

"Thank you."

She sat down and tore her hat off wearily, and it dropped from her hand to the floor. He hurried to pick it up. He walked to the windows and drew the curtains. He said:

"You are safe here, with me. As safe as in one of those castles my ancestors had to protect that which was most precious to them."

"Now give me a cigarette."

He offered his open cigarette case, struck a flame in his dark metal lighter with its golden crest, held it out to her steadily, and his eyes glanced straight into hers, into those wide, pale eyes that looked so calm and open, concealing a mystery he could not pierce.

He sat down, facing her, leaning on the arm of his chair, the light of a lamp on his golden hair. He said:

"Do you know that it is really I who must thank you? Not only for coming, but for coming tonight of all nights."

"Why?"

"It is strange. One might almost think that there is some providence watching over us. Perhaps, you have taken one life in order to save another."

"I have?"

"You have killed a man. Please excuse me for mentioning this, if it is unpleasant to you. But please understand that it is not said in the spirit of reproach. After all, men make entirely too much of the fact of murder. There is more honor in having killed than in being one worth being killed."

"But you did not know Granton Sayers."

"And I do not have to know. I know you. The great mistake has always been in thinking that a life is a precious entity equal to all other lives. When, as a matter of fact, there are lives that cannot be replaced by millions of others through centuries to come. Men hunt a murderer, when the first, the only question, should be whether the murdered one was worth leaving alive. In this case, how could he have been, if *you* found it necessary to kill him? In that alone, whoever he was, whatever he had done, is the justification of what men may call your crime. One thousand lives—what are they beside one hour of yours?"

"But you do not know me."

He was leaning toward her, and the cigarette dropped, unnoticed, from his fingers.

"I know what you can tell me about yourself. I know that world into which you have been thrown and what it has done to you. But I know something that has kept you out of its reach. Something which I wish I did not see. Something I can't help seeing. Only I can't name it."

"What is it?" she asked softly. "My beauty?"

"Beauty is one of those words that seem to mean so much, but when you think of it, it means nothing whatever. I have looked at all that men call beauty—and I've longed for some nonexistent boric acid to wash my eyes."

"My wisdom?"

"I have listened to all that men call wisdom—and I have heard nothing more valuable than how to clean my fingernails."

"My art?"

"I have watched all that men call art—and I have yawned. If I were allowed to make one request to the all-powerful Messiah of this world—if such existed—I would beg him, on my knees, for a cure to stop me from yawning. Only that can never be granted."

"Then what is it?"

"I don't know. Something that needs no name, no explanation. Something to which the proudest, the weariest head bows reverently.

You have given yourself to a graceless world and to many graceless men. I know that. But something has kept you still out of their reach. Something. What is it?"

"A hope," she whispered.

He rose. He paced up and down the room. His steps had the light, exultant swing of youth. His eyes were tired no longer; they were eager, sparkling, alive. He stopped suddenly before her.

"A hope! Who doesn't have that? Man has always known, deep in his heart, that his life is not what it should have been. He has always gone forth on glorious, doomed crusades. But he has always returned empty-handed. Because he has never had a chance. It's a hopeless quest and one gets so tired! I have seen all men call their virtues. I have seen all they call their vices and I have enjoyed the vices to forget their virtues. But I still have that in me which has eyes for the real, the only life possible, that which still keeps me alive. That which is the highest. You."

"Are you sure," she whispered, "are you sure you want me?"

"You'll know the answer," he replied, "tomorrow."

He stood before her, his eyes blazing.

"I've told you you have saved a life tonight. You have. I was ready to end it. But not now. Not now. I have something worth fighting for. We have to flee—both of us. We'll run away to where men's claws will never reach us. I want nothing but to serve you. Nothing, but to be a knight such as my ancestors were. They would envy me, if they could see me. For my Holy Grail is of this earth. It is real, alive, possible. Only even they may not understand. No one will understand. It will remain only for the two of us. Only for you and me."

"Yes," she whispered, and her eyes were on him, and her eyes were open, trusting, surrendering, "only for you and me."

He smiled suddenly, a wide, brilliant smile, his teeth sparkling. He said, very simply:

"I hope I haven't frightened you by being so terribly serious. Please forgive me. You're trembling. Are you cold?"

"A little."

"I'll make a fire."

He threw logs into the marble fireplace, struck a match, and knelt, watching the flames crackle, leap in the air.

She rose and walked across the room, her hands crossed behind her head, and when their eyes met they smiled as if they had known each other for a very long time.

He walked to the table with the glasses.

"May I?" he asked.

She nodded.

He filled the glasses. She took off her coat, threw it on a chair, took her glass. She stood across the table from him, leaning with one knee on the soft, low arm of a chair, swaying back a little, her shoulders very thin under the tight black satin of a long blouse with a stern, high collar. He noticed her breasts, very close to him, under the blouse, covered only by the soft, lustrous black silk.

She raised the glass in her long, slender fingers and drank a little, throwing her head back slightly, her hair very blond on her black shoulders. Then she lowered her glass. He emptied his at once, and refilled it.

"Are you afraid of airplanes?" he asked, smiling. "Because we'll have to travel a great deal."

"Terribly."

"Well, you'll have to get used to them. I'll see to that."

"Will you be very severe with me?"

"Terribly."

"I am very difficult, you know. You will have to get me a lot of chocolate. I love chocolate."

"Only one bar a day."

"No more?"

"Positively not."

"I am terrible on stockings. I ruin four pairs a day."

"You'll have to learn to darn them."

She walked lazily across the room, her glass in hand, as if she felt quite at home. He refilled his glass again, and stood by the fireplace, watching her. Her movements were slow. Her body leaned backward a little. He could see the play of every muscle under the long black blouse. He asked:

"Do you always lose your gloves and handkerchiefs?"

"Always."

"That won't do."

"No?"

"No."

"I also lose my rings. Diamond ones."

"I'll certainly have to put a stop to that. You can lose the pearl ones, well, maybe also the ruby ones. But not the diamonds."

"How about the emeralds?"

"Well, I don't know. I'll think about that."

"Oh, please!"

"No, I can't promise."

She sat down on a davenport by the fire and stretched out her feet, and her slender little heels were red in the glow. He sat down on the floor, crossing his legs, his glass in hand, and little flames twinkled in the glass. They talked, swift words dropping as sparks; they laughed softly, happily.

Somewhere far downstairs, a clock chimed three times.

"Oh, I didn't know it was so late," he said, rising. "You must be tired."

"Yes. Very."

"You must go to bed. At once. You can have my bedroom. I'll sleep here, on the davenport."

"But—"

"But of course. I'll be perfectly comfortable. This way, please. You can use some of my pajamas. They may not fit very well, but I'm afraid there's not much of the night left. And we'll have to get up early."

At the bedroom door, she stopped. She raised her glass.

"Tomorrow," she said.

"Tomorrow," he answered, raising his.

She stood at the door, slender, fragile, her face tranquil, innocent, young, her lips like those of a saint.

"Good night," she whispered.

"Good night."

She extended her hand. He raised it, slowly, hesitantly, and his lips touched lightly, reverently, the soft, transparent blue-white skin. . . .

There was a heavy silence in the building, the silence of deep rugs, soft drapes, and men lost in sleep. There was a heavy silence in the city beyond, the silence of empty pavement and dark houses. Dietrich von Esterhazy lay on the davenport, his hands crossed under his head, and looked at the window. A last red glow breathed, jerking, in the fireplace. He could see a trembling red spot in the darkness, in her glass left on a table. He could breathe, as a shadow, as the ghost of a fragrance, her faint perfume that still remained around him.

He turned restlessly on his couch and drew his steamer rug higher under his arms. He closed his eyes. In the dark waves that rolled vaguely under the eyelids he tried to press down tightly, a lustrous spot shimmered, a spot of light on black silk over a firm young breast.

He opened his eyes. The room was dark. In the shadows of its black corners he could see a long, tight blouse descending to slender hips.

He seized the arm of the couch; he thought he was going to leap up.

He closed his eyes. He could see her walking across the room, he could see the shoulders thrown back, every motion of her legs crossing each other, clearly, precisely, exactly the movement of the hand raising the glass to her lips.

He brushed his hair off a damp forehead.

He buried his face in the pillow, not to smell that perfume he hated suddenly; the pillow where she had sat, still warm with the warmth of her body.

He jumped up. He walked uncertainly to the table, found his glass in the darkness, poured it so full that the cold liquid ran over his trembling fingers, over the table, and he heard heavy drops thudding dully against the carpet.

He drank it all at once, throwing his head back. He stood, clutching the empty glass, his eyebrows drawn grimly together, his eyes on the closed door.

He returned to the couch. He fell down, kicking the rug to the floor. He could not breathe.

Why should he care what would happen then, afterward? Why should he care what she'd think of him? He saw the black satin, soft, lustrous, round. His lips burnt with the touch of that white skin. Why should he care?

He rose. He walked, slowly, steadily, to the closed door. He threw it open.

She lay dressed, on his bed, and her one hand hung over the edge, white in the darkness. She jerked her head up and he could guess her eyes on the pale blot of her face. She felt his teeth sinking into her hand.

She struggled ferociously, her muscles tense, hard, sharp as an animal's.

"Keep still," he whispered hoarsely into her throat. "You can't call for help!"

She did not call for help. . . .

He lay still, limp, exhausted. His eyes were accustomed to the darkness. He saw her face. She laughed suddenly, softly, fearfully. He looked at her. She was no longer the fragile saint with the tranquil, unfathomable eyes. Her glistening lips were parted. Her eyes were half closed. She was the reckless, infamous woman he had seen on the screen. Her hand brushed softly the hair on his forehead. The caress was an insult.

Then she rose. He saw her gathering her clothes, dressing swiftly, silently.

"What are you doing?" he asked.

She did not answer.

"Where are you going? . . . You can't go. . . . You can't go out. . . . Don't you know it's dangerous? . . . Where can you go? . . ."

She did not seem to hear.

He felt suddenly that his voice was weak, that he had no strength to move, that words were hopeless. The darkness beyond the window was spreading slowly, over his room, over his brain, over the coming morning.

He did not move when she crossed the room and he heard the door opening and closing after her.

He did not move when he heard her laughter, loud, reckless, moving away down the corridor.

7

Johnnie Dawes

"Dear Miss Gonda,

This letter is addressed to you, but I am writing it to myself. Perhaps it will answer something that I cannot understand, something I have to know. There are so many things that I don't understand. Sometimes I think that I am a person who should never have been born. This is not a complaint. I am not afraid and I am not sorry. Only I am so bewildered, and I have to know.

I do not understand men, and they do not understand me. They live and seem to be happy. But to me—all they live for, all they talk of is only a vague blot without meaning, a blot that does not even understand the word 'meaning.' To them I say—all I want are sounds from a language they were not born to speak. Which of us is right? Does it matter? Only—can there ever be a bridge?

That for which I'd give—happily—all of the life I may have, to the last day, they forget so easily for the sake of what they call living. That which they call living—I couldn't stand one moment of it, not one second. What are they? Are they muddled, halfhearted, unfinished creatures, a riddle with but one answer: lies? Or are they the sane, the real, the must-be, while I'm only a distorted freak that should not be allowed to exist?

I can't even say what it is I want of life. I know only what I want to feel, but I've never found that which could make me feel it. I want to feel, maybe only for a second, something for which there is no human word, maybe an ecstasy, but that doesn't express it, a feeling that needs no reason and no explanation, a feeling complete, absolute, when one can be the end and the justification of all existence, a moment of life that would be life itself condensed. I want nothing more. I can want nothing less.

But if I spoke of it—what answer would I get? I would hear a lot about children, about dinner, about football, about God. Are they empty words? Or am I an empty creature that can never be filled?

I have often wanted to die. I want it now. It's not despair or rebellion. I want to go calmly and quietly and willingly. There is no place for me in the world. I cannot hope to change it. I have not even the right to want it changed. But I also cannot change myself. I cannot accuse the others. I cannot say that I am right. I don't know. I don't care to know. But I have to leave a place for which I am not fitted.

Only there's something holding me here. Something that I am waiting for. Something that must come to me before I go. I want only to know one living moment, but one moment of that which is *mine*, not theirs, one moment of that which their world has never held. I want only to know that it exists, that it can exist.

Do you wonder why I am writing all this to you? It is because when I look at you on the screen, I know what it is that I want of life. I know what life is not, what it could have been. I know what is possible.

And I want to tell it to you, even though you may not bother to read this, or, reading it, may not understand. I do not know what you are. I am writing to what I think you could have been.

Johnnie Dawes
Main Street
Los Angeles, California"

On the night of May 5th, Johnnie Dawes lost his job of night shipping clerk in a wholesale house.

The manager coughed, cleaned his left eye with his fingernail, rolled something between his fingers, wiped them on his shirt, and said:

"Business being what it is, we find we have to let some of you fellows go. Come again in a couple months or so. But I can't promise nothing."

Johnnie Dawes received his check for the last twelve days. He had been working part-time. The check wasn't much. When he walked out, the manager said to a clerk who had not been fired, a heavy fellow with a red, pimpled face:

"There goes one kid I don't aim to ever see again. Stuck-up little snot. Makes a regular guy feel creepy."

Johnnie Dawes walked out into the street, silent and empty in the early hours of the morning. He raised the collar of his patched coat and pulled his cap low over his eyes. He plunged forward, as if diving into icy water.

It was not the first job he had lost. Johnnie Dawes had lost many jobs in his short twenty years. He always knew his work, but no one seemed to notice. He never laughed and smiled seldom. He never knew any good jokes to tell and never seemed to have anything to say. No one had heard of a girl he had ever taken to the movies, and no one knew what he had had for breakfast, if any. When there was a crowd of fellows celebrating at the corner beer joint, he was never in it. When there was a crowd of fellows laid off, he was always included.

He walked swiftly, his hands in his pockets. His lips were a thin line over a square chin. His cheeks were hollow, with gray shadows under sharp cheekbones. His eyes were clear, quick, astonished.

He was going home, not that he had to go; he could keep on walking, and never come back, and no one, no one in the whole wide world, would ever know the difference. In a few hours, there would be morning. There would be another day. He could lie in his garret and sleep. Or he could get up and start out through the streets, any streets. It would be all the same.

He had to look for another job. He had to spend endless, weary days to find a job to spend endless, weary days without meaning. He had held many of them.

There had been a murky hotel with dim halls that smelt of rotting cloth; he had climbed narrow stairways, in a tight uniform that did not fit, answering sharp bells from musty rooms, his big, clear eyes looking steadily into hot perspiring faces. The manager had said that he was too shy.

There had been a drugstore with a fly-spotted mirror behind a long counter that smelt of stale onions, and he had worn a white cap over one ear, and mixed ice-cream sodas in streaked shakers, the muscles of his face frozen as if under a mask of white wax. The manager had said he was too unfriendly.

There had been a restaurant with spotted, checkered tablecloths and a Special Lunch 20 Cents sign on a faded pasteboard on the wall where people sat with their elbows on the tables; and the hamburgers frying in the kitchen filled the room with a smoky haze; and he had carried trays of greasy dishes high over his head, trudging sideways through the crowd, his elbows aching, his spine numb, Johnnie Dawes who dreamed of life condensed and wondered at the wishes of men. The manager had said he was not a good mixer.

In between, there had been a handful of nickels growing lighter and lighter in his pocket, a cup of coffee, then nothing but a dull ache in his stomach and his belt drawn tight; a bed for fifteen cents a night in a long room smelling of sweat and Lysol; then a park bench and a newspaper over his head, and behind his closed eyes the song of life without answer. There was no one to ask for help, and no one had asked to help him. Once, a lady in a mink coat had suggested dryly that a normal, responsible young man could always work his way through college, provided he worked hard, and become a respectable teacher or dentist, provided he had ambition. He had no ambition.

He walked swiftly. His steps rang against cement, against stone cubes piled high to a black abyss above. In the gray tunnels with long bands of graying floor streaked with morning dampness, in the silence of a city that seemed to twist its dead passageways underground, no whisper rustled to meet him, no echo, no movement. He was alone.

He stopped at a narrow brick building. Greenish streaks spread like whiskers under its blackened sills, like traces of refuse poured out of its narrow windows. On the dark bricks of a side wall, white letters spoke of a chewing tobacco, and rags of a faded poster spoke of a circus. Over the door was a sign with letters missing: Ro ms a d beds. Under it was a dusty glass plaque with a faded inscription: De Luxe Beds 20 cents.

There was no elevator. There were no lights on the stairs. He went up slowly, his hand following a cold iron bannister. He rose many floors, stopping once in a while, choking.

On the second landing from the top, a door opened and a crack of light fell across the stairs. The old landlady stood, shivering in a faded bathrobe, greasy at the elbows, gray hair hanging over swollen eyes, a gnarled hand on the doorknob.

"So it's ye, is it?" she hissed in a high, cracked voice. "Don't think ye can sneak upstairs. I've been waitin' for ye, Ay'ave. It's me rent Ay'm after, and ye know it. Come across now or ye don't go up."

The rent had been due for ten days. He drew the check from his pocket and handed it to her. It was all he had. He was too weary to argue. He knew the check was not enough.

"Ye been fired?"

"Yes, Mrs. Mulligan."

"No good, that's what ye are, no good. It's a born bum, ye are. Ye get outta here in the mornin'. Out ye go. Hear me?"

"Yes, Mrs. Mulligan."

He had passed her, he had risen three steps, when she croaked:

"It's small wonder ye ain't got no money never. Runnin' around with wimmen!"

He stopped.

"Women?" he asked. "What women?"

"Aw, it ain't no use playin' the wooden saint with me!"

"What are you talking about?"

"Well," she spluttered, spitting hair out of her mouth, "there's one waitin' for ye up in yer room right now!"

"A . . . what?"

"A dame."

"You mean . . . a woman?"

"Ay mean a woman. What d'ye think? A elephant? A swell dame, too."

"You don't mean in *my* room?"

"Well, Ay let her in meself. She asked for ye."

"Who is she?"

"Ay'll ask ye that! She stinks like a lady, too."

He swung up the stairs, up two more landings, to his garret. He threw the door open.

A candle was burning on the table. The woman rose slowly and her head almost touched the low, slanting ceiling. Her hair seemed to light the room.

Johnnie Dawes recognized her. He was not surprised. He said, no hesitation and no question in his voice:

"Good evening, Miss Gonda."

"Good evening."

Her eyes were fixed on his, her glance like an anchor flung into his dark pupils, groping for support. It was Kay Gonda's eyes that looked surprised.

He asked simply, as if the matter of her presence were not unusual at all:

"Did you have a hard time climbing those stairs?"

She answered, "A little. All climbing is hard. But it's usually worth it."

He took off his coat. He was very calm, only his movements were slow, as if his muscles were unreal, as if his hands were floating, without weight, like in a dream.

He sat down, and she walked toward him suddenly, and took his face in her hands, her long fingers on his cheeks, raising it slowly, and she asked:

"What's the matter, Johnnie?"

He answered:

"Nothing—now."

"You must not be so glad to see me."

"I'm not—glad. It isn't that. I knew you'd come."

"When you wrote to me?"

"Yes."

"Why?"

"Because I need you."

"I've seen many people tonight, Johnnie. And I'm glad I did. But now . . . I don't know . . . perhaps I'm sorry that I came here."

"Why?"

"Perhaps . . . I'd rather you had not seen me."

"Why?"

"Your eyes, Johnnie. . . . They see too much of what is not."

"Of what could be."

"I don't know, Johnnie. . . . I am so tired! Of everything."

"I knew that when I looked at you on the screen."

"Do you still think so?"

"Yes. More than ever."

She walked across the room. She fell wearily on his narrow iron cot with its coarse gray blanket. She said, looking at him, her lips smiling, a smile that was not gay, not friendly:

"People say I am a great star, Johnnie."

"Yes."

"People say I have everything one can wish."

"Have you?"

"No. But why do you know it?"

"Why do you know I know it?"

"You are never afraid when you speak to people, are you, Johnnie?"

"Yes. I am very afraid. Always. I don't know what to say to them. But I am not afraid—now."

"I am a very bad woman, Johnnie. Everything you've heard about me is true. Everything—and more. I came to tell you that you must not think of me what you said in your letter."

"You came to tell me that everything I said in my letter was true. Everything—and more."

She threw her hat on the bed and ran her fingers through her hair, her long, white fingers on her high, white temples.

"I've been the mistress of every man in the studio. Every one that wanted me. The lower, the better."

"I know."

"Once, very long ago, I was a servant. Do you know what that means? You get up in the morning and you don't know why you must live that day. But you don't die. And you don't live. But you hear something, a strange thing, life calling to you. And you have no answer. Then I thought I must forget. Everything. Close my ears and go straight through. Take everything from men, everything they had to offer, and laugh at them and at myself. I took it. All of it. The lowest they had. To make me like they were. To make me forget. But I still hear it. I still hear that which no one can give me. Why do I hear it? What's crying it to me?"

"Yourself."

"Myself! I am nothing. Nothing anymore! . . . Do you know that I get fifteen thousand a week?"

"Yes."

"Do you know that I have two hundred pairs of shoes?"

"I suppose so."

"And diamonds. By the handful?"

"I suppose so."

"Do you know that my pictures are shown in every town in the world?"

"And people look at them, people whom you don't want to see you."

"They pay money, millions to see me. But do I mean anything to them?"

"No. You know it."

"I work. I tell them of something they have never had, of something I have never had, of life as it could be lived. I cry to them—but I get no answer. They pay millions to see me. They write to me. But do they want me? Do they really want me?"

"No. You know it."

"I know it now—tonight. I thought I knew it—an hour ago. . . . Oh, why don't you ask me for something?"

"What do you want me to ask you?"

"Why don't you ask me to give you a job in the movies?"

"The only thing I could ask you, you've given to me already."

She got up. She paced furiously up and down the room. Her hands grasped her elbows, and her elbows knocked against walls striped with streaks of peeling paint. She stopped before him, and her lips were hard, pitiless.

"You're a fool!" she hissed. "You're a damn fool!"

"Why are you so angry?"

"Why are you living? What do you want?"

"I don't think I'll be living much longer. I don't have to. I've seen everything I want."

"What?"

"You."

She looked at him, her eyes pleading. She whispered:

"What is it we want, Johnnie, you and I?"

He answered, and each word seemed to be reflected in his eyes, and his eyes were as a song:

"Have you ever been in a temple and seen men kneeling silently, reverently, their souls raised to the greatest height they can reach? To the height where they know they are clean, and clear, and perfect? When their spirit is the end and the reason of all things? Then have you wondered why that has to exist only in a temple? Why men can't carry it also into their lives? Why, if they can know the height, they can still want to live less than the highest? That's what we want to live, you and I. And if we can dream, we must also see our dreams in life. If not—of what account are dreams?"

"Ah, Johnnie, Johnnie, of what account is life?"

"None. But who made it so?"

"Those who cannot dream."

"No. Those who can only dream."

She stood silently, looking at him. He said:

"Sit down. We have a few hours left. What happened before—and what will happen afterwards—does it matter?"

She sat obediently. They sat far from each other. Between them stood a broken table, and a soapbox, and a candle in a bottle. The candle was a shivering glow over dark walls with beams showing through cracked paint. They talked as if the world had existed but for half an hour. Their eyes did not leave each other. Their eyes were locked as if in a long embrace. They talked, the woman who had seen all of life and the boy who had seen none, and they understood each other.

"Johnnie," she asked suddenly, softly, "you said we had only a few hours left. Why?"

He answered without looking at her:

"It was something I was thinking."

"What?"

"Nothing. Not now."

Beyond the dusty skylight in the slanting roof, the sky was turning a soft, deep blue, a blue dark in a last effort. Then . . . Johnnie Dawes asked suddenly:

"You killed him?"

"We don't have to talk about that, do we, Johnnie?"

"I knew Granton Sayers. I worked for him once, caddying, at a golf club in Santa Barbara. A hard kind of a man."

"He was a very unhappy man, Johnnie."

"Was anyone present?"

"Where?"

"When you killed him?"

"Do we have to discuss that?"

"It's something I must know. Did anyone see you kill him?"

"No. No one saw me kill him."

He rose. He looked at her blond hair drooping wearily to one shoulder. He said:

"It's very late. You must be tired."

"Yes, Johnnie. Very tired."

"You must go to sleep. Here, on my bed. I'll climb out on the roof."

"On the roof?"

"Why, yes. I've slept there often in hot weather."

"But it is very cold."

"I don't mind. I'm used to it. Try to sleep for a while. Forget everything. Don't worry. I have a way out for you."

"*You* have a way out? For *me*?"

"Yes. Out of the murder trouble. Only we won't discuss that now. Tomorrow. Try to sleep."

"Yes, Johnnie."

He pushed the table under the skylight, climbed up on it, opened the dusty pane, swung his body up to the frame, raising himself on two strong, young arms. He knelt by the skylight and whispered:

"Don't think of anything now. Just sleep. Good night."

"Good night, Johnnie," she whispered, looking up, her eyes curious. He closed the pane softly.

He sat on the roof, his shoulders drawn together, his hands clasping his knees. He sat without moving for a long time.

Beyond a sea of rooftops, a rusty band of smoke rose slowly, and over the dark band the bright blue was ripped suddenly, and a crack of soft pink hung over the city, soft, radiant, untouched. Around him, under his feet, the houses slept, dark, soot-streaked, and only a few windows sparkled, scattered over the city, as dewdrops, pink in a coming light. There was no sun. Only the blue above was growing darker and brighter, and behind the black shadows of skyscrapers flung into the clouds, sheaves of rays streamed up, hazy, pale, colorless rays, like a halo. Johnnie Dawes sat motionless and watched the dawn rising over the city.

When he heard wheels screeching somewhere far below, and a streetcar shrieked, rattling on cold tracks, and dots of light flickered in windows, he glanced cautiously into the darkness of his garret, a darkness that guarded a pale, golden treasure on a white pillow. Then he opened the skylight and slipped down into the room.

Kay Gonda was asleep.

Her coat was thrown over her feet, and her black satin shoulders were huddled tight against the pillow, and her blond hair hung over the edge of the bed.

He touched her shoulder and called softly: "Miss Gonda!"

She opened her eyes and rolled back on the pillow, her lips parting lazily, soft and swollen a little with sleep, and said docilely, like a child:

"Good morning."

"Good morning, Miss Gonda. I'm sorry to disturb you. But you have to get up."

She sat up on the bed, and threw her hair back with a long, slow movement, unruly threads tangled in her fingers. She blinked, and asked lazily:

"I have to get up?"

"Yes. There's no time to lose."

"What's on your mind, Johnnie?"

"I have a plan. To save you. No, I can't tell you now. You must trust me."

"I trust you, Johnnie."

"Will you do exactly as I say?"

"Yes, Johnnie."

"Have you brought a car?"

"Yes. It is parked around the corner."

"Now go to your car and drive away. Anywhere. Just keep on driving, out of the city, where no one can follow you. Drive all day. Toward evening you can come back. To your house. It will be all right then. You will be safe."

She watched him fixedly, curiously. She said nothing.

"Will you do that?" he asked.

"Yes, Johnnie."

When she was ready to go, she stopped at the door for a second. He stood looking at her. He said:

"One moment or many lifetimes—does it matter? Just to have seen you, to know that you exist, that you can exist. . . . There's only one thing I want you to remember: that I thank you."

She repeated slowly:

"Just to know that it exists, that it can exist."

He stood for a long time after her steps had died far downstairs. Then he walked to his table, sat down and wrote a letter. He sealed the envelope and propped it against the bottle.

Then he opened the door and listened. He heard Mrs. Mulligan shuffling up the stairs, the trash can she carried rattling against the steps. He heard her groaning in her kitchen, its door left open.

He left his door open, too. Mrs. Mulligan would hear. He wanted her to hear. . . .

Kay Gonda drove, at seventy miles an hour, down long smooth country roads, her hands on the wheel, her hair flying in the wind. The long, low, sparkling roadster went hurtling past rose hedges and alfalfa fields and farmhouses where bewildered eyes followed it and sunburned heads shook slowly. Her brows were drawn tightly together, her eyes steady on the flying road. In her eyes was a last question, still to be answered.

In was late, and on street corners the first lights were fighting with the glow of a red sky, when she drove back into the city. Newsboys were waving white sheets, yelling extras. She paid no attention.

She drove to her mansion and stopped her car at full speed, brakes screaming, under the white colonnade of the entrance. She ran swiftly up the steps, her heels clicking on white marble. In the dim spacious lobby inside, a nervous figure pacing furiously up and down stopped short when she entered. It was Mick Watts.

Mick Watts was sober. His shirt collar was torn open. His hair was disheveled. His eyes were bloodshot. His fists were crumpling a newspaper ferociously.

"So it's you, isn't it?" he roared. "So here you are! I knew you'd be back! I knew you'd be back now!"

"Phone the studio, Mick," she said calmly, pulling her gloves off, finger by finger. "Tell them to be ready to shoot at nine tomorrow. Have the wardrobe girl in my bungalow at seven-thirty and be sure she has the skirt well pressed, no wrinkles around the pockets."

"Well, I hope you've had a good time! I hope you've enjoyed it! But I'm through! I wish I could quit!"

"You know you won't quit, Mick."

"That's the hell of it! That you know it, too! Why did I ever meet you? Why do I have to serve you like a dog, and will go on serving you like a dog for the rest of my days? Why can't I resist any crazy whim of yours? Why did I have to go and spread those insane rumors about a murder you had never committed—just because you wanted to find out something! Well, have you found it out?"

"Yes, Mick."

"Well, I hope you're satisfied! I hope you're satisfied with what you've done!"

And he flung the newspaper into her face.

She opened the paper slowly. The headline read: "Amazing Development in Sayers 'Murder.'" Under it was the story:

A young man identified as Johnnie Dawes committed suicide early this morning at his home at South Main Street. The body was discovered by Mrs. Martha Mulligan, the landlady, who heard the shot and notified the police. A letter addressed to the police was found, in which the boy confessed that he had killed Granton Sayers, Santa Barbara millionaire, on the night of May 3rd, explaining the action by an old grudge against Sayers who had caused him to lose a job at a golf club some time ago, and asking the police to stop the investigation of the crime as he did not want innocent persons to be implicated. The police are baffled by the "confession" and can explain it only as the act of a crank, in view of the statement given out by Miss Frederica Sayers, sister of the deceased millionaire, when she was questioned by the police officers.

Johnnie Dawes

Miss Sayers' statement follows:

"I am utterly amazed by the confession of this boy, whose name I have never heard before, and I am completely at a loss to explain it, since there was nothing of the nature of a murder connected with my brother's death. My brother, Granton Sayers, committed suicide on the night of May 3rd, after he had dinner with Miss Kay Gonda. He left a letter addressed to me, the contents of which I can now make public. It is no longer necessary to keep secret the fact that my brother's business was on the verge of bankruptcy and the only thing that could save it was a deal with a powerful concern, negotiations for which were then in progress. My brother wrote that he was tired of life and had no desire to struggle any longer; that the only woman he had ever loved and who could have inspired him to live had again refused to marry him, that night. I realized that the news of my brother's suicide would be liable to break off these business negotiations, indicating as it did the desperate state of his firm. Therefore, I decided to keep the manner of his death a secret for a while. I visited Miss Gonda at her home, that night, and explaining the situation, asked her not to disclose the truth, for she alone could have guessed the circumstances of my brother's sudden death. She was gracious enough to promise this. The business deal was successfully concluded this morning and I am able to reveal the truth. I must add that I was surprised by the rumors that ascribed my brother's 'murder' to Miss Gonda. I am completely dumbfounded by the suicide and 'confession' of that unknown boy."

"Well?" said Mick Watts.

"Do you mind going home, Mick? I am very tired."

"You *are* a murderess, Kay Gonda! You killed that boy!"

"No, Mick, not I alone."

"How can you stand there and stare at me like that? Do you know, do you realize what you have done?!"

Kay Gonda looked through the open door at the sun sinking behind brown hills, at the lights of the city twinkling on dark winding roads.

"That," said Kay Gonda, "was the kindest thing I have ever done."

PART II

Ideal: The Play

Introduction to *Ideal: The Play*

I deal was written in 1934, at a time when Ayn Rand had cause to be unhappy with the world. *We the Living* was being rejected by a succession of publishers for being "too intellectual" and too opposed to Soviet Russia (this was the time of America's Red Decade); *Night of January 16th* had not yet found a producer; and Miss Rand's meager savings were running out. The story was written originally as a novelette and then, probably within a year or two, was extensively revised and turned into a stage play. It has never been produced.

After the political themes of her first professional work, Ayn Rand now returns to the subject matter of her early stories: the role of values in men's lives. The focus in this case, as in "Her Second Career," is negative, but this time the treatment is not jovial; dominantly, it is sober and heartfelt. The issue now is men's lack of integrity, their failure to act according to the ideals they espouse. The theme is the evil of divorcing ideals from life.

An acquaintance of Miss Rand's, a conventional middle-aged woman, told her once that she worshiped a certain famous actress and would give her life to meet her. Miss Rand was dubious about the authenticity of the woman's emotion, and this suggested a dramatic idea: a story in which a famous actress, so beautiful that she comes to represent to men the embodiment of their deepest ideals, actually enters the lives of her admirers. She comes in a context suggesting that she is in grave danger. Until this point, her worshipers have professed their reverence for her—in words, which cost them nothing. Now, however, she is no longer a distant dream, but a reality demanding action on their part, or betrayal.

"What do you dream of?" Kay Gonda, the actress, asks one of the characters, in the play's thematic statement.

"Nothing," he answers. "Of what account are dreams?"

"Of what account is life?"

"None. But who made it so?"

"Those who cannot dream."

"No. Those who can *only* dream."

In a journal entry written at the time (dated April 9, 1934), Miss Rand elaborates this viewpoint:

> I believe—and I want to gather all the facts to illustrate this—that the worst curse on mankind is the ability to consider ideals as something quite abstract and detached from one's everyday life. The ability of *living* and *thinking* quite differently, in other words eliminating thinking from your actual life. This applied not to deliberate and conscious hypocrites, but to those more dangerous and hopeless ones who, alone with themselves and to themselves, tolerate a complete break between their convictions and their lives, and still believe that they have convictions. To them—either their ideals or their lives are worthless—and usually both.

Such "dangerous and hopeless ones" may betray their ideal in the name of "social respectability" (the small businessman in this story) or in the name of the welfare of the masses (the Communist) or the will of God (the evangelist) or the pleasure of the moment (the playboy count)—or they may do it for the license of claiming that the good is impossible and therefore the struggle for it unnecessary (the painter). *Ideal* captures eloquently the essence of each of these diverse types and demonstrates their common denominator. In this regard, it is an intellectual tour de force. It is a philosophical guide to hypocrisy, a dramatized inventory of the kinds of ideas and attitudes that lead to the impotence of ideals—that is, to their detachment from life.

(The inventory, however, is not offered in the form of a developed plot structure. In the body of the play, there is no progression of events, no necessary connection between one encounter and the next. It is a series of evocative vignettes, often illuminating and ingenious, but as theater, I think, unavoidably somewhat static.)

Dwight Langley, the painter, is the pure exponent of the evil the play is attacking; he is, in effect, the spokesman for Platonism, who explicitly preaches that beauty is unreachable in this world and perfection unattainable. Since he insists that ideals are impossible on earth, he cannot, logically enough, believe in the reality of any ideal, even when it actually confronts him. Thus, although he knows every facet of Kay Gonda's face, he (alone among the characters) does not recognize her when she appears in his life. This philosophically induced blindness, which motivates his betrayal of her, is a particularly brilliant concretization of the play's theme, and makes a dramatic Act I curtain.

In her journal of the period, Miss Rand singles out religion as the main cause of men's lack of integrity. The worst of the characters, accordingly, the one who evokes her greatest indignation, is Hix, the evangelist, who preaches earthly suffering as a means to heavenly happiness. In an excellently worked-out scene, we see that it is not his vices, but his religion, including his definition of virtue, that brings him to demand the betrayal of Kay Gonda, her deliberate sacrifice to the lowest of creatures. By gaining a stranglehold on ethics, then preaching sacrifice as an ideal, religion, no matter what its intentions, systematically inculcates hypocrisy: it teaches men that achieving values is low ("selfish"), but that giving them up is noble. "Giving them up," in practice, means betraying them.

"None of us," one of the characters complains, "ever chooses the bleak, hopeless life he is forced to lead." Yet, as the play demonstrates, all these men do choose the lives they lead. When confronted by the ideal they profess to desire, they do not want it. Their vaunted "idealism" is largely a form of self-deception, enabling them to pretend to themselves and others that they aspire to something higher. In fact and in reality, however, they don't.

Kay Gonda, by contrast, is a passionate valuer; like Irene in "The Husband I Bought," she cannot accept anything less than the ideal. Her exalted sense of life cannot accept the ugliness, the pain, the "dismal little pleasures" that she sees all around her, and she feels a desperate need to know that she is not alone in this regard. There is no doubt that Ayn Rand herself shared Kay Gonda's sense of life, and often her loneliness, too—and that Kay's cry in the play is her own:

> I want to see, real, living, and in the hours of my own days, that glory I create as an illusion! I want it real! I want to know that there is someone, somewhere, who wants it, too! Or else what is the use of seeing it, and working, and burning oneself for an impossible vision? A spirit, too, needs fuel. It can run dry.

Introduction to *Ideal: The Play*

Emotionally, *Ideal* is unique among Ayn Rand's works. It is the polar opposite of "Good Copy." "Good Copy" was based on the premise of the impotence and insignificance of evil. But *Ideal* focuses almost exclusively on evil or mediocrity (in a way that even *We the Living* does not); it is pervaded by Kay Gonda's feeling of alienation from mankind, the feeling, tinged by bitterness, that the true idealist is in a minuscule minority amid an earthful of value-betrayers with whom no communication is possible. In accordance with this perspective, the hero, Johnnie Dawes, is not a characteristic Ayn Rand figure, but a misfit utterly estranged from the world, a man whose virtue is that he does not know how to live today (and has often wanted to die). If Leo feels this in Soviet Russia, the explanation is political, not metaphysical. But Johnnie feels it in the United States.

In her other works, Ayn Rand herself gave the answer to such a "malevolent universe" viewpoint, as she called it. Dominique Francon in *The Fountainhead,* for instance, strikingly, resembles Kay and Johnnie in her idealistic alienation from the world, yet she eventually discovers how to reconcile evil with the "benevolent universe" approach. "You must learn," Roark tells her, "not to be afraid of the world. Not to be held by it as you are now. Never to be hurt by it as you were in that courtroom." Dominique does learn it; but Kay and Johnnie do not, or at least not fully. The effect is untypical Ayn Rand: a story written *approvingly* from Dominique's initial viewpoint.

Undoubtedly, the intensity of Miss Rand's personal struggle at the time—her intellectual and professional struggle against a seemingly deaf, even hostile culture—helps to account for the play's approach. Dominique, Miss Rand has said, is "myself in a bad mood." The same may be said of this aspect of *Ideal.*

Despite its somber essence, however, *Ideal* is not entirely a malevolent story. The play does have its lighter, even humorous side, such as its witty satire of Chuck Fink, the "selfless" radical, and of the Elmer Gantry–like Sister Essie Twomey, with her Service Station of the Spirit. The ending, moreover, however unhappy, is certainly not intended as tragedy or defeat. Johnnie's final action is *action*—that is the whole point—action to protect the ideal, as against empty words or dreams. *His* idealism, therefore, is genuine, and Kay Gonda's search ends on a positive note. In this respect, even *Ideal* may be regarded as an affirmation (albeit in an unusual form) of the benevolent universe.

Leonard Peikoff

CHARACTERS

BILL MCNITT, screen director

CLAIRE PEEMOLLER, scenario writer

SOL SALZER, associate producer

ANTHONY FARROW, president of the Farrow Film Studios

FREDERICA SAYERS

MICK WATTS, press agent

MISS TERRENCE, Kay Gonda's secretary

GEORGE S. PERKINS, assistant manager of the Daffodil Canning Co.

MRS. PERKINS, his wife

MRS. SHLY, her mother

KAY GONDA

CHUCK FINK, sociologist

JIMMY, Chuck's friend

FANNY FINK, Chuck's wife

DWIGHT LANGLEY, artist

EUNICE HAMMOND

CLAUDE IGNATIUS HIX, evangelist

SISTER ESSIE TWOMEY, evangelist

EZRY

COUNT DIETRICH VON ESTERHAZY

LALO JANS

MRS. MONAGHAN

JOHNNIE DAWES

SECRETARIES, LANGLEY'S GUESTS, POLICEMEN

Place   Los Angeles, California
Time   Present; from afternoon to early evening of the following day

SYNOPSIS OF SCENES

PROLOGUE—Office of Anthony Farrow in the Farrow Film Studios

ACT I
Scene 1—Living room of George S. Perkins
Scene 2—Living room of Chuck Fink
Scene 3—Studio of Dwight Langley

ACT II
Scene 1—Temple of Claude Ignatius Hix
Scene 2—Drawing room of Dietrich von Esterhazy
Scene 3—Garret of Johnnie Dawes
Scene 4—Entrance hall in the residence of Kay Gonda

PROLOGUE

*L*ate afternoon. Office of ANTHONY FARROW *in the Farrow Film Studios. A spacious, luxurious room in an overdone modernistic style, which looks like the dream of a second-rate interior decorator with no limit set to the bill.*

Entrance door is set diagonally in the upstage Right corner. Small private door downstage in wall Right. Window in wall Left. A poster of KAY GONDA, *on wall Center; she stands erect, full figure, her arms at her sides, palms up, a strange woman, tall, very slender, very pale; her whole body is stretched up in such a line of reverent, desperate aspiration that the poster gives a strange air to the room, an air that does not belong in it. The words* "KAY GONDA IN FORBIDDEN ECSTASY" *stand out on the poster.*

The curtain rises to disclose CLAIRE PEEMOLLER, SOL SALZER, *and* BILL MCNITT. SALZER, *forty, short, stocky, stands with his back to the room, looking hopelessly out of the window, his fingers beating nervously, monotonously, against the glass pane.* CLAIRE PEEMOLLER, *in her early forties, tall, slender, with a sleek masculine haircut and an exotically tailored outfit, reclines in her chair, smoking a cigarette in a lengthy holder.* MCNITT, *who looks like a brute of a man and acts it, lies rather than sits in a deep armchair, his legs stretched out, picking his teeth with a match. No one moves. No one speaks. No one looks at the others. The silence is tense, anxious, broken only by the sound of* SALZER's *fingers on the glass.*

MCNITT: [*Exploding suddenly*] Stop it, for Christ's sake!

[SALZER *turns slowly to look at him and turns away again, but stops the beating. Silence*]

CLAIRE: [*Shrugging*] Well? [*No one answers*] Hasn't anyone here a suggestion to offer?

SALZER: [*Wearily*] Aw, shut up!

CLAIRE: I see absolutely no sense in behaving like this. We can talk about something *else,* can't we?

MCNITT: Well, talk about something else.

CLAIRE: [*With unconvincing lightness*] I saw the rushes of *Love Nest* yesterday. It's a smash, *but* a smash! You should see Eric in that scene where he kills the old man and . . . [*A sudden jerk from the others. She stops short*] Oh, I see. I beg your pardon. [*Silence. She resumes uneasily*] Well, I'll tell you about my new car. The gorgeous thing is so chic! It's simply dripping, *but* dripping with chromium! I was doing eighty yesterday and not a bump! They say this new Sayers Gas is . . . [*There is a stunned, involuntary gasp from the others. She looks at two tense faces*] Well, what on earth is the matter?

SALZER: Listen, Peemoller, for God's sake, Peemoller, don't mention it!

CLAIRE: What?

MCNITT: The name!

CLAIRE: What name?

SALZER: *Sayers,* for God's sake!

CLAIRE: Oh! [*Shrugs with resignation*] I'm sorry.

[*Silence.* MCNITT *breaks the match in his teeth, spits it out, produces a match folder, tears off another match, and continues with his dental work. A man's voice is heard in the next room. They all whirl toward the entrance door*]

SALZER: [*Eagerly*] There's Tony! He'll tell us! He must know something!

[ANTHONY FARROW *opens the door, but turns to speak to someone offstage before entering. He is tall, stately, middle-aged, handsomely tailored and offensively distinguished*]

FARROW: [*Speaking into the next room*] Try Santa Barbara again. Don't hang up until you get her personally. [*Enters, closing the door. The three look at him anxiously, expectantly*] My friends, has any of you seen Kay Gonda today? [*A great sigh, a moan of disappointment, rises from the others*]

SALZER: Well, that's that. You, too. And I thought you knew something!

FARROW: Discipline, my friends. Let us keep our heads. The Farrow Studios expect each man to do his duty.

SALZER: Skip it, Tony! What's the latest?

CLAIRE: It's preposterous! *But* preposterous!

MCNITT: I've always expected something like this from Gonda!

FARROW: No panic, please. There is no occasion for panic. I have called you here in order to formulate our policy in this emergency, coolly and calmly and . . . [*The interoffice communicator on his desk buzzes sharply. He leaps forward, his great calm forgotten, clicks the switch, speaks anxiously*] Yes? . . . You did? Santa Barbara? . . . Give it to me! . . . *What?!* Miss Sayers won't speak to *me*?! . . . She *can't* be out—it's an evasion! Did you tell them it was Anthony Farrow? Of the Farrow Films? . . . Are you sure you made it clear? *President* of the Farrow Films? . . . [*His voice falling dejectedly*] I see. . . . When did Miss Sayers leave? . . . It's an evasion. Try again in half an hour. . . . And try again to get the chief of police.

SALZER: [*Desperately*] That I could have told you! The Sayers dame won't talk. If the papers could get nothing out of her—we can't!

FARROW: Let us be systematic. We cannot face a crisis without a system. Let us have discipline, calm. Am I understood? . . . [*Breaks in two a pencil he has been playing with nervously*] Calm!

SALZER: Calm he wants at a time like this!

FARROW: Let us . . . [*The intercom buzzes. He leaps to it*] Yes? . . . Fine! Put him on! . . . [*Very jovially*] Hel-lo, Chief! How are you? I . . . [*Sharply*] What do you mean you have nothing to say? This is *Anthony Farrow* speaking! . . . Well, it usually *does* make a difference. Hell . . . I mean, Chief, there's only one question I have to ask you, and I think I'm entitled to an answer. Have there or have there not been any charges filed in Santa Barbara? [*Through his teeth*] Very well. . . . Thank you. [*Switches off, trying to control himself*]

SALZER: [*Anxiously*] Well?

FARROW: [*Hopelessly*] He won't talk. No one will talk. [*Turns to the intercom again*] Miss Drake? . . . Have you tried Miss Gonda's home once more? . . . Have you tried all her friends? . . . I know she hasn't any, but try them anyway! [*Is about to switch off, then adds*] And get Mick Watts, if you can find the bast—if you can find him. If anyone knows, *he* knows!

MCNITT: That one won't talk, either.

FARROW: And that is precisely the thing for us to do. Silence. Am I

understood? *Silence.* Do not answer any questions on the lot or
outside. Avoid all references to this morning's papers.

SALZER: *Us* the papers should avoid!

FARROW: They haven't said much so far. It's only rumors. Idle gossip.

CLAIRE: But it's all over town! Hints, whispers, questions. If I could
see any point in it, I'd say someone was spreading it intentionally.

FARROW: Personally, I do not believe the story for a minute. However,
I want all the information you can give me. I take it that none of
you has seen Miss Gonda since yesterday?

[*The others shrug hopelessly, shaking their heads*]

SALZER: If the papers couldn't find her—we can't.

FARROW: Had she mentioned to any of you that she was going to have
dinner with Granton Sayers last night?

CLAIRE: When has she ever told anyone anything?

FARROW: Did you notice anything suspicious in her behavior when
you saw her last?

CLAIRE: I . . .

MCNITT: I should say I did! I thought at the time it was damn funny.
Yesterday morning, it was. I drove up to her beach home and there
she was, out at sea, tearing through the rocks in a motorboat till I
thought I'd have heart failure watching it.

SALZER: My God! That's against our contracts!

MCNITT: What? My having heart failure?

SALZER: To hell with you! Gonda driving her motorboat!

MCNITT: Try and stop her! So she climbs up to the road, finally, wet all
over. "You'll get killed someday," I say to her, and she looks straight
at me and she says, "That won't make any difference to me," she
says, "nor to anyone else anywhere."

FARROW: She said that?

MCNITT: She did. "Listen," I said, "I don't give a damn if you break your neck, but you'll get pneumonia in the middle of my next picture!" She looks at me in that damnable way of hers and she says, "Maybe there won't be any next picture." And she walks straight back to the house and her damn flunky wouldn't let me in!

FARROW: She actually said that? Yesterday?

MCNITT: She did—damn the slut! I never wanted to direct her, anyway. I . . .

[*Intercom buzzes*]

FARROW: [*Clicking the switch*] Yes? . . . *Who?* Who is Goldstein and Goldstein? . . . [*Exploding*] Tell them to go to hell! . . . Wait! Tell them Miss Gonda does *not* need any attorneys! Tell them you don't know what on earth made them think she did! [*Switches off furiously*]

SALZER: God! I wish we'd never signed her! A headache we should have ever since she came on the lot!

FARROW: Sol! You're forgetting yourself! After all! Our greatest star!

SALZER: Where did we find her? In the gutter we found her! In the gutter in Vienna! What do we get for our pains? Gratitude we get?

CLAIRE: Down-to-earthiness, that's what she lacks. You know. No finer feelings. *But* none! No sense of human brotherhood. Honestly, I don't understand what they all see in her, anyway!

SALZER: Five million bucks net per each picture—that's what *I* see!

CLAIRE: I don't know why she draws them like that. She's completely heartless. I went down to her house yesterday afternoon—to discuss her next script. And what's the use? She wouldn't let me put in a baby or a dog, as I wanted to. Dogs have such human appeal. You know, we're all brothers under the skin, and . . .

SALZER: Peemoller's right. She's got something there.

CLAIRE: And furthermore . . . [*Stops suddenly*] Wait! That's funny! I haven't thought of this before. She did mention the dinner.

FARROW: [*Eagerly*] What did she say?

CLAIRE: She got up and left me flat, saying she had to dress. "I'm going to Santa Barbara tonight," she said. Then she added, "I do not like missions of charity."

SALZER: My God, what did she mean by that?

CLAIRE: What does she mean by anything? So then I just couldn't resist it, *but* couldn't! I said, "Miss Gonda, do you really think you're so much better than everybody else?" And what did she have the nerve to answer? "Yes," she said, "I do. I wish I didn't have to."

FARROW: Why didn't you tell me this sooner?

CLAIRE: I had forgotten. I really didn't know there was anything between Gonda and Granton Sayers.

MCNITT: An old story. I thought she was through with him long ago.

CLAIRE: What did *he* want with her?

FARROW: Well, Granton Sayers—you know Granton Sayers. A reckless fool. Fifty million dollars, three years ago. Today—who knows? Perhaps, fifty thousand. Perhaps, fifty cents. But cut-crystal swimming pools and Greek temples in his garden, and . . .

CLAIRE: And Kay Gonda.

FARROW: Ah, yes, and Kay Gonda. An expensive little plaything or artwork, depending on how you want to look at it. Kay Gonda, that is, two years ago. Not today. I know that she had not seen Sayers for over a year, previous to that dinner in Santa Barbara last night.

CLAIRE: Had there been any quarrel between them?

FARROW: None. Never. That fool had proposed to her three times, to my knowledge. She could have had him, Greek temples and oil wells and all, anytime she winked an eyelash.

CLAIRE: Has she had any trouble of any kind lately?

FARROW: None. None whatever. In fact, you know, she was to sign her new contract with us today. She promised me faithfully to be here at five, and . . .

SALZER: [*Clutching his head suddenly*] Tony! It's the contract!

FARROW: What about the contract?

SALZER: Maybe she's changed her mind again, and quit for good.

CLAIRE: A pose, Mr. Salzer, just a pose. She's said that after every picture.

SALZER: Yeah? You should laugh if you had to crawl after her on your knees like we've done for two months. "I'm through," she says. "Does it really mean anything?" Five million net per each picture—does it mean anything! "Is it really worth doing?" Ha! Twenty thousand a week we offer her and she asks is it worth doing!

FARROW: Now, now, Sol. Control your subconscious. You know, I have an idea that she will come here at five. It would be just like her. She is so utterly unpredictable. We cannot judge her actions by the usual standards. With her—anything is possible.

SALZER: Say, Tony, how about the contract? Did she insist again . . . is there anything in it again about Mick Watts?

FARROW: [*Sighing*] There is, unfortunately. We had to write it in again. So long as she is with us, Mick Watts will be her personal press agent. Most unfortunate.

CLAIRE: That's the kind of trash she gathers around her. But the rest of us aren't good enough for her! Well, if she's got herself into a mess now—I'm glad. Yes, glad! I don't see why we should all worry ourselves sick over it.

MCNITT: I don't give a damn myself! I'd much rather direct Joan Tudor anyway.

CLAIRE: And I'd just as soon write for Sally Sweeney. She's such a sweet kid. And . . .

[*The entrance door flies open.* MISS DRAKE *rushes in, slamming it behind her, as if holding the door against someone*]

MISS DRAKE: She's here!
FARROW: [*Leaping to his feet*] Who? Gonda?!
MISS DRAKE: No! Miss Sayers! Miss Frederica Sayers!

[*They all gasp*]

FARROW: What?! Here?!
MISS DRAKE: [*Pointing at the door foolishly*] In there! Right in there!
FARROW: Good Lord!
MISS DRAKE: She wants to see you, Mr. Farrow. She *demands* to see you!
FARROW: Well, let her in! Let her right in, for God's sake! [*As* MISS DRAKE *is about to rush out*] Wait! [*To the others*] You'd better get out of here! It may be confidential. [*Rushes them to private door Right*]
SALZER: [*On his way out*] Make her talk, Tony! For God's sake, make her talk!
FARROW: Don't worry!

[SALZER, CLAIRE, *and* MCNITT *exit Right.* FARROW *whirls on* MISS DRAKE]

FARROW: Don't stand there shaking! Bring her right in!

[MISS DRAKE *exits hurriedly.* FARROW *flops down behind his desk and attempts a nonchalant attitude. The entrance door is thrown open as* FREDERICA SAYERS *enters. She is a tall, sparse, stern lady of middle age, gray-haired, erect in her black clothes of mourning.* MISS DRAKE *hovers anxiously behind her.* FARROW *jumps to his feet*]

MISS DRAKE: Miss Frederica Sayers, Mr. Far—

MISS SAYERS: [*Brushing her aside*] Abominable discipline in your studio, Farrow! That's no way to run the place. [MISS DRAKE *slips out, closing the door*] Five reporters pounced on me at the gate and trailed me to your office. I suppose it will all appear in the evening papers, the color of my underwear included.

FARROW: My *dear* Miss Sayers! How do you do? So kind of you to come here! Rest assured that I . . .

MISS SAYERS: Where's Kay Gonda? I must see her. At once.

FARROW: [*Looks at her, startled. Then:*] Do sit down, Miss Sayers. Please allow me to express my deepest sympathy for your grief at the untimely loss of your brother, who . . .

MISS SAYERS: My brother was a fool. [*Sits down*] I've always known he'd end up like this.

FARROW: [*Cautiously*] I must admit I have not been able to learn all the unfortunate details. How *did* Mr. Sayers meet his death?

MISS SAYERS: [*Glancing at him sharply*] Mr. Farrow, your time is valuable. So is mine. I did not come here to answer questions. In fact, I did not come here to speak to you at all. I came to find Miss Gonda. It is most urgent.

FARROW: Miss Sayers, let us get this clear. I have been trying to get in touch with you since early this morning. You must know who started these rumors. And you must realize how utterly preposterous it is. Miss Gonda happens to have dinner with your brother last night. He is found dead, this morning, with a bullet through him. . . . Most unfortunate and I do sympathize, believe me, but is this ground enough for a suspicion of murder against a lady of Miss Gonda's standing? Merely the fact that she happened to be the last one seen with him?

MISS SAYERS: And the fact that nobody has seen her since.

FARROW: Did she . . . did she really do it?

MISS SAYERS: I have nothing to say about that.

FARROW: Was there anyone else at your house last night?

MISS SAYERS: I have nothing to say about that.

FARROW: But good God! [*Controlling himself*] Look here, Miss Sayers, I can well understand that you may not wish to give it out to the press, but you can tell me, in strict confidence, can't you? What were the exact circumstances of your brother's death?

MISS SAYERS: I have given my statement to the police.

FARROW: The police refuse to disclose anything!

MISS SAYERS: They must have their reasons.

FARROW: Miss Sayers! Please try to understand the position I'm in! I'm entitled to know. What actually happened at that dinner?

MISS SAYERS: I have never spied on Granton and his mistresses.

FARROW: But . . .

MISS SAYERS: Have you asked Miss Gonda? What did she say?

FARROW: Look here, if you don't talk—I don't talk, either.

MISS SAYERS: I have not asked you to talk. In fact, I haven't the slightest interest in anything you may say. I want to see Miss Gonda. It is to her own advantage. To yours also, I suppose.

FARROW: May I give her the message?

MISS SAYERS: Your technique is childish, my good man.

FARROW: But in heaven's name, what is it all about? If you've accused her of murder, you have no right to come here demanding to see her! If she's hiding, wouldn't she be hiding from you above all people?

MISS SAYERS: Most unfortunate, if she is. Highly ill advised. Highly.

FARROW: Look here, I'll offer you a bargain. You tell me everything and I'll take you to Miss Gonda. Not otherwise.

MISS SAYERS: [*Rising*] I have always been told that picture people had abominable manners. Most regrettable. Please tell Miss Gonda that I have tried. I shall not be responsible for the consequences now.

FARROW: [*Rushing after her*] Wait! Miss Sayers! Wait a moment! [*She turns to him*] I'm so sorry! Please forgive me! I'm . . . I'm quite upset, as you can well understand. I beg of you, Miss Sayers, consider what it means! The greatest star of the screen! The dream woman of the world! They worship her, millions of them. It's practically a cult.

MISS SAYERS: I have never approved of motion pictures. Never saw one. The pastime of morons.

FARROW: You wouldn't say that if you read her fan mail. Do you think it comes from shopgirls and schoolkids, like the usual kind of trash? No. Not Kay Gonda's mail. From college professors and authors and judges and ministers! Everybody! Dirt farmers and international names! It's extraordinary! I've never seen anything like it in my whole career.

MISS SAYERS: Indeed?

FARROW: I don't know what she does to them all—but she does something. She's not a movie star to them—she's a goddess. [*Correcting himself hastily*] Oh, forgive me. I understand how you must feel about her. Of course, you and I know that Miss Gonda is not exactly above reproach. She is, in fact, a very objectionable person who . . .

MISS SAYERS: I thought she was a rather charming young woman. A bit anemic. A vitamin deficiency in her diet, no doubt. [*Turning to him suddenly*] Was she happy?

FARROW: [*Looking at her*] Why do you ask that?

MISS SAYERS: I don't think she was.

FARROW: That, Miss Sayers, is a question I've been asking myself for years. She's a strange woman.

MISS SAYERS: She is.

FARROW: But surely you can't hate her so much as to want to ruin her!

MISS SAYERS: I do not hate her at all.

FARROW: Then for heaven's sake, help me to save her name! Tell me what happened. One way or the other, only let's stop these rumors! Let's stop these rumors!

MISS SAYERS: This is getting tiresome, my good man. For the last time, will you let me see Miss Gonda or won't you?

FARROW: I'm so sorry, but it is impossible, and . . .

MISS SAYERS: Either you are a fool or you don't know where she is yourself. Regrettable, in either case. I wish you a good day.

[*She is at the entrance door when the private door Right is thrown open violently.* SALZER *and* MCNITT *enter, dragging and pushing* MICK WATTS *between them.* MICK WATTS *is tall, about thirty-five, with disheveled platinum-blond hair, the ferocious face of a thug, and the blue eyes of a baby. He is obviously, unquestionably drunk*]

MCNITT: There's your precious Mick Watts for you!

SALZER: Where do you think we found him? He was . . . [*Stops short seeing* MISS SAYERS] Oh, I beg your pardon! We thought Miss Sayers had left!

MICK WATTS: [*Tearing himself loose from them*] Miss *Sayers*?! [*Reels ferociously toward her*] What did you tell them?

MISS SAYERS: [*Looking at him coolly*] And who are you, young man?

MICK WATTS: *What did you tell them?*

MISS SAYERS: [*Haughtily*] I have told them nothing.

MICK WATTS: Well, keep your mouth shut! Keep your mouth shut!

MISS SAYERS: That, young man, is precisely what I am doing. [*Exits*]

MCNITT: [*Lurching furiously at* MICK WATTS] Why, you drunken fool!

FARROW: [*Interfering*] Wait a moment! What happened? Where did you find him?

SALZER: Down in the publicity department! Just think of that! He walked right in and there's a mob of reporters pounced on him and started filling him up with liquor and—

FARROW: Oh, my Lord!

SALZER: —and here's what he was handing out for a press release! [*Straightens out a slip of paper he has crumpled in his hand, reads:*] "Kay Gonda does not cook her own meals or knit her own underwear. She does not play golf, adopt babies, or endow hospitals for homeless horses. She is not kind to her dear old mother—she *has* no dear old mother. She is not just like you and me. She never was like you and me. She's like nothing you bastards ever dreamt of!"

FARROW: [*Clutching his head*] Did they get it?

SALZER: A fool you should think I am? We dragged him out of there just in time!

FARROW: [*Approaching* MICK WATTS, ingratiatingly] Sit down, Mick, do sit down. There's a good boy.

[MICK WATTS *flops down on a chair and sits motionless, staring into space*]

MCNITT: If you let me punch the bastard just once, he'll talk all right.

Prologue

[SALZER *nudges him frantically to keep quiet.* FARROW *hurries to a cabinet, produces a glass and a decanter, pours*]

FARROW: [*Bending over* MICK WATTS, *solicitously, offering him the glass*] A drink, Mick? [MICK WATTS *does not move or answer*] Nice weather we're having, Mick. Nice, but hot. Awfully hot. Supposing you and I have a drink together?

MICK WATTS: [*In a dull monotone*] I don't know a thing. Save your liquor. Go to hell.

FARROW: What *are* you talking about?

MICK WATTS: I'm talking about nothing—and that goes for everything.

FARROW: You could stand a drink once in a while, couldn't you? You look thirsty to me.

MICK WATTS: I don't know a thing about Kay Gonda. Never heard of her. . . . Kay Gonda. It's a funny name, isn't it? I went to confession once, long ago—and they talked about the redemption of all sins. It's useless to yell "Kay Gonda" and to think that all your sins are washed away. Just pay two bits in the balcony—and come out pure as snow.

[*The others exchange glances and shrug hopelessly*]

FARROW: On second thought, Mick, I won't offer you another drink. You'd better have something to eat.

MICK WATTS: I'm not hungry. I stopped being hungry many years ago. But she is.

FARROW: Who?

MICK WATTS: Kay Gonda.

FARROW: [*Eagerly*] Any idea where she's having her next meal?

IDEAL

MICK WATTS: In heaven. [FARROW *shakes his head helplessly*] In a blue heaven with white lilies. Very white lilies. Only she'll never find it.

FARROW: I don't understand you, Mick.

MICK WATTS: [*Looking at him slowly for the first time*] You don't understand? She doesn't, either. Only it's no use. It's no use trying to unravel, because if you try, you end up with more dirt on your hands than you care to wipe off. There are not enough towels in the world to wipe it off. Not enough towels. That's the trouble.

SALZER: [*Impatiently*] Look here, Watts, you must know something. You'd better play ball with us. Remember, you've been fired from every newspaper on both coasts—

MICK WATTS: —and from many others in between.

SALZER: —so that if anything should happen to Gonda, you won't have a job here unless you help us now and . . .

MICK WATTS: [*His voice emotionless*] Do you think I'd want to stay with the lousy bunch of you if it weren't for her?

MCNITT: Jesus, it beats me what they all see in that bitch!

[MICK WATTS *turns and looks at* MCNITT *fixedly, ominously*]

SALZER: [*Placatingly*] Now, now, Mick, he doesn't mean it. He's kidding, he's—

[MICK WATTS *rises slowly, deliberately, walks up to* MCNITT *without hurry, then strikes him flat on the face, a blow that sends him sprawling on the floor.* FARROW *rushes to help the stunned* MCNITT. MICK WATTS *stands motionless, with perfect indifference, his arms limp*]

MCNITT: [*Raising his head slowly*] The damn . . .

FARROW: [*Restraining him*] Discipline, Bill, discipline, control your . . .

[*The door is flung open as* CLAIRE PEEMOLLER *rushes in breath-lessly*]

CLAIRE: She's coming! She's coming!

FARROW: Who?!

CLAIRE: Kay Gonda! I just saw her car turning the corner!

SALZER: [*Looking at his wristwatch*] By God! It's five o'clock! Can you beat that!

FARROW: I knew she would! I knew it! [*Rushes to intercom, shouts:*] Miss Drake! Bring in the contract!

CLAIRE: [*Tugging at* FARROW'*s sleeve*] Tony, you won't tell her what I said, will you, Tony? I've always been her best friend! I'll do anything to please her! I've always . . .

SALZER: [*Grabbing a telephone*] Get the publicity department! Quick!

MCNITT: [*Rushing to* MICK WATTS] I was only kidding, Mick! You know I was only kidding. No hard feelings, eh, pal?

[MICK WATTS *does not move or look at him.* WATTS *is the only one motionless amid the frantic activity*]

SALZER: [*Shouting into the phone*] Hello, Meagley? . . . Call all the papers! Reserve the front pages! Tell you later! [*Hangs up*]

[MISS DRAKE *enters, carrying a batch of legal documents*]

FARROW: [*At his desk*] Put it right here, Miss Drake! Thank you! [*Steps are heard approaching*] Smile, all of you! Smile! Don't let her think that we thought for a minute that she . . .

[*Everyone obeys, save* MICK WATTS, *all eyes turned to the door. The door opens.* MISS TERRENCE *enters and steps on the threshold. She is a prim, ugly little shrimp of a woman*]

MISS TERRENCE: Is Miss Gonda here?

[*A moan rises from the others*]

SALZER: Oh, God!

MISS TERRENCE: [*Looking at the stunned group*] Well, what is the matter?

CLAIRE: [*Choking*] Did you . . . did *you* drive up in Miss Gonda's car?

MISS TERRENCE: [*With hurt dignity*] Why, certainly. Miss Gonda had an appointment here at five o'clock, and I thought it a secretary's duty to come and tell Mr. Farrow that it looks as if Miss Gonda will not be able to keep it.

FARROW: [*Dully*] So it does.

MISS TERRENCE: There is also something rather peculiar I wanted to check on. Has anyone from the studio been at Miss Gonda's home since last night?

FARROW: [*Perking up*] No. Why, Miss Terrence?

MISS TERRENCE: This is *most* peculiar.

SALZER: *What* is?

MISS TERRENCE: I'm sure I can't understand it. I've questioned the servants, but they have not taken them.

FARROW: Taken what?

MISS TERRENCE: If no one else took them, then Miss Gonda must have been back at home late last night.

FARROW: [*Eagerly*] Why, Miss Terrence?

MISS TERRENCE: Because I saw them on her desk yesterday after she left for Santa Barbara. And when I entered her room this morning, they were gone.

FARROW: What was gone?

MISS TERRENCE: Six letters from among Miss Gonda's fan mail.

[*A great sigh of disappointment rises from all*]

SALZER: Aw, nuts!

MCNITT: And I thought it was something!

[MICK WATTS *bursts out laughing suddenly, for no apparent reason*]

FARROW: [*Angrily*] What are you laughing at?

MICK WATTS: [*Quietly*] Kay Gonda.

MCNITT: Oh, throw the drunken fool out!

MICK WATTS: [*Without looking at anyone*] A great quest. The quest of the hopeless. Why do we hope? Why do we seek it, when we'd be luckier if we didn't think that it could exist? Why does she? Why does she have to be hurt? [*Whirls suddenly upon the others with ferocious hatred*] Goddamn you all! [*Rushes out, slamming the door*]

CURTAIN

ACT I

SCENE I

When the curtain rises, a motion-picture screen is disclosed and a letter is flashed on the screen, unrolling slowly. It is written in a neat, precise, respectable handwriting:

Dear Miss Gonda,

I am not a regular movie fan, but I have never missed a picture of yours. There is something about you which I can't give a name to, something I had and lost, but I feel as if you're keeping it for me, for all of us. I had it long ago, when I was very young. You know how it is: when you're very young, there's something ahead of you, so big that you're afraid of it, but you wait for it and you're so happy waiting. Then the years pass and it never comes. And then you find, one day, that you're not waiting any longer. It seems foolish, because you didn't even know what it was you were waiting for. I look at myself and I don't know. But when I look at you—I do.

And if ever, by some miracle, you were to enter my life, I'd drop everything, and follow you, and gladly lay down my life for you, because, you see, I'm still a human being.

Very truly yours,

George S. Perkins

. . . S. Hoover Street

Los Angeles, California

When the letter ends, all lights go out, and when they come on again, the screen has disappeared and the stage reveals the living room of GEORGE S. PERKINS.

It is a room such as thousands of other rooms in thousands of other homes whose owners have a respectable little income and a respectable little character.

Center back, a wide glass door opening on the street. Door into the rest of the house in wall Left.

When the curtain rises, it is evening. The street outside is dark. MRS. PERKINS *stands in the middle of the room, tense, erect, indignant, watching with smoldering emotion the entrance door where* GEORGE S. PERKINS *is seen outside turning the key in the lock.* MRS. PERKINS *looks like a dried-out bird of prey that has never been young.* GEORGE S. PERKINS *is short, blond, heavy, helpless, and over forty. He is whistling a gay tune as he enters. He is in a very cheerful mood.*

MRS. PERKINS: [*Without moving, ominously*] You're late.

PERKINS: [*Cheerfully*] Well, dovey, I have a good excuse for being late.

MRS. PERKINS: [*Speaking very fast*] I have no doubt about that. But listen to me, George Perkins, you'll have to do something about Junior. That boy of yours got a D again in arithmetic. If a father don't take the proper interest in his children, what can you expect from a boy who . . .

PERKINS: Aw, honeybunch, we'll excuse the kid for once—just to celebrate.

MRS. PERKINS: Celebrate what?

PERKINS: How would you like to be Mrs. Assistant Manager of the Daffodil Canning Company?

MRS. PERKINS: I would like it very much. Not that I have any hopes of ever being.

PERKINS: Well, dovey, you are. As of today.

MRS. PERKINS: [*Noncommittally*] Oh. [*Calls into house*] Mama! Come here!

[MRS. SHLY *waddles in from door Left. She is fat and looks chronically dissatisfied with the whole world.* MRS. PERKINS *speaks, half-boasting, half-bitter*]

Mama, Georgie's got a promotion.

MRS. SHLY: [*Dryly*] Well, we've waited for it long enough.

PERKINS: But you don't understand. I've been made *Assistant Manager*—[*Looks for the effect on her face, finds none, adds lamely*]—of the Daffodil Canning Company.

MRS. SHLY: Well?

PERKINS: [*Spreading his hands helplessly*] Well . . .

MRS. SHLY: All I gotta say is it's a fine way to start off on your promotion, coming home at such an hour, keeping us waiting with dinner and . . .

PERKINS: Oh, I . . .

MRS. SHLY: Oh, we ate all right, don't you worry! Never seen a man that cared two hoops about his family, not two hoops!

PERKINS: I'm sorry. I had dinner with the boss. I should've phoned, only I couldn't keep him waiting, you know, the boss asking me to dinner, in person.

MRS. PERKINS: And here I was waiting for you. I had something to tell you, a nice surprise for you, and . . .

MRS. SHLY: Don't you tell him, Rosie. Don't you tell him now. Serves him right.

PERKINS: But I figured you'd understand. I figured you'd be happy— [*Corrects his presumption hastily*]—well, *glad* that I've been made—

MRS. PERKINS: —Assistant Manager! Lord, do we have to hear it for the rest of our lives?

PERKINS: [*Softly*] Rosie, it's twenty years I've waited for it.

MRS. SHLY: That, my boy, is nothing to brag about!

PERKINS: It's a long time, twenty years. One gets sort of tired. But now we can take it easy . . . light . . . [*With sudden eagerness*] . . . you know, *light* . . . [*Coming down to earth, apologetically*] . . . easy, I mean.

MRS. SHLY: Listen to him! How much you got, Mr. Rock*a*feller?

PERKINS: [*With quiet pride*] One hundred and sixty-five dollars.

MRS. PERKINS: A *week*?

PERKINS: Yes, dovey, a week. Every single week.

MRS. SHLY: [*Impressed*] Well! [*Gruffly*] Well, what're you standing there for? Sit down. You must be all tired out.

PERKINS: [*Removing his coat*] Mind if I slip my coat off? Sort of stuffy tonight.

MRS. PERKINS: I'll fetch your bathrobe. Don't you go catching a cold. [*Exits Left*]

MRS. SHLY: We gotta think it over careful. There's lots a man can do with one-sixty-five a week. Not that there ain't some men what get around two hundred. Still, one-sixty-five ain't to be sneezed at.

PERKINS: I've been thinking . . .

MRS. PERKINS: [*Returning with a flashy striped flannel bathrobe*] Now, put it on like a good boy, nice and comfy.

PERKINS: [*Obeying*] Thanks. . . . Dovey, I was sort of planning . . . I've been thinking of it for a long time, nights, you know . . . making plans . . .

MRS. PERKINS: Plans? But your wife's not let in on it?

PERKINS: Oh, it was only sort of like dreaming . . . I wanted to . . .

[*There is a thunderous crash upstairs, the violent scuffle of a battle and a child's shrill scream*]

BOY'S VOICE: [*Offstage*] No, ya don't! No, ya don't! Ya dirty snot!

GIRL'S VOICE: Ma-a-a!

BOY'S VOICE: I'll learn ya! I'll . . .

GIRL'S VOICE: Ma-a! He bit me on the pratt!

MRS. PERKINS: [*Throws the door Left open, yells upstairs*] Keep quiet up there and march straight to bed, or I'll beat the living Jesus out of the both of you! [*Slams the door. The noise upstairs subsides to thin whimpers*] For the life of me, I don't see why of all the children in the world I had to get these!

PERKINS: Please, dovey, not tonight. I'm tired. I wanted to talk about . . . the plans.

MRS. PERKINS: What plans?

PERKINS: I was thinking . . . if we're very careful, we could take a vacation maybe . . . in a year or two . . . and go to Europe, you know, like Switzerland or Italy . . . [*Looks at her hopefully, sees no reaction, adds*] . . . It's where they have mountains, you know.

MRS. PERKINS: Well?

PERKINS: Well, and lakes. And snow high up on the peaks. And sunsets.

MRS. PERKINS: And what would we do?

PERKINS: Oh . . . well . . . just rest, I guess. And look around, sort of. You know, at the swans and the sailboats. Just the two of us.

MRS. SHLY: Uh-huh. Just the *two* of you.

MRS. PERKINS: Yes, you were always a great one for making up ways of wasting good money, George Perkins. And me slaving and skimping and saving every little penny. Swans, indeed! Well, before you go thinking of any swans, you'd better get us a new Frigidaire, that's all I've got to say.

MRS. SHLY: And a mayonnaise mixer. And a 'lectric washing machine. And it's about time to be thinking of a new car, too. The old one's a sight. And . . .

PERKINS: Look, you don't understand. I don't want anything that we need.

MRS. PERKINS: What?

PERKINS: I want something I don't need at all.

MRS. PERKINS: George Perkins! Have you been drinking?

PERKINS: Rosie, I . . .

MRS. SHLY: [*Resolutely*] Now, I've had just about enough of this nonsense! Now, you come down to earth, George Perkins. There's something bigger to think about. Rosie has a surprise for you. A pretty surprise. Tell him, Rosie.

MRS. PERKINS: I just found it out today, Georgie. You'll be glad to hear it.

MRS. SHLY: He'll be tickled pink. Go on.

MRS. PERKINS: Well, I . . . I've been to the doctor's this morning. We have a baby coming.

Act I

[*Silence. The two women look, with bright smiles, at* PERKINS' *face, a face that distorts slowly before their eyes into an expression of stunned horror*]

PERKINS: [*In a choked voice*] Another one?

MRS. PERKINS: [*Brightly*] Uh-huh. A brand-new little baby. [*He stares at her silently*] Well? [*He stares without moving*] Well, what's the matter with you? [*He does not move*] Aren't you glad?

PERKINS: [*In a slow, heavy voice*] You're not going to have it.

MRS. PERKINS: Mama! What's he saying?

PERKINS: [*In a dull, persistent monotone*] You know what I'm saying. You can't have it. You won't.

MRS. SHLY: Have you gone plumb outta your mind? Are you thinking of . . . of . . .

PERKINS: [*Dully*] Yes.

MRS. PERKINS: Mama!!

MRS. SHLY: [*Ferociously*] D'you know who you're talking to? It's my daughter you're talking to, not a street woman! To come right out with a thing like that . . . to his own wife . . . to his own . . .

MRS. PERKINS: What's happened to you?

PERKINS: Rosie, I didn't mean to insult you. It's not even dangerous nowadays and . . .

MRS. PERKINS: Make him stop, Mama!

MRS. SHLY: Where did you pick that up? Decent people don't even know about such things! You hear about it maybe with gangsters and actresses. But in a respectable married home!

MRS. PERKINS: What's happened to you today?

PERKINS: It's not today, Rosie. It's for a long, long time back. . . . But I'm set with the firm now. I can take good care of you and the children. But the rest— Rosie, I can't throw it away for good.

MRS. PERKINS: What are you talking about? What better use can you find for your extra money than to take care of a baby?

PERKINS: That's just it. Take care of it. The hospital and the doctors. The strained vegetables—at two bits a can. The school and the measles. All over again. And nothing else.

MRS. PERKINS: So that's how you feel about your duties! There's nothing holier than to raise a family. There's no better blessing. Haven't I spent my life making a home for you? Don't you have everything every decent man struggles for? What else do you want?

PERKINS: Rosie, it's not that I don't like what I've got. I like it fine. Only . . . Well, it's like this bathrobe of mine. I'm glad I have it, it's warm and comfortable, and I like it, just the same as I like the rest of it. Just like that. And no more. There should be more.

MRS. PERKINS: Well, I like that! The swell bathrobe I picked out for your birthday! Well, if you didn't like it, why didn't you exchange it?

PERKINS: Oh, Rosie, it's not that! It's only that a man can't live his whole life for a bathrobe. Or for things that he feels the same way about. Things that do nothing to him—inside, I mean. There should be something that he's afraid of—afraid and happy. Like going to church—only not in a church. Something he can look up to. Something—high, Rosie . . . that's it, *high*.

MRS. PERKINS: Well, if it's culture you want, didn't I subscribe to the Book-of-the-Month Club?

PERKINS: Oh, I know I can't explain it! All I ask is, don't let's have that baby, Rosie. That would be the end of it all for me. I'll be an old man, if I give those things up. I don't want to be old. Not yet. God, not yet! Just leave me a few years, Rosie!

MRS. PERKINS: [*Breaking down into tears*] Never, never, never did I think I'd live to hear this!

MRS. SHLY: [*Rushing to her*] Rosie, sweetheart! Don't cry like that, baby! [*Whirling upon* PERKINS] See what you've done? Now, don't let me hear another word out of that filthy mouth of yours! Do you want to kill your wife? Take the Chinese, for instance. They go in for abortions, that's why all the Chinks have rickets.

PERKINS: Now, Mother, who ever told you that?

MRS. SHLY: Well, I suppose I don't know what I'm talking about? I suppose the big businessman is the only one to tell us what's what?

PERKINS: I didn't mean . . . I only meant that . . .

MRS. PERKINS: [*Through her sobs*] You leave Mama alone, George.

PERKINS: [*Desperately*] But I didn't . . .

MRS. SHLY: I understand. I understand perfectly, George Perkins. An old mother, these days, is no good for anything but to shut up and wait for the graveyard!

PERKINS: [*Resolutely*] Mother, I wish you'd stop trying to . . . [*Bravely*] . . . to make trouble.

MRS. SHLY: So? So that's it? So I'm making trouble? So I'm a burden to you, am I? Well, I'm glad you came out with it, Mr. Perkins! And here I've been, poor fool that I am, slaving in this house like if it was my own! That's the gratitude I get. Well, I won't stand for it another minute. Not one minute. [*Rushes out Left, slamming the door*]

MRS. PERKINS: [*With consternation*] George! . . . George, if you don't apologize, Mama will leave us!

PERKINS: [*With sudden, desperate courage*] Well, let her go.

MRS. PERKINS: [*Stares at him incredulously, then:*] So it's come to that? So that's what it does to you, your big promotion? Coming home, picking a fight with everybody, throwing his wife's old mother out into the gutter! If you think I'm going to stand for . . .

PERKINS: Listen, I've stood about as much of her as I'm going to stand. She'd better go. It was coming to this, sooner or later.

MRS. PERKINS: You just listen to me, George Perkins! If you don't apologize to Mama, if you don't apologize to her before tomorrow morning, I'll never speak to you again as long as I live!

PERKINS: [*Wearily*] How many times have I heard that before?

[MRS. PERKINS *runs to door Left and exits, slamming the door.* PERKINS *sits wearily, without moving. An old-fashioned clock strikes nine. He rises slowly, turns out the lights, pulls the shade down over the glass entrance door. The room is dim but for one lamp burning by the fireplace. He leans against the mantelpiece, his head on his arm, slumped wearily. The doorbell rings. It is a quick, nervous, somehow furtive sound.* PERKINS *starts, looks at the entrance door, surprised, hesitates, then crosses to door and opens it. Before we can see the visitor, his voice a stunned explosion:*] Oh, my God!! [PERKINS *steps aside.* KAY GONDA *stands on the threshold. She wears an exquisitely plain black suit, very modern, austerely severe; a black hat, black shoes, stockings, bag, and gloves. The sole and startling contrast to her clothes is the pale, luminous gold of her hair and the whiteness of her face. It is a strange face with eyes that make one uncomfortable. She is tall and very slender. Her movements are slow, her steps light, soundless. There is a feeling of unreality about her, the feeling of a being that does not belong on this earth. She looks more like a ghost than a woman*]

KAY GONDA: Please keep quiet. And let me in.

PERKINS: [*Stuttering foolishly*] You . . . you are . . .

KAY GONDA: Kay Gonda. [*She enters and closes the door behind her*]

PERKINS: W-why . . .

KAY GONDA: Are you George Perkins?

Act I

PERKINS: [*Foolishly*] Yes, ma'am. George Perkins. George S. Perkins . . . Only how . . .

KAY GONDA: I am in trouble. Have you heard about it?

PERKINS: Y-yes . . . oh, my God! . . . Yes . . .

KAY GONDA: I have to hide. For the night. It is dangerous. Can you let me stay here?

PERKINS: *Here?*

KAY GONDA: Yes. For one night.

PERKINS: But how . . . That is . . . Why did you . . .

KAY GONDA: [*Opens her bag and shows him the letter*] I read your letter. And I thought that no one would look for me here. And I thought you would want to help me.

PERKINS: I . . . Miss Gonda, you'll excuse me, please, you know it's enough to make a fellow . . . I mean, if I don't seem to make sense or . . . I mean, if you need help, you can stay here the rest of your life, Miss Gonda.

KAY GONDA: [*Calmly*] Thank you. [*She throws her bag on a table, takes off her hat and gloves, indifferently, as if she were quite at home. He keeps staring at her*]

PERKINS: You mean . . . they're really after you?

KAY GONDA: The police. [*Adds*] For murder.

PERKINS: I won't let them get you. If there's anything I can . . . [*He stops short. Steps are heard approaching, behind the door Left*]

MRS. PERKINS' VOICE: [*Offstage*] George!

PERKINS: Yes . . . dovey?

MRS. PERKINS' VOICE: Who was that who rang the bell?

PERKINS: No . . . no one, dovey. Somebody had the wrong address. [*He listens to the steps moving away, then whispers:*] That was my wife. We'd better keep quiet. She's all right. Only . . . she wouldn't understand.

KAY GONDA: It will be dangerous for you, if they find me here.

PERKINS: I don't care. [*She smiles slowly. He points to the room helplessly*] Just make yourself at home. You can sleep right here, on the davenport, and I'll stay outside and watch to see that no one . . .

KAY GONDA: No. I don't want to sleep. Stay here. You and I, we have so much to talk about.

PERKINS: Oh, yes. Sure . . . that is . . . about what, Miss Gonda?

[*She sits down without answering. He sits down on the edge of a chair, gathering his bathrobe, miserably uncomfortable. She looks at him expectantly, a silent question in her eyes. He blinks, clears his throat, says resolutely:*]

Pretty cold night, this is.

KAY GONDA: Yes.

PERKINS: That's California for you . . . the Golden West . . . Sunshine all day, but cold as the . . . but very cold at night.

KAY GONDA: Give me a cigarette.

[*He leaps to his feet, produces a package of cigarettes, strikes three matches before he can light one. She leans back, the lit cigarette between her fingers*]

PERKINS: [*He mutters helplessly*] I . . . I smoke this kind. Easier on your throat, they are. [*He looks at her miserably. He has so much to tell her. He fumbles for words. He ends with:*] Now, Joe Tucker—that's a friend of mine—Joe Tucker, he smokes cigars. But I never took to them, never did.

KAY GONDA: You have many friends?

PERKINS: Yes, sure. Sure I have. Can't complain.

KAY GONDA: You like them?

PERKINS: Yes, I like them fine.

KAY GONDA: And they like you? They approve of you, and they bow to you on the street?

PERKINS: Why . . . I guess so.

KAY GONDA: How old are you, George Perkins?

PERKINS: I'll be forty-three this coming June.

KAY GONDA: It will be hard to lose your job and to find yourself in the street. In a dark, lonely street, where you'll see your friends passing by and looking past you, as if you did not exist. Where you will want to scream and tell them of the great things you know, but no one will hear and no one will answer. It will be hard, won't it?

PERKINS: [Bewildered] Why . . . When should that happen?

KAY GONDA: [Calmly] When they find me here.

PERKINS: [Resolutely] Don't worry about that. No one will find you here. Not that I'm afraid for myself. Suppose they learn I helped you? Who wouldn't? Who'd hold that against me? Why should they?

KAY GONDA: Because they hate me. And they hate all those who take my side.

PERKINS: Why should they hate you?

KAY GONDA: [Calmly] I am a murderess, George Perkins.

PERKINS: Well, if you ask me, I don't believe it. I don't even want to ask you whether you've done it. I just don't believe it.

KAY GONDA: If you mean Granton Sayers . . . No, I do not want to speak about Granton Sayers. Forget that. But I am still a murderess. You see, I came here and, perhaps, I will destroy your life— everything that has been your life for forty-three years.

PERKINS: [In a low voice] That's not much, Miss Gonda.

KAY GONDA: Do you always go to see my pictures?

PERKINS: Always.

KAY GONDA: Are you happy when you come out of the theater?

PERKINS: Yes. Sure. . . . No, I guess I'm not. That's funny, I never thought of it that way. . . . Miss Gonda, you won't laugh at me if I tell you something?

KAY GONDA: Of course not.

PERKINS: Miss Gonda, I . . . I cry when I come home after seeing a picture of yours. I just lock myself in the bathroom and I cry, every time. I don't know why.

KAY GONDA: I knew that.

PERKINS: How?

KAY GONDA: I told you I am a murderess. I kill so many things in people. I kill the things they live by. But they come to see me because I am the only one who makes them realize that they want those things to be killed. Or they think they do. And it's their whole pride, that they think and say they do.

PERKINS: I'm afraid I don't follow you, Miss Gonda.

KAY GONDA: You'll understand someday.

PERKINS: Did you really do it?

KAY GONDA: What?

PERKINS: Did you kill Granton Sayers? [*She looks at him, smiles slowly, shrugs*] I was only wondering why you could have done it.

KAY GONDA: Because I could not stand it any longer. There are times when one can't stand it any longer.

PERKINS: Yes. There are.

KAY GONDA: [*Looking straight at him*] Why do you want to help me?

PERKINS: I don't know . . . only that . . .

KAY GONDA: Your letter, it said . . .

PERKINS: Oh! I never thought you'd read the silly thing.

KAY GONDA: It was not silly.

PERKINS: I bet you have plenty of them, fans, I mean, and letters.

KAY GONDA: I like to think that I mean something to people.

PERKINS: You must forgive me if I said anything fresh, you know, or personal.

KAY GONDA: You said you were not happy.

PERKINS: I . . . I didn't mean to complain, Miss Gonda, only . . . I guess I've missed something along the way. I don't know what it is, but I know I've missed it. Only I don't know why.

KAY GONDA: Perhaps it is because you wanted to miss it.

PERKINS: No. [*His voice is suddenly firm*] No. [*He rises and stands looking straight at her*] You see, I'm not unhappy at all. In fact, I'm a very happy man—as happiness goes. Only there's something in me that knows of a life I've never lived, the kind of life no one has ever lived, but should.

KAY GONDA: You know it? Why don't you live it?

PERKINS: Who does? Who can? Who ever gets a chance at the . . . the very best possible to him? We all bargain. We take the second best. That's all there is to be had. But the . . . the God in us, it knows the other . . . the very best . . . which never comes.

KAY GONDA: And . . . if it came?

PERKINS: We'd grab it because there *is* a God in us.

KAY GONDA: And . . . the God in you, you really want it?

PERKINS: [*Fiercely*] Look, I know this: let them come, the cops, let them come now and try to get you. Let them tear this house down. I built it—took me fifteen years to pay for it. Let them tear it down, before I let them take you. Let them come, whoever it is that's after you . . . [*The door Left is flung open.* MRS. PERKINS *stands on the threshold; she wears a faded corduroy bathrobe and a long nightgown of grayish-pink cotton*]

MRS. PERKINS: [*Gasping*] George! . . .

[KAY GONDA *rises and stands looking at them*]

PERKINS: Dovey, keep quiet! For God's sake, keep quiet . . . Come
in . . . Close the door!

MRS. PERKINS: I thought I heard voices . . . I . . . [*She chokes, unable to
continue*]

PERKINS: Dovey . . . this . . . Miss Gonda, may I present—my wife?
Dovey, this is Miss Gonda, Miss Kay Gonda! [KAY GONDA *inclines
her head, but* MRS. PERKINS *remains motionless, staring at her.*
PERKINS *says desperately*:] Don't you understand? Miss Gonda's in
trouble, you know, you've heard about it, the papers said . . . [*He
stops.* MRS. PERKINS *shows no reaction. Silence. Then:*]

MRS. PERKINS: [*To* KAY GONDA, *her voice unnaturally emotionless*] Why
did you come here?

KAY GONDA: [*Calmly*] Mr. Perkins will have to explain that.

PERKINS: Rosie, I . . . [*Stops*]

MRS. PERKINS: Well?

PERKINS: Rosie, there's nothing to get excited about, only that Miss
Gonda is wanted by the police and—

MRS. PERKINS: Oh.

PERKINS: —and it's for murder and—

MRS. PERKINS: Oh!

PERKINS: —and she just has to stay here overnight. That's all.

MRS. PERKINS: [*Slowly*] Listen to me, George Perkins: either she goes
out of the house this minute, or else I go.

PERKINS: But let me explain . . .

MRS. PERKINS: I don't need any explanations. I'll pack my things, and

I'll take the children, too. And I'll pray to God we never see you again. [*She waits. He does not answer*] Tell her to get out.

PERKINS: Rosie . . . I can't.

MRS. PERKINS: We've struggled together pretty hard, haven't we, George? Together. For fifteen years.

PERKINS: Rosie, it's just one night. . . . If you knew . . .

MRS. PERKINS: I don't want to know. I don't want to know why my husband should bring such a thing upon me. A fancy woman or a murderess, or both. I've been a faithful wife to you, George. I've given you the best years of my life. I've borne your children.

PERKINS: Yes, Rosie . . .

MRS. PERKINS: It's not just for me. Think of what will happen to you. Shielding a murderess. Think of the children. [*He doesn't answer*] And your job, too. You just got that promotion. We were going to get new drapes for the living room. The green ones. You always wanted them.

PERKINS: Yes . . .

MRS. PERKINS: And that golf club you wanted to join. They have the best of members, solid, respectable members, not men with their fingerprints in the police files.

PERKINS: [*His voice barely audible*] No . . .

MRS. PERKINS: Have you thought of what will happen when people learn about this?

PERKINS: [*Looks desperately for a word, a glance from* KAY GONDA. *He wants her to decide. But* KAY GONDA *stands motionless, as if the scene did not concern her at all. Only her eyes are watching him. He speaks to her, his voice a desperate plea*] What will happen when people learn about this?

[KAY GONDA *does not answer*]

MRS. PERKINS: I'll tell you what will happen. No decent person will ever want to speak to you again. They'll fire you, down at the Daffodil Company, they'll throw you right out in the street!

PERKINS: [*Repeats softly, dazedly, as if from far away*] . . . in a dark, lonely street where your friends will be passing by and looking straight past you . . . and you'll want to scream . . . [*He stares at* KAY GONDA, *his eyes wide. She does not move*]

MRS. PERKINS: That will be the end of everything you've ever held dear. And in exchange for what? Back roads and dark alleys, fleeing by night, hunted and cornered, and forsaken by the whole wide world! . . . [*He does not answer or turn to her. He is staring at* KAY GONDA *with a new kind of understanding*] Think of the children, George. . . . [*He does not move*] We've been pretty happy together, haven't we, George? Fifteen years. . . .

[*Her voice trails off. There is a long silence. Then* PERKINS *turns slowly away from* KAY GONDA *to look at his wife. His shoulders droop; he is suddenly old*]

PERKINS: [*Looking at his wife*] I'm sorry, Miss Gonda, but under the circumstances . . .

KAY GONDA: [*Calmly*] I understand.

[*She puts on her hat, picks up her bag and gloves. Her movements are light, unhurried. She walks to the door Center. When she passes* MRS. PERKINS, *she stops to say calmly:*]

I'm sorry. I had the wrong address.

[*She walks out.* PERKINS *and his wife stand at the open door and watch her go*]

Act I

PERKINS: [*Putting his arm around his wife's waist*] Is Mother asleep?

MRS. PERKINS: I don't know. Why?

PERKINS: I thought I'd go in and talk to her. Make up, sort of. She knows all about raising babies.

CURTAIN

SCENE 2

*W*hen the curtain rises, another letter is projected on the screen. This one is written in a small, uneven, temperamental handwriting:

Dear Miss Gonda,

    The determinism of duty has conditioned me to pursue the relief of my fellow men's suffering. I see daily before me the wrecks and victims of an outrageous social system. But I gain courage for my cause when I look at you on the screen and realize of what greatness the human race is capable. Your art is a symbol of the hidden potentiality which I see in my derelict brothers. None of them chose to be what he is. None of us ever chooses the bleak, hopeless life he is forced to lead. But in our ability to recognize you and bow to you lies the hope of mankind.

    Sincerely yours,

    Chuck Fink

    . . . Spring Street

    Los Angeles, California

Lights go out, screen disappears, and stage reveals living room in the home of CHUCK FINK. *It is a miserable room in a run-down furnished bungalow. Entrance door upstage in wall Right; large open window next to it, downstage; door to bedroom in wall Center. Late evening. Although there are electric fixtures in the room, it is lighted by a single kerosene lamp smoking in a corner. The tenants are moving out; two battered trunks and a number of grocery cartons stand in the middle of the room; closets and chests gape open, half emptied; clothes, books, dishes, every conceivable piece of household junk are piled indiscriminately into great heaps on the floor.*

At curtain rise, CHUCK FINK *is leaning anxiously out of the window; he is a young man of about thirty, slight, anemic, with a rich mane of dark hair, a cadaverous face, and a neat little mustache. He is watching the people seen hurrying past the window in great agitation; there is a dim confusion of voices outside. He sees someone outside and calls:*

FINK: Hey, Jimmy!

JIMMY'S VOICE: [*Offstage*] Yeah?

FINK: Come here a minute!

[JIMMY *appears at the window outside; he is a haggard-looking youth, his clothes torn, his eyes swollen, blood running down the side of his face from a gash on his forehead*]

JIMMY: Oh, that you, Chuck? Thought it was a cop. What d'you want?

FINK: Have you seen Fanny down there?

JIMMY: Huh! Fanny!

FINK: Have you seen her?

JIMMY: Not since it started.

FINK: Is she hurt?

JIMMY: Might be. I seen her when it started. She threw a brick plumb through their window.

Act I

FINK: What's happened out there?

JIMMY: Tear gas. They've arrested a bunch of the pickets. So we beat it.

FINK: But hasn't anyone seen Fanny?

JIMMY: Oh, to hell with your Fanny! There's people battered all over the place. Jesus, that was one swell free-for-all!

[JIMMY *disappears down the street.* FINK *leaves the window. Paces nervously, glancing at his watch. The noise subsides in the street.* FINK *tries to continue his packing, throws a few things into cartons halfheartedly. The entrance door flies open.* FANNY FINK *enters. She is a tall, gaunt, angular girl in her late twenties, with a sloppy masculine haircut, flat shoes, a man's coat thrown over her shoulders. Her hair is disheveled, her face white. She leans against the doorjamb for support*]

FINK: Fanny! [*She does not move*] Are you all right? What happened? Where have you been?

FANNY: [*In a flat, husky voice*] Got any Mercurochrome?

FINK: What?

FANNY: Mercurochrome. [*Throws her coat off. Her clothes are torn, her bare arms bruised; there is a bleeding cut on one forearm*]

FINK: Jesus!

FANNY: Oh, don't stand there like an idiot! [*Walks resolutely to a cabinet, rummages through the shelves, produces a tiny bottle*] Stop staring at me! Nothing to get hysterical over!

FINK: Here, let me help.

FANNY: Never mind. I'm all right. [*Dabs her arm with Mercurochrome*]

FINK: Where have you been so late?

FANNY: In jail.

FINK: Huh?!

FANNY: All of us. Pinky Thomlinson, Bud Miller, Mary Phelps, and all the rest. Twelve of us.

FINK: What happened?

FANNY: We tried to stop the night shift from going in.

FINK: And?

FANNY: Bud Miller started it by cracking a scab's skull. But the damn Cossacks were prepared. Biff just sprung us out on bail. Got a cigarette? [*She finds one and lights it; she smokes nervously, continuously throughout the scene*] Trial next week. They don't think the scab will recover. It looks like a long vacation in the cooler for yours truly. [*Bitterly*] You don't mind, do you, sweetheart? It will be a nice, quiet rest for you here without me.

FINK: But it's outrageous! I won't allow it! We have some rights . . .

FANNY: Sure. Rights. C.O.D. rights. Not worth a damn without cash. And where will you get that?

FINK: [*Sinking wearily into a chair*] But it's unthinkable!

FANNY: Well, don't think of it, then. . . . [*Looks around*] You don't seem to have done much packing, have you? How are we going to finish with all this damn junk tonight?

FINK: What's the hurry? I'm too upset.

FANNY: What's the hurry! If we're not out of here by morning, they'll dump it all, right out on the sidewalk.

FINK: If that wasn't enough! And now this trial! Now you had to get into this! What are we going to do?

FANNY: I'm going to pack. [*Starts gathering things, hardly looking at them, and flinging them into the cartons with ferocious hatred*] Shall we move to the Ambassador or the Beverly-Sunset, darling? [*He does not answer. She flings a book into the carton*] The Beverly-Sunset would be nice, I think. . . . We shall need a suite of seven rooms—do you think we could manage in seven rooms? [*He does not move.*

She flings a pile of underwear into the carton] Oh, yes, and a private swimming pool. [*Flings a coffeepot into the carton viciously*] And a two-car garage! For the Rolls-Royce! [*Flings a vase down; it misses the carton and shatters against a chair leg. She screams suddenly hysterically*] Goddamn them! Why do some people have all of that!

FINK: [*Languidly, without moving*] Childish escapism, my dear.

FANNY: The heroics is all very well, but I'm so damn sick of standing up to make speeches about global problems and worrying all the time whether the comrades can see the runs in my stockings!

FINK: Why don't you mend them?

FANNY: Save it, sweetheart! Save the brilliant sarcasm for the magazine editors—maybe it will sell an article for you someday.

FINK: That was uncalled for, Fanny.

FANNY: Well, it's no use fooling yourself. There's a name for people like us. At least, for one of us, I'm sure. Know it? Does your brilliant vocabulary include it? Failure's the word.

FINK: A relative conception, my love.

FANNY: Sure. What's rent money compared to infinity? [*Flings a pile of clothing into a carton*] Do you know it's number five, by the way?

FINK: Number five what?

FANNY: Eviction number five for us, Socrates! I've counted them. Five times in three years. All we've ever done is paid the first month and waited for the sheriff.

FINK: That's the way most people live in Hollywood.

FANNY: You might *pretend* to be worried—just out of decency.

FINK: My dear, why waste one's emotional reserves in blaming oneself for what is the irrevocable result of an inadequate social system?

FANNY: You could at least refrain from plagiarism.

FINK: Plagiarism?

FANNY: You lifted that out of *my* article.

FINK: Oh, yes. *The* article. I beg your pardon.

FANNY: Well, at least it was published.

FINK: So it was. Six years ago.

FANNY: [*Carrying an armful of old shoes*] Got any acceptance checks to show since then? [*Dumps her load into a carton*] Now what? Where in hell are we going to go tomorrow?

FINK: With thousands homeless and jobless—why worry about an individual case?

FANNY: [*Is about to answer angrily, then shrugs, and turning away stumbles over some boxes in the semidarkness*] Goddamn it! It's enough that they're throwing us out. They didn't have to turn off the electricity!

FINK: [*Shrugging*] Private ownership of utilities.

FANNY: I wish there was a kerosene that didn't stink.

FINK: Kerosene is the commodity of the poor. But I understand they've invented a new, odorless kind in Russia.

FANNY: Sure. Nothing stinks in Russia. [*Takes from a shelf a box full of large brown envelopes*] What do you want to do with these?

FINK: What's in there?

FANNY: [*Reading from the envelopes*] Your files as trustee of the Clark Institute of Social Research . . . Correspondence as Consultant to the Vocational School for Subnormal Children . . . Secretary to the Free Night Classes of Dialectic Materialism . . . Adviser to the Workers' Theater . . .

FINK: Throw the Workers' Theater out. I'm through with them. They wouldn't put my name on their letterheads.

FANNY: [*Flings one envelope aside*] What do you want me to do with the rest? Pack it or will you carry it yourself?

FINK: Certainly I'll carry it myself. It might get lost. Wrap them up for me, will you?

FANNY: [*Picks up some newspapers, starts wrapping the files, stops, attracted by an item in a paper, glances at it*] You know, it's funny, this business about Kay Gonda.

FINK: What business?

FANNY: In this morning's paper. About the murder.

FINK: Oh, that? Rubbish. She had nothing to do with it. Yellow press gossip.

FANNY: [*Wrapping up the files*] That Sayers guy sure had the dough.

FINK: Used to have. Not anymore. I know from that time when I helped to picket Sayers Oil last year that the big shot was going by the board even then.

FANNY: It says here that Sayers Oil was beginning to pick up.

FINK: Oh, well, one plutocrat less. So much the better for the heirs.

FANNY: [*Picks up a pile of books*] Twenty-five copies of *Oppress the Oppressors*—[*Adds with a bow*]—by Chuck Fink! . . . What the hell are we going to do with them?

FINK: [*Sharply*] What do you *think* we're going to do with them?

FANNY: God! Lugging all that extra weight around! Do you think there are twenty-five people in the United States who bought one copy each of your great masterpiece?

FINK: The number of sales is no proof of a book's merit.

FANNY: No, but it sure does help!

FINK: Would you like to see me pandering to the middle-class rabble, like the scribbling lackeys of capitalism? You're weakening, Fanny. You're turning petty bourgeois.

FANNY: [*Furiously*] Who's turning petty bourgeois? I've done more than you'll ever hope to do! I don't go running with manuscripts to third-rate publishers. I've had an article printed in *The Nation*! Yes, in *The Nation*! If I didn't bury myself with you in this mudhole of a . . .

FINK: It's in the mudholes of the slums that the vanguard trenches of social reform are dug, Fanny.

FANNY: Oh, Lord, Chuck, what's the use? Look at the others. Look at Miranda Lumkin. A column in the *Courier* and a villa at Palm Springs! And she couldn't hold a candle to me in college! Everybody always said I was an advanced thinker. [*Points at the room*] *This* is what one gets for being an advanced thinker.

FINK: [*Softly*] I know, dear. You're tired. You're frightened. I can't blame you. But, you see, in our work one must give up everything. All thought of personal gain or comfort. I've done it. I have no private ego left. All I want is that millions of men hear the name of Chuck Fink and come to regard it as that of their leader!

FANNY: [*Softening*] I know. You mean it all right. You're real, Chuck. There aren't many unselfish men in the world.

FINK: [*Dreamily*] Perhaps, five hundred years from now, someone will write my biography and call it *Chuck Fink the Selfless*.

FANNY: And it will seem so silly, then, that here we were worried about some piddling California landlord!

FINK: Precisely. One must know how to take a long view on things. And . . .

FANNY: [*Listening to some sound outside, suddenly*] Sh-sh! I think there's someone at the door.

FINK: Who? No one'll come here. They've deserted us. They've left us to . . . [*There is a knock at the door. They look at each other.* FINK *walks to the door*] Who's there? [*There is no answer. The knock is repeated. He throws the door open angrily*] What do you . . . [*He stops short as* KAY GONDA *enters; she is dressed as in the preceding scene. He gasps*] Oh! . . . [*He stares at her, half frightened, half incredulous.* FANNY *makes a step forward and stops. They can't make a sound*]

KAY GONDA: Mr. Fink?

FINK: [*Nodding frantically*] Yes. Chuck Fink. In person. . . . But you . . . you're *Kay Gonda*, aren't you?

KAY GONDA: Yes. I am hiding. From the police. I have no place to go. Will you let me stay here for the night?

FINK: Well, I'll be damned! . . . Oh, excuse me!

FANNY: You want us to hide you here?

KAY GONDA: Yes. If you are not afraid of it.

FANNY: But why on earth did you pick . . .

KAY GONDA: Because no one would find me here. And because I read Mr. Fink's letter.

FINK: [*Quite recovering himself*] But of course! My letter. I knew you'd notice it among the thousands. Pretty good, wasn't it?

FANNY: I helped him with it.

FINK: [*Laughing*] What a glorious coincidence! I had no idea when I wrote it, that . . . But how wonderfully things work out!

KAY GONDA: [*Looking at him*] I am wanted for murder.

FINK: Oh, don't worry about that. We don't mind. We're broad-minded.

FANNY: [*Hastily pulling down the window shade*] You'll be perfectly safe here. You'll excuse the . . . informal appearance of things, won't you? We were considering moving out of here.

FINK: Please sit down, Miss Gonda.

KAY GONDA: [*Sitting down, removing her hat*] Thank you.

FINK: I've dreamt of a chance to talk to you like this. There are so many things I've always wanted to ask you.

KAY GONDA: There are many things I've always wanted to be asked.

FINK: Is it true, what they say about Granton Sayers? You ought to know. They say he was a regular pervert and what he didn't do to women . . .

FANNY: Chuck! That's entirely irrelevant and . . .

KAY GONDA: [*With a faint smile at her*] No. It isn't true.

FINK: Of course, I'm not one to censure anything. I despise morality. Then there's another thing I wanted to ask you: I've always been interested, as a sociologist, in the influence of the economic factor on the individual. How much does a movie star actually get?

KAY GONDA: Fifteen or twenty thousand a week on my new contract— I don't remember.

[FANNY *and* FINK *exchange startled glances*]

FINK: What an opportunity for social good! I've always believed that you were a great humanitarian.

KAY GONDA: Am I? Well, perhaps I am. I hate humanity.

FINK: You don't mean that, Miss Gonda!

KAY GONDA: There are some men with a purpose in life. Not many, but there are. And there are also some with a purpose—and with integrity. These are very rare. I like them.

FINK: But one must be tolerant! One must consider the pressure of the economic factor. Now, for instance, take the question of a star's salary . . .

KAY GONDA: [*Sharply*] I do not want to talk about it. [*With a note that sounds almost like pleading in her voice*] Have you nothing to ask me about my work?

FINK: Oh, God, so much! . . . [*Suddenly earnest*] No. Nothing. [KAY GONDA *looks at him closely, with a faint smile. He adds, suddenly simple, sincere for the first time:*] Your work . . . one shouldn't talk about it. I can't. [*Adds*] I've never looked upon you as a movie star. No one does. It's not like looking at Joan Tudor or Sally Sweeney, or the rest of them. And it's not the trashy stories you make—you'll excuse me, but they are trash. It's something else.

KAY GONDA: [*Looking at him*] What?

FINK: The way you move, and the sound of your voice, and your eyes. Your eyes.

FANNY: [*Suddenly eager*] It's as if you were not a human being at all, not the kind we see around us.

FINK: We all dream of the perfect being that man could be. But no one has ever seen it. You have. And you're showing it to us. As if you knew a great secret, lost by the world, a great secret and a great hope. Man washed clean. Man at his highest possibility.

FANNY: When I look at you on the screen, it makes me feel guilty, but it also makes me feel young, new and proud. Somehow, I want to raise my arms like this. . . . [*Raises her arms over her head in a triumphant, ecstatic gesture; then, embarrassed:*] You must forgive us. We're being perfectly childish.

FINK: Perhaps we are. But in our drab lives, we have to grasp at any ray of light, anywhere, even in the movies. Why not in the movies, the great narcotic of mankind? You've done more for the damned than any philanthropist ever could. How do you do it?

KAY GONDA: [*Without looking at him*] One can do it just so long. One can keep going on one's own power, and wring dry every drop of hope—but then one has to find help. One has to find an answering voice, an answering hymn, an echo. I am very grateful to you. [*There is a knock at the door. They look at one another.* FINK *walks to the door resolutely*]

FINK: Who's there?

WOMAN'S VOICE: [*Offstage*] Say, Chuck, could I borrow a bit of cream?

FINK: [*Angrily*] Go to hell! We haven't any cream. You got your nerve disturbing people at this hour! [*A muffled oath and retreating steps are heard offstage. He returns to the others*] God, I thought it was the police!

FANNY: We mustn't let anyone in tonight. Any of those starving bums around here would be only too glad to turn you in for a—[*Her voice changes suddenly, strangely, as if the last word had dropped out accidentally*]—a reward.

KAY GONDA: Do you realize what chance you are taking if they find me here?

FINK: They'll get you out of here over my dead body.

KAY GONDA: You don't know what danger . . .

FINK: We don't have to know. We know what your work means to us. Don't we, Fanny?

FANNY: [*She has been standing aside, lost in thought*] What?

FINK: We know what Miss Gonda's work means to us, don't we?

FANNY: [*In a flat voice*] Oh, yes . . . yes . . .

KAY GONDA: [*Looking at FINK intently*] And that which means to you . . . you will not betray it?

FINK: One doesn't betray the best in one's soul.

KAY GONDA: No. One doesn't.

FINK: [*Noticing FANNY's abstraction*] Fanny!

FANNY: [*With a jerk*] Yes? What?

FINK: Will you tell Miss Gonda how we've always . . .

FANNY: Miss Gonda must be tired. We should really allow her to go to bed.

KAY GONDA: Yes. I am very tired.

FANNY: [*With brisk energy*] You can have our bedroom. . . . Oh, yes, please don't protest. We'll be very comfortable here, on the couch. We'll stay here on guard, so that no one will try to enter.

KAY GONDA: [*Rising*] It is very kind of you.

FANNY: [*Taking the lamp*] Please excuse this inconvenience. We're having a little trouble with our electricity. [*Leading the way to the bedroom*] This way, please. You'll be comfortable and safe.

Act I

FINK: Good night, Miss Gonda. Don't worry. We'll stand by you.

KAY GONDA: Thank you. Good night. [*She exits with* FANNY *into the bedroom.* FINK *lifts the window shade. A broad band of moonlight falls across the room. He starts clearing the couch of its load of junk.* FANNY *returns into the room, closing the door behind her*]

FANNY: [*In a low voice*] Well, what do you think of that? [*He stretches his arms wide, shrugging*] And they say miracles don't happen!

FINK: We'd better keep quiet. She may hear us. . . . [*The band of light goes out in the crack of the bedroom door*] How about the packing?

FANNY: Never mind the packing now. [*He fishes for sheets and blankets in the cartons, throwing their contents out again.* FANNY *stands aside, by the window, watching him silently. Then, in a low voice:*] Chuck . . .

FINK: Yes?

FANNY: In a few days, I'm going on trial. Me and eleven of the kids.

FINK: [*Looking at her, surprised*] Yeah.

FANNY: It's no use fooling ourselves. They'll send us all up.

FINK: I know they will.

FANNY: Unless we can get money to fight it.

FINK: Yeah. But we can't. No use thinking about it. [*A short silence. He continues with his work*]

FANNY: [*In a whisper*] Chuck . . . do you think she can hear us?

FINK: [*Looking at the bedroom door*] No.

FANNY: It's a murder that she's committed.

FINK: Yeah.

FANNY: It's a millionaire that she's killed.

FINK: Right.

FANNY: I suppose his family would like to know where she is.

FINK: [*Raising his head, looking at her*] What are you talking about?

FANNY: I was thinking that if his family were told where she's hiding, they'd be glad to pay a reward.

FINK: [*Stepping menacingly toward her*] You lousy . . . what are you trying to . . .

FANNY: [*Without moving*] Five thousand dollars, probably.

FINK: [*Stopping*] Huh?

FANNY: Five thousand dollars, probably.

FINK: You lousy bitch! Shut up before I kill you! [*Silence. He starts to undress. Then:*] Fanny . . .

FANNY: Yes?

FINK: Think they'd—hand over five thousand?

FANNY: Sure they would. People pay more than that for ordinary kidnappers.

FINK: Oh, shut up! [*Silence. He continues to undress*]

FANNY: It's jail for me, Chuck. Months, maybe years in jail.

FINK: Yeah . . .

FANNY: And for the others, too. Bud, and Pinky, and Mary, and the rest. Your friends. Your comrades. [*He stops his undressing*] You need them. The cause needs them. Twelve of our vanguard.

FINK: Yes . . .

FANNY: With five thousand, we'd get the best lawyer from New York. He'd beat the case. . . . And we wouldn't have to move out of here. We wouldn't have to worry. You could continue your great work. . . . [*He does not answer*] Think of all the poor and helpless who need you. . . . [*He does not answer*] Think of twelve human beings you're sending to jail . . . twelve to one, Chuck. . . . [*He does not answer*] Think of your duty to millions of your brothers. Millions to one. [*Silence*]

FINK: Fanny . . .

FANNY: Yes?

FINK: How would we go about it?

Act I

FANNY: Easy. We get out while she's asleep. We run to the police station. Come back with the cops. Easy.

FINK: What if she hears?

FANNY: She won't hear. But we got to hurry. [*She moves to the door. He stops her*]

FINK: [*In a whisper*] She'll hear the door opening. [*Points to the open window*] This way . . .

[*They slip out through the window. The room is empty for a brief moment. Then the bedroom door opens.* KAY GONDA *stands on the threshold. She stands still for a moment, then walks across the room to the entrance door and goes out, leaving the door open*]

CURTAIN

SCENE 3

*T*he screen unrolls a letter written in a bold, aggressive handwriting:

Dear Miss Gonda,

I am an unknown artist. But I know to what heights I
shall rise, for I carry a sacred banner which cannot fail—and
which is you. I have painted nothing that was not you. You
stand as a goddess on every canvas I've done. I have never
seen you in person. I do not need to. I can draw your face
with my eyes closed. For my spirit is but a mirror of yours.

Someday you shall hear men speak of me. Until then,
this is only a first tribute from your devoted priest—

Dwight Langley

. . . Normandie Avenue

Los Angeles, California

Lights go out, screen disappears, and stage reveals studio of DWIGHT
LANGLEY. *It is a large room, flashy, dramatic, and disreputable. Center
back, large window showing the dark sky and the shadows of treetops; entrance door center Left; door into next room upstage Right. A profusion of
paintings and sketches on the walls, on the easels, on the floor; all are of* KAY
GONDA; *heads, full figures, in modern clothes, in flowering drapes, naked.*

IDEAL

A mongrel assortment of strange types fills the room: men and women in all kinds of outfits, from tails and evening gowns to beach pajamas and slacks, none too prosperous-looking, all having one attribute in common— a glass in hand—and all showing signs of its effect.

DWIGHT LANGLEY lies stretched in the middle of a couch; he is young, with a tense, handsome, sunburned face, dark, disheveled hair, and a haughty, irresistible smile. EUNICE HAMMOND keeps apart from the guests, her eyes returning constantly, anxiously, to LANGLEY; she is a beautiful young girl, quiet, reticent, dressed in a smart, simple dark dress obviously more expensive than any garment in the room.

As the curtain rises, the guests are lifting their glasses in a grand toast to LANGLEY, their voices piercing the raucous music coming over the radio.

MAN IN DRESS SUIT: Here's to Lanny!

MAN IN SWEATER: To Dwight Langley of California!

WOMAN IN EVENING GOWN: To the winner and the best of us—from the cheerful losers!

TRAGIC GENTLEMAN: To the greatest artist ever lived!

LANGLEY: [*Rising, waving his hand curtly*] Thanks.

[ALL *drink. Someone drops a glass, breaking it resonantly. As* LANGLEY *steps aside from the others,* EUNICE *approaches him*]

EUNICE: [*Extending her glass to his, whispers softly*] To the day we've dreamt of for such a long time, dear.

LANGLEY: [*Turning to her indifferently*] Oh . . . oh, yes . . . [*Clinks glass to hers automatically, without looking at her*]

WOMAN IN SLACKS: [*Calling to her*] No monopoly on him, Eunice. Not anymore. From now on—Dwight Langley belongs to the world!

WOMAN IN EVENING GOWN: Well, not that I mean to minimize

Lanny's triumph, but I must say that for the greatest exhibition of the decade, it was rather a fizz, wasn't it? Two or three canvases with some idea of something, but the rest of the trash people have the nerve to exhibit these days . . .

EFFEMINATE YOUNG MAN: Dear me! It is positively preposterous!

MAN IN DRESS SUIT: But Lanny beat them all! First prize of the decade!

LANGLEY: [*With no trace of modesty*] Did it surprise you?

TRAGIC GENTLEMAN: Because Lanny's a geniush!

EFFEMINATE YOUNG MAN: Oh, my, yes! Positively a genius!

[LANGLEY *walks over to a sideboard to refill his glass.* EUNICE, *standing beside him, slips her hand over his*]

EUNICE: [*In a low voice, tenderly*] Dwight, I haven't had a moment with you to congratulate you. And I do want to say it tonight. I'm too happy, too proud of you to know how to say it, but I want you to understand . . . my dearest . . . how much it means to me.

LANGLEY: [*Jerking his hand away, indifferently*] Thanks.

EUNICE: I can't help thinking of the years past. Remember, how discouraged you were at times, and I talked to you about your future, and . . .

LANGLEY: You don't have to bring that up now, do you?

EUNICE: [*Trying to laugh*] I shouldn't. I know. Utterly bad form. [*Breaking down involuntarily*] But I can't help it. I love you.

LANGLEY: I know it. [*Walks away from her*]

BLOND GIRL: [*Sitting on the couch, next to the woman in slacks*] Come here, Lanny! Hasn't anyone got a chance with a real genius?

LANGLEY: [*Flopping down on the couch, between the two girls*] Hello.

WOMAN IN SLACKS: [*Throwing her arms around his shoulders*] Langley, I can't get over that canvas of yours. I still see it as it hung there tonight. The damn thing haunts me.

LANGLEY: [*Patronizingly*] Like it?

WOMAN IN SLACKS: Love it. You do get the damnedest titles, though. What was it called? Hope, faith, or charity? No. Wait a moment. Liberty, equality, or . . .

LANGLEY: *Integrity*.

WOMAN IN SLACKS: That's it. "Integrity." Just what did you really mean by it, darling?

LANGLEY: Don't try to understand.

MAN IN DRESS SUIT: But the woman! The woman in your painting, Langley! Ah, that, my friend, is a masterpiece!

WOMAN IN SLACKS: That white face. And those eyes. Those eyes that look straight through you!

WOMAN IN EVENING GOWN: You know, of course, who she is?

MAN IN DRESS SUIT: Kay Gonda, as usual.

MAN IN SWEATSHIRT: Say, Lanny, will you ever paint any other female? Why do you always have to stick to that one?

LANGLEY: An artist *tells*. He does not *explain*.

WOMAN IN SLACKS: You know, there's something damn funny about Gonda and that Sayers affair.

MAN IN DRESS SUIT: I bet she did it, all right. Wouldn't put it past her.

EFFEMINATE YOUNG MAN: Imagine Kay Gonda being hanged! The blond hair and the black hood and the noose. My, it would be *perfectly* thrilling!

WOMAN IN EVENING GOWN: There's a new theme for you, Lanny. *Kay Gonda on the Gallows*.

LANGLEY: [*Furiously*] Shut up, all of you! She didn't do it! I won't have you discussing her in my house!

Act I

[*The guests subside for a brief moment*]

MAN IN DRESS SUIT: Wonder how much Sayers actually left.

WOMAN IN SLACKS: The papers said he was just coming into a swell setup. A deal with United California Oil or some such big-time stuff. But I guess it's off now.

MAN IN SWEATER: No, the evening papers said his sister is rushing the deal through.

WOMAN IN EVENING GOWN: But what're the police doing? Have they issued any warrants?

MAN IN DRESS SUIT: Nobody knows.

WOMAN IN EVENING GOWN: Damn funny . . .

MAN IN SWEATER: Say, Eunice, any more drinks left in this house? No use asking Lanny. He never knows where anything is.

MAN IN DRESS SUIT: [*Throwing his arm around* EUNICE] The greatest little mother-sister-and-all-the-rest combination an artist ever had!

[EUNICE *disengages herself, not too brusquely, but obviously displeased*]

EFFEMINATE YOUNG MAN: Do you know that Eunice darns his socks? Oh, my, yes! I've seen a pair. Positively the cutest things!

MAN IN SWEATER: The woman behind the throne! The woman who guided his footsteps, washed his shirts, and kept up his courage in his dark years of struggle.

WOMAN IN EVENING GOWN: [*To the* WOMAN IN SLACKS, *in a low voice*] Kept up his courage—and his bank account.

WOMAN IN SLACKS: No. Really?

WOMAN IN EVENING GOWN: My dear, it's no secret. Where do you suppose the money came from for the "dark years of struggle"? The Hammond millions. Not that old man Hammond didn't kick her out of the house. He did. But she had some money of her own.

EFFEMINATE YOUNG MAN: Oh, my, yes. The Social Register dropped her, too. But she didn't care one bit, not one bit.

MAN IN SWEATER: [*To* EUNICE] How about it, Eunice? Where are the drinks?

EUNICE: [*Hesitating*] I'm afraid . . .

LANGLEY: [*Rising*] She's afraid she doesn't approve. But we're going to drink whether she approves of it or not. [*Searches through the cupboards frantically*]

WOMAN IN SLACKS: Really, folks, it's getting late and . . .

MAN IN DRESS SUIT: Oh, just one more drink, and we'll all toddle home.

LANGLEY: Hey, Eunice, where's the gin?

EUNICE: [*Opening a cabinet and producing two bottles, quietly*] Here.

MAN IN SWEATER: Hurrah! Wait for baby!

[*There is a general rush to the bottles*]

MAN IN DRESS SUIT: Just one last drink and we'll scram. Hey, everybody! Another toast. To Dwight Langley and Eunice Hammond!

EUNICE: To Dwight Langley and his future!

[*All roar approval and drink*]

EVERYONE: [*Roaring at once*] Speech, Lanny! . . . Yes! . . . Come on, Lanny! . . . Speech! . . . Come on!

LANGLEY: [*Climbs up on a chair, stands a little unsteadily, speaks with a kind of tortured sincerity*] The bitterest moment of an artist's life is the moment of his triumph. The artist is but a bugle calling to a battle no one wants to fight. The world does not see and does not want to see. The artist begs men to throw the doors of their lives open to grandeur and beauty, but those doors will remain closed forever . . . forever . . . [*Is about to add something, but drops his hand in a gesture of hopelessness and ends in a tone of quiet sadness*] . . . forever. . . . [*Applause. The general noise is cut short by a knock at the door.* LANGLEY *jumps off his chair*] Come in!

[*The door opens, disclosing an irate* LANDLADY *in a soiled Chinese kimono*]

LANDLADY: [*In a shrill whine*] Mr. Langley, this noise will have to stop! Don't you know what time it is?

LANGLEY: Get out of here!

LANDLADY: The lady in 315 says she'll call the police! The gentleman in . . .

LANGLEY: You heard me! Get out! Think I have to stay in a lousy dump like this?

EUNICE: Dwight! [*To* LANDLADY] We'll keep quiet, Mrs. Johnson.

LANDLADY: Well, you'd better! [*She exits angrily*]

EUNICE: Really, Dwight, we shouldn't . . .

LANGLEY: Oh, leave me alone! No one's going to tell *me* what to do from now on!

EUNICE: But I only . . .

LANGLEY: You're turning into a damnable, nagging, middle-class female!

[EUNICE *stares at him, frozen*]

WOMAN IN SLACKS: Going a bit too far, Langley!

LANGLEY: I'm sick and tired of people who can't outgrow their possessiveness! You know the hypocritical trick—the chains of *gratitude*!

EUNICE: Dwight! You don't think that I . . .

LANGLEY: I know damn well what *you* think! Think you've bought me, don't you? Think you own me for the rest of my life in exchange for some grocery bills?

EUNICE: What did you say? [*Screaming suddenly*] I didn't hear you right!

MAN IN SWEATER: Look here, Langley, take it easy. You don't know what you're saying, you're . . .

LANGLEY: [*Pushing him aside*] Go to hell! You can all go to hell if you don't like it! [*To* EUNICE] And as for you . . .

EUNICE: Dwight . . . please . . . not now . . .

LANGLEY: Yes! Right here and now! I want them all to hear! [*To the guests*] So you think I can't get along without her? I'll show you! I'm through! [*To* EUNICE] Do you hear that? I'm through! [EUNICE *stands motionless*] I'm free! I'm going to rise in the world! I'm going places none of you ever dreamt of! I'm ready to meet the only woman I've ever wanted—Kay Gonda! I've waited all these years for the day when I would meet her! That's all I've lived for! And no one's going to stand in my way!

EUNICE: [*She walks to door Left, picks up her hat and coat from a pile of clothing in a corner, turns to him again, quietly*] Good-bye, Dwight . . . [*Exits*]

[*There is a second of strained silence in the room: the* WOMAN IN SLACKS *is the first one to move; she goes to pick up her coat, then turns to* LANGLEY]

WOMAN IN SLACKS: I thought you had just done a painting called *Integrity*.

LANGLEY: If that was intended for a dirty crack . . . [*The* WOMAN IN SLACKS *exits, slamming the door*] Well, go to hell! [*To the others*] Get out of here! All of you! Get out!

[*There is a general shuffle for hats and coats*]

WOMAN IN EVENING GOWN: Well, if we're being kicked out . . .

MAN IN DRESS SUIT: That's all right. Lanny's a bit upset.

LANGLEY: [*Somewhat gentler*] I'm sorry. I thank you all. But I want to be alone. [*The guests are leaving, waving halfhearted good-byes*]

BLOND GIRL: [*She is one of the last to leave. She hesitates, whispering tentatively:*] Lanny . . .

LANGLEY: Out! All of you! [*She exits. The stage is empty but for* LANGLEY *surveying dazedly the havoc of his studio. There is a knock at the door*] Out, I said! Don't want any of you! [*The knock is repeated. He walks to the door, throws it open.* KAY GONDA *enters. She stands looking at him without a word. He asks impatiently:*] Well? [*She does not answer*] What do you want?

KAY GONDA: Are you Dwight Langley?

LANGLEY: Yes.

KAY GONDA: I need your help.

LANGLEY: What's the matter?

KAY GONDA: Don't you know?

LANGLEY: How should I know? Just who are you?

KAY GONDA: [*After a pause*] Kay Gonda.

LANGLEY: [*Looks at her and bursts out laughing*] So? Not Helen of Troy? Nor Madame Du Barry? [*She looks at him silently*] Come on, out with it. What's the gag?

KAY GONDA: Don't you know me?

LANGLEY: [*Looks her over contemptuously, his hands in his pockets, grinning*] Well, you do look like Kay Gonda. So does her stand-in. So do dozens of extra girls in Hollywood. What is it you're after? I can't get you into pictures, my girl. I'm not even the kind to promise you a screen test. Drop the racket. Who are you?

KAY GONDA: Don't you understand? I am in danger. I have to hide. Please let me stay here for the night.

LANGLEY: What do you think this is? A flophouse?

KAY GONDA: I have no place to go.

LANGLEY: That's an old one in Hollywood.

KAY GONDA: They will not look for me here.

LANGLEY: Who?

KAY GONDA: The police.

LANGLEY: Really? And why would Kay Gonda pick my house to hide in of all places? [*She starts to open her handbag, but closes it again and says nothing*] How do I know you're Kay Gonda? Have you any proof?

KAY GONDA: None, but the honesty of your vision.

LANGLEY: Oh, cut the tripe! What are you after? Taking me for a . . . [*There is a loud knock at the door*] What's this? A frame-up? [*Walks to door and throws it open. A uniformed* POLICEMAN *enters.* KAY GONDA *turns away quickly, her back to the others*]

POLICEMAN: [*Good-naturedly*] Evening. [*Looking about him, helplessly*] Where's the drunken party we got a complaint about?

LANGLEY: Of all the nerve! There's no party, Officer. I had a few friends here, but they left long ago.

POLICEMAN: [*Looking at* KAY GONDA *with some curiosity*] Between you and me, it's a lotta cranks that call up complaining about noise. As I see it, there's no harm in young people having a little fun.

Act I

LANGLEY: [*Watching curiously the* POLICEMAN'*s reaction to* KAY GONDA] We really weren't disturbing anyone. I'm sure there's nothing you want here, *is there,* Officer?

POLICEMAN: No, sir. Sorry to have bothered you.

LANGLEY: We are really alone here—[*Points to* KAY GONDA]—*this lady* and I. But you're welcome to *look around.*

POLICEMAN: Why, no, sir. No need to. Good night. [*Exits*]

LANGLEY: [*Waits to hear his steps descending the stairs. Then turns to* KAY GONDA *and bursts out laughing*] That gave the show away, didn't it, my girl?

KAY GONDA: What?

LANGLEY: The cop. If you were Kay Gonda and if the police were looking for you, wouldn't he have grabbed you?

KAY GONDA: He did not see my face.

LANGLEY: He would have looked. Come on, what kind of racket are you really working?

KAY GONDA: [*Stepping up to him, in full light*] Dwight Langley! Look at me! Look at all these pictures of me that you've painted! Don't you know me? You've lived with me in your hours of work, your best hours. Were you lying in those hours?

LANGLEY: Kindly leave my art out of it. My art has nothing to do with your life or mine.

KAY GONDA: Of what account is an art that preaches things it does not want to exist?

LANGLEY: [*Solemnly*] Listen. Kay Gonda is the symbol of all the beauty I bring to the world, a beauty we can never reach. We can only sing of her, who is the unattainable. That is the mission of the artist. We can only strive, but never succeed. Attempt, but never achieve. That is our tragedy, but our hopelessness is our glory. Get out of here!

KAY GONDA: I need your help.

LANGLEY: Get out!!

[*Her arms fall limply. She turns and walks out.* DWIGHT LANGLEY *slams the door*]

CURTAIN

ACT II

SCENE I

*T*he letter projected on the screen is written in an ornate, old-
fashioned handwriting:

Dear Miss Gonda,

    Some may call this letter a sacrilege. But as I write it, I
do not feel like a sinner. For when I look at you on the
screen, it seems to me that we are working for the same
cause, you and I. This may surprise you, for I am only a
humble Evangelist. But when I speak to men about the
sacred meaning of life, I feel that you hold the same Truth
which my words struggle in vain to disclose. We are

traveling different roads, Miss Gonda, but we are bound to
the same destination.

Respectfully yours,

Claude Ignatius Hix

. . . Slosson Blvd.

Los Angeles, California

*Lights go out, screen disappears. When the curtain rises on the temple
of* CLAUDE IGNATIUS HIX, *the stage is almost completely black. Nothing can
be seen of the room save the dim outline of a door, downstage Right, open
upon a dark street. A small cross of electric lights burns high on wall Center.
It throws just enough light to show the face and shoulders of* CLAUDE IGNA-
TIUS HIX *high above the ground (he is standing in the pulpit, but this
cannot be distinguished in the darkness). He is tall, gaunt, clothed in black;
his hair is receding off a high forehead. His hands rise eloquently as he
speaks into the darkness.*

HIX: . . . but even in the blackest one of us, there is a spark of the
sublime, a single drop in the desert of every barren soul. And all the
suffering of men, all the twisted agonies of their lives, come from
their treason to that hidden flame. All commit the treason, and
none can escape the payment. None can . . . [*Someone sneezes loudly
in the darkness, by the door Right.* HIX *stops short, calls in a startled
voice:*] Who's there?

[*He presses a switch that lights two tall electric tapers by the sides
of his pulpit. We can now see the temple. It is a long, narrow
barn with bare rafters and unpainted walls. There are no windows and only a single door. Rows of old wooden benches fill the
room, facing the pulpit*]

Act II

[SISTER ESSIE TWOMEY *stands downstage Right, by the door. She is a short, plump woman nearing forty, with bleached blond hair falling in curls on her shoulders, from under the brim of a large pink picture hat trimmed with lilies-of-the-valley. Her stocky little figure is draped in the long folds of a sky-blue cape*]

ESSIE TWOMEY: [*She raises her right arm solemnly*] Praise the Lord! Good evening, Brother Hix. Keep going. Don't let me interrupt you.

HIX: [*Startled and angry*] *You?* What are *you* doing here?

ESSIE TWOMEY: I heard you way from the street—it's a blessed voice you have, though you don't control your belly tones properly—and I didn't want to intrude. I just slipped in.

HIX: [*Icily*] And of what service may I be to *you?*

ESSIE TWOMEY: Go ahead with the rehearsal. It's an inspiring sermon you have there, a peach of a sermon. Though a bit on the old-fashioned side. Not modern enough, Brother Hix. That's not the way I do it.

HIX: I do not recall having solicited advice, Sister Twomey, and I should like to inquire for the reason of this sudden visitation.

ESSIE TWOMEY: Praise the Lord! I'm a harbinger of good news. Yes, indeed. I got a corker for you.

HIX: I shall point out that we have never had any matters of common interest.

ESSIE TWOMEY: Verily, Brother Hix. You smacked the nail right on the head. That's why you'll be overjoyed at the proposition. [*Settling herself comfortably down on a bench*] It's like this, brother: there's no room in this neighborhood for you and me both.

HIX: Sister Twomey, these are the first words of truth I have ever heard emerging from your mouth.

ESSIE TWOMEY: The poor dear souls in these parts are heavily laden, indeed. They cannot support two temples. Why, the mangy bums haven't got enough to feed the fleas on a dog!

HIX: Dare I believe, sister, that your conscience has spoken at last, and you are prepared to leave this neighborhood?

ESSIE TWOMEY: Who? *Me* leave this neighborhood? [*Solemnly*] Why, Brother Hix, you have no idea of the blessed work my temple is doing. The lost souls milling at its portals—praise the Lord! . . . [*Sharply*] No, brother, keep your shirt on. I'm going to buy you out.

HIX: What?!

ESSIE TWOMEY: Not that I really have to. You're no competition. But I thought I might as well clear it up once and for all. I want this territory.

HIX: [*Beside himself*] You had the infernal presumption to suppose that the Temple of Eternal Truth was for sale?

ESSIE TWOMEY: Now, now, Brother Hix, let's be modern. That's no way to talk business. Just look at the facts. You're washed up here, brother.

HIX: I will have you understand . . .

ESSIE TWOMEY: What kind of a draw do you get? Thirty or fifty heads on a big night. Look at me. Two thousand souls every evening, seeking the glory of God! *Two thousand* noses, actual count! I'm putting on a Midnight Service tonight—"The Night Life of the Angels"—and I'm expecting three thousand.

HIX: [*Drawing himself up*] There come moments in a man's life when he is sorely pressed to remember the lesson of charity to all. I have no wish to insult you. But I have always considered you a tool of the Devil. My temple has stood in this neighborhood for . . .

ESSIE TWOMEY: I know. For twenty years. But times change, brother.

You haven't got what it takes anymore. You're still in the horse-and-buggy age—praise the Lord!

HIX: The faith of my fathers is good enough for me.

ESSIE TWOMEY: Maybe so, brother, maybe so. But not for the customers. Now, for instance, take the name of your place: Temple of Eternal Truth. Folks don't go for that nowadays. What have I got? The Little Church of the Cheery Corner. That draws 'em, brother. Like flies.

HIX: I do not wish to discuss it.

ESSIE TWOMEY: Look at what you were just rehearsing here. That'll put 'em to sleep. Verily. You can't hand out that line anymore. Now take my last sermon—"The Service Station of the Spirit." There's a lesson for you, brother! I had a whole service station built—[*Rises, walks to pulpit*]—right there, behind my pulpit. Tall pumps, glass and gold, labeled PURITY, PRAYER, PRAYER WITH FAITH SUPER-MIXTURE. And young boys in white uniforms—good-lookers, every one of 'em!—with gold wings, and caps inscribed CREED OIL, INC. Clever, eh?

HIX: It's a sacrilege!

ESSIE TWOMEY: [*Stepping up on the pulpit*] And the pulpit here was—[*Looks at her fingers*]—hm, dust, Brother Hix. Bad business! . . . And the pulpit was made up like a gold automobile. [*Greatly inspired*] Then I preached to my flock that when you travel the hard road of life, you must be sure that your tank is filled with the best gas of Faith, that your tires are inflated with the air of Charity, that your radiator is cooled with the sweet water of Temperance, that your battery is charged with the power of Righteousness, and that you beware of treacherous Detours which lead to perdition! [*In her normal voice*] Boy, did that wow 'em! Praise the Lord! It brought the house down! And we had no trouble at all when we passed the collection box made up in the shape of a gasoline can!

HIX: [*With controlled fury*] Sister Twomey, you will please step down from my pulpit!

ESSIE TWOMEY: [*Coming down*] Well, brother, to make a long story short, I'll give you five hundred bucks and you can move your junk out.

HIX: *Five hundred dollars for the Temple of Eternal Truth?*

ESSIE TWOMEY: Well, what's the matter with five hundred dollars? It's a lot of money. You can buy a good secondhand car for five hundred dollars.

HIX: Never, in twenty years, have I shown the door to anyone in this temple. But I am doing it now. [*He points to the door*]

ESSIE TWOMEY: [*Shrugging*] Well, have it your own way, brother. They have eyes, but they see not! . . . I should worry, by Jesus! [*Raising her arm*] Praise the Lord! [*Exits*]

[*The minute she is out,* EZRY's *head comes peering cautiously from behind the door.* EZRY *is a lanky, gangling youth, far from bright*]

EZRY: [*Calls in a whisper*] Oh, Brother Hix!

HIX: [*Startled*] Ezry! What are you doing there? Come in.

EZRY: [*Enters, awed*] Gee, it was better'n a movie show!

HIX: Have you been listening?

EZRY: Gee! Was that Sister Essie Twomey?

HIX: Yes, Ezry, it was Sister Essie Twomey. Now, you mustn't tell anyone about what you heard here.

EZRY: No, sir. Cross my heart, Brother Hix. [*Looking at the door with admiration*] My, but Sister Twomey talks pretty!

HIX: You mustn't say that. Sister Twomey is an evil woman.

EZRY: Yes, sir. . . . Gee, but she's got such pretty curls!

HIX: Ezry, do you believe in me? Do you like to come here for the services?

EZRY: Yes, sir. . . . The Crump twins, they said Sister Twomey had a airyplane in her temple, honest to goodness!

HIX: [*Desperately*] My boy, listen to me, for the sake of your immortal soul . . . [*He stops short.* KAY GONDA *enters*]

KAY GONDA: Mr. Hix?

HIX: [*Without taking his eyes from her, in a choked voice*] Ezry. Run along.

EZRY: [*Frightened*] Yes, sir. [*Exits hurriedly*]

HIX: You're not . . .

KAY GONDA: Yes. I am.

HIX: To what do I owe the great honor of . . .

KAY GONDA: To a murder.

HIX: Do you mean that those rumors are true?

KAY GONDA: You can throw me out, if you wish. You can call the police, if you prefer. Only do so now.

HIX: You are seeking shelter?

KAY GONDA: For one night.

HIX: [*Walks to the open door, closes it, and locks it*] This door has not been closed for twenty years. It shall be closed tonight. [*He returns to her and silently hands her the key*]

KAY GONDA: [*Astonished*] Why are you giving it to me?

HIX: The door will not be opened, until you wish to open it.

KAY GONDA: [*She smiles, takes the key, and slips it into her bag. Then*:] Thank you.

HIX: [*Sternly*] No. Do not thank me. I do not want you to stay here.

KAY GONDA: [*Without understanding*] You—don't?

HIX: But you are safe—if this is the safety you want. I have turned the place over to you. You may stay here as long as you like. The decision will be yours.

KAY GONDA: You do not want me to hide here?

HIX: I do not want you to hide.

KAY GONDA: [*She looks at him thoughtfully, then walks to a bench and sits down, watching him. She asks slowly:*] What would you have me do?

HIX: [*He stands before her, austerely erect and solemn*] You have taken a heavy burden upon your shoulders.

KAY GONDA: Yes. A heavy burden. And I wonder how much longer I will be able to carry it.

HIX: You may hide from the men who threaten you. But of what importance is that?

KAY GONDA: Then you do not want to save me?

HIX: Oh, yes. I want to save you. But not from the police.

KAY GONDA: From whom?

HIX: From yourself. [*She looks at him for a long moment, a fixed, steady glance, and does not answer*] You have committed a mortal sin. You have killed a human being. [*Points to the room*] Can this place—or any place—give you protection from that?

KAY GONDA: No.

HIX: You cannot escape from your crime. Then do not try to run from it. Give up. Surrender. Confess.

KAY GONDA: [*Slowly*] If I confess, they will take my life.

HIX: If you don't, you will lose your life—the eternal life of your soul.

KAY GONDA: Is it a choice, then? Must it be one or the other?

HIX: It has always been a choice. For all of us.

KAY GONDA: Why?

HIX: Because the joys of this earth are paid for by damnation in the

Kingdom of Heaven. But if we choose to suffer, we are rewarded with eternal happiness.

KAY GONDA: Then we are on earth only in order to suffer?

HIX: And the greater the suffering, the greater our virtue. [*Her head drops slowly*] You have a sublime chance before you. Accept, of your own will, the worst that can be done to you. The infamy, the degradation, the prison cell, the scaffold. Then your punishment will become your glory.

KAY GONDA: How?

HIX: It will let you enter the Kingdom of Heaven.

KAY GONDA: Why should I want to enter it?

HIX: If you know that a life of supreme beauty is possible—how can you help but want to enter it?

KAY GONDA: How can I help but want it here, on earth?

HIX: Ours is a dark, imperfect world.

KAY GONDA: Why is it not perfect? Because it cannot be? Or because we do not want it to be?

HIX: This world is of no consequence. Whatever beauty it offers us is here only that we may sacrifice it—for the greater beauty beyond. [*She is not looking at him. He stands watching her for a moment; then, his voice low with emotion:*] You don't know how lovely you are at this moment. [*She raises her head*] You don't know the hours I've spent watching you across the infinite distance of a screen. I would give my life to keep you here in safety. I would let myself be torn to shreds, rather than see you hurt. Yet I am asking you to open this door and walk out to martyrdom. That is my chance of sacrifice. I am giving up the greatest thing that ever came to me.

KAY GONDA: [*Her voice soft and low*] And after you and I have made our sacrifice, what will be left on this earth?

HIX: Our example. It will light the way for all the miserable souls who flounder in helpless depravity. They, too, will learn to renounce. Your fame is great. The story of your conversion will be heard the world over. You will redeem the scrubby wretches who come to this temple and all the wretches in all the slums.

KAY GONDA: Such as that boy who was here?

HIX: Such as that boy. Let him be the symbol, not a nobler figure. That, too, is part of the sacrifice.

KAY GONDA: [*Slowly*] What do you want me to do?

HIX: Confess your crime. Confess it publicly, to a crowd, to the hearing of all!

KAY GONDA: Tonight?

HIX: Tonight!

KAY GONDA: But there is no crowd anywhere at this hour.

HIX: At this hour . . . [*With sudden inspiration*] Listen. At this hour, a large crowd is gathered in a temple of error, six blocks away. It is a dreadful place, run by the most contemptible woman I've ever known. I'll take you there. I'll let you offer that woman the greatest gift—the kind of sensation she's never dared to imagine for her audience. You will confess to her crowd. Let her take the credit and the praise for your conversion. Let her take the fame. She is the one least worthy of it.

KAY GONDA: That, too, is part of the sacrifice?

HIX: Yes.

[KAY GONDA *rises. She walks to the door, unlocks it, and flings it open. Then she turns to* HIX *and throws the key in his face. It strikes him as she goes out. He stands motionless, only his head dropping and his shoulders sagging*]

CURTAIN

SCENE 2

The letter projected on the screen is written in a sharp, precise, cultured handwriting:

Dear Miss Gonda,

    I have had everything men ask of life. I have seen it all, and I feel as if I were leaving a third-rate show on a disreputable side street. If I do not bother to die, it is only because my life has all the emptiness of the grave and my death would have no change to offer me. It may happen, any day now, and nobody—not even the one writing these lines—will know the difference.

    But before it happens, I want to raise what is left of my soul in a last salute to you, you who are that which the world should have been. *Morituri te salutamus.*

    Dietrich von Esterhazy
    Beverly-Sunset Hotel
    Beverly Hills, California

Lights go out, screen disappears, and stage reveals drawing room in the hotel suite of DIETRICH VON ESTERHAZY. *It is a large, luxurious room, modern, exquisitely simple. Wide entrance door in center wall Left. Smaller door to bedroom in wall Right, upstage. Large window in wall Left, show-ing the dark view of a park far below. Downstage Right a fireplace. One single lamp burning.*

As the curtain rises the entrance door opens to admit DIETRICH VON ESTERHAZY *and* LALO JANS. DIETRICH VON ESTERHAZY *is a tall, slender man in his early forties, whose air of patrician distinction seems created for the trim elegance of his full dress suit.* LALO JANS *is an exquisite female, hidden in the soft folds of an ermine wrap over a magnificent evening gown. She walks in first and falls, exhausted, on a sofa downstage, stretch-ing out her legs with a gesture of charming lassitude.* DIETRICH VON ESTER-HAZY *follows her silently. She makes a little gesture, expecting him to take her wrap. But he does not approach her or look at her, and she shrugs, throwing her wrap back, letting it slide halfway down her bare arms.*

LALO: [*Looking at a clock on the table beside her, lazily*] Only two
    o'clock. . . . Really, we didn't have to leave so early, darling. . . .
    [ESTERHAZY *does not answer. He does not seem to hear. There is no*
    hostility in his attitude, but a profound indifference and a strange
    tension. He walks to the window and stands looking out thoughtfully,
    unconscious of LALO'*s presence. She yawns, lighting a cigarette*] I think
    I'll go home. . . . [*No answer*] I said, I think I'll go home. . . .
    [*Coquettishly*] Unless, of course, you insist. . . . [*No answer. She*
    shrugs and settles down more comfortably. She speaks lazily, watching
    the smoke of her cigarette] You know, Rikki, we'll just have to go to
    Agua Caliente. And this time I'll put it all on Black Rajah. It's a
    cinch. . . . [*No answer*] By the way, Rikki, my chauffeur's wages
    were due yesterday. . . . [*Turns to him. Slightly impatient:*] Rikki?
ESTERHAZY: [*Startled, turning to her abruptly, polite and completely*
    indifferent] What were you saying, my dear?
LALO: [*Impatiently*] I said my chauffeur's wages were due yesterday.

ESTERHAZY: [*His thoughts miles away*] Yes, of course. I shall take care of it.

LALO: What's the matter, Rikki? Just because I lost that money?

ESTERHAZY: Not at all, my dear. Glad you enjoyed the evening.

LALO: But then you know I've always had the damnedest luck at roulette. And if we hadn't left so early, I'm sure I'd have won it back.

ESTERHAZY: I'm sorry. I was a little tired.

LALO: And anyway, what's one thousand and seventy something?

ESTERHAZY: [*Stands looking at her silently. Then, with a faint smile of something like sudden decision, he reaches into his pocket and calmly hands her a checkbook*] I think you might as well see it.

LALO: [*Taking the book indifferently*] What's that? Some bankbook?

ESTERHAZY: See what's left . . . at some bank.

LALO: [*Reading*] Three hundred and sixteen dollars. . . . [*Looks quickly through the check stubs*] Rikki! You wrote that thousand-dollar check on this bank! [*He nods silently, with the same smile*] You'll have to transfer the money from another bank, first thing in the morning.

ESTERHAZY: [*Slowly*] I have no other bank.

LALO: Huh?

ESTERHAZY: I have no other money. You're holding there all that's left.

LALO: [*Her lazy nonchalance gone*] Rikki! You're kidding me!

ESTERHAZY: Far be it from me, my dear.

LALO: But . . . but you're crazy! Things like that don't happen like . . . like that! One sees . . . in advance . . . One knows.

ESTERHAZY: [*Calmly*] I've known it. For the last two years. But a fortune does not vanish without a few last convulsions. There has always been something to sell, to pawn, to borrow on. Always someone to borrow from. But not this time. This time, it's done.

LALO: [*Aghast*] But . . . but where did it go?

ESTERHAZY: [*Shrugging*] How do I know? Where did all the rest of it go, those other things, inside, that you start life with? Fifteen years is a long time. When they threw me out of Austria, I had millions in my pocket, but the rest—the rest, I think, was gone already.

LALO: That's all very beautiful, but what are you going to do?

ESTERHAZY: Nothing.

LALO: But tomorrow . . .

ESTERHAZY: Tomorrow, Count Dietrich von Esterhazy will be called upon to explain the matter of a bad check. *May* be called upon.

LALO: Stop grinning like that! Do you think it's funny?

ESTERHAZY: I think it's curious. . . . The first Count Dietrich von Esterhazy died fighting under the walls of Jerusalem. The second died on the ramparts of his castle, defying a nation. The last one wrote a bad check in a gambling casino with chromium and poor ventilation. . . . It's curious.

LALO: What are you talking about?

ESTERHAZY: About what a peculiar thing it is—a leaking soul. You go through your days and it slips away from you, drop by drop. With each step. Like a hole in your pocket and coins dropping out, bright little coins, bright and shining, never to be found again.

LALO: To hell with that! What's to become of me?

ESTERHAZY: I've done all I could, Lalo. I've warned you before the others.

LALO: You're not going to stand there like a damn fool and let things . . .

ESTERHAZY: [*Softly*] You know, I think I'm glad it happened like this. A few hours ago I had problems, a thick web of problems I was much too weary to untangle. Now I'm free. Free at one useless stroke I did not intend striking.

LALO: Don't you care at all?

ESTERHAZY: I would not be frightened if I still cared.

LALO: Then you are frightened?

ESTERHAZY: I should like to be.

LALO: Why don't you do something? Call your friends!

ESTERHAZY: Their reaction, my dear, would be precisely the same as yours.

LALO: You're blaming *me*, now!

ESTERHAZY: Not at all. I appreciate you. You make my prospect so simple—and so easy.

LALO: But good God! What about the payments on my new Cadillac? And those pearls I charged to you? And . . .

ESTERHAZY: And my hotel bill. And my florist's bill. And that last party I gave. And the mink coat for Colette Dorsay.

LALO: [*Jumping up*] What?!

ESTERHAZY: My dear, you really didn't think you were . . . the only one?

LALO: [*Looks at him, her eyes blazing. Is on the point of screaming something. Laughs suddenly instead, a dry insulting laughter*] Do you think I care—*now*? Do you think I'm going to cry over a worthless . . .

ESTERHAZY: [*Quietly*] Don't you think you'd better go home now?

LALO: [*Tightens her wrap furiously, rushes to the door, turns abruptly*] Call me up when you come to your senses. I'll answer—if I feel like it tomorrow.

ESTERHAZY: And if I'm here to call—*tomorrow*.

LALO: Huh?

ESTERHAZY: I said, if I'm here to call—tomorrow.

LALO: Just what do you mean? Do you intend to run away or . . .

ESTERHAZY: [*With quiet affirmation*] Or.

LALO: Oh, don't be a melodramatic fool! [*Exits, slamming the door*]

[ESTERHAZY *stands motionless, lost in thought. Then he shudders slightly, as if recovering himself. Shrugs. Walks into bedroom Right, leaving the door open. The telephone rings. He returns, his evening coat replaced by a trim lounging jacket*]

ESTERHAZY: [*Picking up receiver*] Hello? . . . [*Astonished*] At this hour? What's her name? . . . She won't? . . . All right, have her come up. [*Hangs up. Lights a cigarette. There is a knock at the door. He smiles*] Come in!

[KAY GONDA *enters. His smile vanishes. He does not move. He stands looking at her for a moment, two motionless fingers holding the cigarette at his mouth. Then he flings the cigarette aside with a violent jerk of his wrist—his only reaction—and bows calmly, formally*]

Good evening, *Miss Gonda.*

KAY GONDA: Good evening.

ESTERHAZY: A veil or black glasses?

KAY GONDA: What?

ESTERHAZY: I hope you didn't let the clerk downstairs recognize you.

KAY GONDA: [*Smiles suddenly, pulling her glasses out of her pocket*] Black glasses.

ESTERHAZY: It was a brilliant idea.

KAY GONDA: What?

ESTERHAZY: Your coming here to hide.

KAY GONDA: How did you know that?

ESTERHAZY: Because it could have occurred only to you. Because you're the only one capable of the exquisite sensitiveness to recognize the only sincere letter I've ever written in my life.

KAY GONDA: [*Looking at him*] Was it?

ESTERHAZY: [*Studying her openly, speaking casually, matter-of-factly*] You look taller than you do on the screen—and less real. Your hair is blonder than I thought. Your voice about a tone higher. It is a pity that the camera does not photograph the shade of your lipstick. [*In a different voice, warm and natural*] And now that I've done my duty as a fan reacting, sit down and let's forget the unusual circumstances.

KAY GONDA: Do you really want me to stay here?

ESTERHAZY: [*Looking at the room*] The place is not too uncomfortable. There's a slight draft from the window at times, and the people upstairs become noisy occasionally, but not often. [*Looking at her*] No, I won't tell you how glad I am to see you here. I never speak of the things that mean much to me. The occasions have been too rare. I've lost the habit.

KAY GONDA: [*Sitting down*] Thank you.

ESTERHAZY: For what?

KAY GONDA: For what you didn't say.

ESTERHAZY: Do you know that it is really I who must thank you? Not only for coming, but for coming tonight of all nights.

KAY GONDA: Why?

ESTERHAZY: Perhaps you have taken a life in order to save another. [*Pause*] A long time ago—no, isn't that strange?—it was only a few minutes ago—I was ready to kill myself. Don't look at me like that. It isn't frightening. But what did become frightening was that feeling of utter indifference, even to death, even to my own indifference. And then you came. . . . I think I could hate you for coming.

KAY GONDA: I think you will.

ESTERHAZY: [*With sudden fire, the first, unexpected emotion*] I don't want to be proud of myself again. I had given it up. Yet now I am. Just because I see you here. Just because a thing has happened which is like nothing I thought possible on earth.

KAY GONDA: You said you would not tell me how glad you were to see me. Don't tell me. I do not want to hear it. I have heard it too often. I have never believed it. And I do not think I shall come to believe it *tonight*.

ESTERHAZY: Which means that you have always believed it. It's an incurable disease, you know—to have faith in the better spirit of man. I'd like to tell you to renounce it. To destroy in yourself all hunger for anything above the dry rot that others live by. But I can't. Because you will never be able to do it. It's your curse. And mine.

KAY GONDA: [*Angry and imploring at once*] I do not want to hear it!

ESTERHAZY: [*Sitting down on the arm of a chair, speaking softly, lightly*] You know, when I was a boy—a very young boy—I thought my life would be a thing immense and shining. I wanted to kneel to my own future. . . . [*Shrugs*] One gets over that.

KAY GONDA: Does one?

ESTERHAZY: Always. But never completely.

KAY GONDA: [*Breaking down, suddenly eager and trusting*] I saw a man once, when I was very young. He stood on a rock, high in the mountains. His arms were spread out and his body bent backward, and I could see him as an arc against the sky. He stood still and tense, like a string trembling to a note of ecstasy no man had ever heard. . . . I have never known who he was. I knew only that this was what life should be. . . . [*Her voice trails off*]

ESTERHAZY: [*Eagerly*] And?

KAY GONDA: [*In a changed voice*] And I came home, and my mother was serving supper, and she was happy because the roast had a thick gravy. And she gave a prayer of thanks to God for it. . . . [*Jumps up, whirls to him suddenly, angrily*] Don't listen to me! Don't look at me like that! . . . I've tried to renounce it. I thought I must close my eyes and bear anything and learn to live like the others. To make me as they were. To make me forget. I bore it. All of it. But I can't forget the man on the rock. I can't!

ESTERHAZY: We never can.

KAY GONDA: [*Eagerly*] You understand? I'm not alone? . . . Oh, God! I can't be alone! [*Suddenly quiet*] Why did you give it up?

ESTERHAZY: [*Shrugging*] Why does anyone give it up? Because it never comes. What did I get instead? Racing boats, and horses, and cards, and women—all those blind alleys—the pleasures of the moment. All the things I never wanted.

KAY GONDA: [*Softly*] Are you certain?

ESTERHAZY: There was nothing else to take. But if it came, if one had a chance, a last chance . . .

KAY GONDA: Are you certain?

ESTERHAZY: [*Looks at her, then walks resolutely to the telephone and picks up the receiver*] Gladstone 2-1018 . . . Hello, Carl? . . . Those two staterooms on the *Empress of Panama* that you told me about—do you still want to get rid of them? Yes . . . yes, I do . . . At seven thirty a.m.? . . . I'll meet you there. . . . I understand. . . . Thank you. [*Hangs up.* KAY GONDA *looks at him questioningly. He turns to her, his manner calm, matter-of-fact*] The *Empress of Panama* leaves San Pedro at seven thirty in the morning. For Brazil. No extradition laws there.

KAY GONDA: What are you attempting?

ESTERHAZY: We're escaping together. We're outside the law—both of us. I have something worth fighting for now. My ancestors would envy me if they could see me. For my Holy Grail is of this earth. It is real, alive, possible. Only they would not understand. It is our secret. Yours and mine.

KAY GONDA: You have not asked me whether I want to go.

ESTERHAZY: I don't have to. If I did—I would have no right to go with you.

KAY GONDA: [*Smiles softly; then:*] I want to tell you.

ESTERHAZY: [*Stops, faces her, earnestly*] Tell me.

KAY GONDA: [*Looking straight at him, her eyes trusting, her voice a whisper*] Yes, I want to go.

ESTERHAZY: [*Holds her glance for an instant; then, as if deliberately refusing to underscore the earnestness of the moment, glances at his wristwatch and speaks casually again*] We have just a few hours to wait. I'll make a fire. We'll be more comfortable. [*He speaks gaily as he proceeds to light the fire*] I'll pack a few things. . . . You can get what you need aboard ship. . . . I haven't much money, but I'll raise a few thousands before morning. . . . I don't know where, as yet, but I'll raise it. . . . [*She sits down in an armchair by the fire. He sits down on the floor at her feet, facing her*] The sun is terrible down in Brazil. I hope your face doesn't get sunburned.

KAY GONDA: [*Happily, almost girlishly*] It always does.

ESTERHAZY: We'll build a house somewhere in the jungle. It will be curious to start chopping trees down—that's another experience I've missed. I'll learn it. And you'll have to learn to cook.

KAY GONDA: I will. I'll learn everything we'll need. We'll start from scratch, from the beginning of the world—our world.

ESTERHAZY: You're not afraid?

KAY GONDA: [*Smiling softly*] I'm terribly afraid. I have never been happy before.

ESTERHAZY: The work will ruin your hands . . . your lovely hands. . . . [*He takes her hand, then drops it hurriedly. Speaks with a little effort, suddenly serious*:] I'll be only your architect, your valet, and your watchdog. And nothing else—until I deserve it.

KAY GONDA: [*Looking at him*] What were you thinking?

ESTERHAZY: [*Absently*] I was thinking about tomorrow and all the days thereafter. . . . They seem such a long way off. . . .

KAY GONDA: [*Gaily*] I'll want a house by the seashore. Or by a great river.

ESTERHAZY: With a balcony off your room, over the water, facing the sunrise. . . . [*Involuntarily*] And the moonlight streaming in at night. . . .

KAY GONDA: We'll have no neighbors . . . nowhere . . . not for miles around. . . . No one will look at me . . . No one will pay to look at me. . . .

ESTERHAZY: [*His voice low*] I shall allow no one to look at you. . . . In the morning, you will swim in the sea . . . alone . . . in the green water . . . with the first sun rays on your body. . . . [*He rises, bends over her, whispers*] And then I'll carry you up to the house . . . up the rocks . . . in my arms . . . [*He seizes her and kisses her violently. She responds. He raises his head and chuckles with a sound of cynical intimacy*] That's all we're really after, you and I, aren't we? Why pretend?

KAY GONDA: [*Not understanding*] What?

ESTERHAZY: Why pretend that we're important? We're no better than the others. [*Tries to kiss her again*]

KAY GONDA: Let me go! [*She tears herself away*]

ESTERHAZY: [*Laughing harshly*] Where? You have no place to go! [*She stares at him, wide-eyed, incredulous*] After all, what difference does it make, whether it's now or later? Why should we take it so seriously? [*She whirls toward the door. He seizes her. She screams, a muffled scream, stopped by his hand on her mouth*] Keep still! You can't call for help! . . . It's a death sentence—or this. . . . [*She starts laughing hysterically*] Keep still! . . . Why should I care what you'll think of me afterwards? . . . Why should I care about tomorrow?

[*She tears herself away, runs to the door, and escapes. He stands still. He hears her laughter, loud, reckless, moving away*]

CURTAIN

SCENE 3

T *he letter projected on the screen is written in a sharp, uneven hand-writing:*

Dear Miss Gonda,

This letter is addressed to you, but I am writing it to myself.

I am writing and thinking that I am speaking to a woman who is the only justification for the existence of this earth, and who has the courage to want to be. A woman who does not assume a glory of greatness for a few hours, then return to the children-dinner-friends-football-and-God reality. A woman who seeks that glory in her every minute and her every step. A woman in whom life is not a curse, nor a bargain, but a hymn.

I want nothing except to know that such a woman exists. So I have written this, even though you may not bother to read it, or reading it, may not understand. I do not know what you are. I am writing to what you could have been.

Johnnie Dawes

. . . Main Street

Los Angeles, California

IDEAL

Lights go out, screen disappears, and stage reveals garret of JOHNNIE
DAWES. *It is a squalid, miserable room with a low, slanting ceiling, with
dark walls showing beams under cracked plaster. The room is so bare that
it gives the impression of being uninhabited, a strange, intangible impression of unreality. A narrow iron cot, at wall Right; a broken table, a few
boxes for chairs. A narrow door opens diagonally in the Left upstage corner.
The entire wall Center is a long window checkered into small panes. It
opens high over the skyline of Los Angeles. Behind the black shadows of
skyscrapers, there is a first hint of pink in the dark sky. When the curtain
rises, the stage is empty, dark. One barely distinguishes the room and sees
only the faintly luminous panorama of the window. It dominates the stage,
so that one forgets the room, and it seems as if the setting is only the city and
the sky. (Throughout the scene, the sky lightens slowly, the pink band of
dawn grows, rising.)*

*Steps are heard coming up the stairs. A quivering light shows in the
cracks of the door. The door opens to admit* KAY GONDA. *Behind her,* MRS.
MONAGHAN, *an old landlady, shuffles in, with a lighted candle in hand.
She puts the candle down on the table, and stands panting as after a long
climb, studying* KAY GONDA *with a suspicious curiosity.*

MRS. MONAGHAN: Here ye are. This is it.

KAY GONDA: [*Looking slowly over the room*] Thank you.

MRS. MONAGHAN: And ye're a relative of him, ye are?

KAY GONDA: No.

MRS. MONAGHAN: [*Maliciously*] Sure, and I was thinking that.

KAY GONDA: I have never seen him before.

MRS. MONAGHAN: Well, I'm after tellin' ye he's no good, that's what he
is, no good. It's a born bum he is. No rent never. He can't keep a
job more'n two weeks.

KAY GONDA: When will he be back?

MRS. MONAGHAN: Any minute at all—or never, for all I know. He runs around all night, the good Lord only knows where. Just walks the streets like the bum he is, just walks. Comes back drunk like, only he's not drunk, 'cause I know he don't drink.

KAY GONDA: I will wait for him.

MRS. MONAGHAN: Suit yerself. [*Looks at her shrewdly*] Maybe ye got a job for him?

KAY GONDA: No. I have no job for him.

MRS. MONAGHAN: He's got himself kicked out again, three days ago it was. He had a swell job bellhoppin'. Did it last? It did not. Same as the soda counter. Same as the waitin' at Hamburger Looey's. He's no good, I'm tellin' ye. I know him. Better'n ye do.

KAY GONDA: I do not know him at all.

MRS. MONAGHAN: And I can't say I blame his bosses, either. He's a strange one. Never a laugh, never a joke out of him. [*Confidentially*] Ye know what Hamburger Looey said to me? He said, "Stuck up little snot," said Hamburger Looey, "makes a regular guy feel creepy."

KAY GONDA: So Hamburger Looey said that?

MRS. MONAGHAN: Faith and he did. [*Confidentially*] And d'ye know? He's been to college, that boy. Ye'd never believe it from the kind of jobs he can't keep, but he has. What he learned there the good Lord only knows. It's no good it done him. And . . . [*Stops, listening. Steps are heard rising up the stairs*] That's him now! Nobody else'd be shameless enough to come home at this hour of the night. [*At the door*] Ye think it over. Maybe ye could do somethin' for him. [*Exits*]

[JOHNNIE DAWES *enters. He is a tall, slender boy in his late twenties; a gaunt face, prominent cheekbones, a hard mouth, clear, steady eyes. He sees* KAY GONDA *and stands still. They look at each other for a long moment*]

JOHNNIE: [*Slowly, calmly, no astonishment and no question in his voice*]
Good evening, Miss Gonda.

KAY GONDA: [*She cannot take her eyes from him, and it is her voice that
sounds astonished*] Good evening.

JOHNNIE: Please sit down.

KAY GONDA: You do not want me to stay here.

JOHNNIE: You're staying.

KAY GONDA: You have not asked me why I came.

JOHNNIE: You're here. [*He sits down*]

KAY GONDA: [*She approaches him suddenly, takes his face in her hands
and raises it*] What's the matter, Johnnie?

JOHNNIE: Nothing—now.

KAY GONDA: You must not be so glad to see me.

JOHNNIE: I knew you'd come.

KAY GONDA: [*She walks away from him, falls wearily down on the cot.
She looks at him and smiles; a smile that is not gay, not friendly*]
People say I am a great star, Johnnie.

JOHNNIE: Yes.

KAY GONDA: They say I have everything one can wish for.

JOHNNIE: Have you?

KAY GONDA: No. But how do you know it?

JOHNNIE: How do you know that I know it?

KAY GONDA: You are never afraid when you speak to people, are you,
Johnnie?

JOHNNIE: Yes. I am very much afraid. Always. I don't know what to
say to them. But I'm not afraid—now.

KAY GONDA: I am a very bad woman, Johnnie. Everything you've
heard about me is true. Everything—and more. I came to tell you
that you must not think of me what you said in your letter.

JOHNNIE: You came to tell me that everything I said in my letter was true. Everything—and more.

KAY GONDA: [*With a harsh little laugh*] You're a fool! I'm not afraid of you. . . . Do you know that I get twenty thousand dollars a week?

JOHNNIE: Yes.

KAY GONDA: Do you know that I have fifty pairs of shoes and three butlers?

JOHNNIE: I suppose so.

KAY GONDA: Do you know that my pictures are shown in every town on earth?

JOHNNIE: Yes.

KAY GONDA: [*Furiously*] Stop looking at me like that! . . . Do you know that people pay millions to see me? I don't need your approval! I have plenty of worshipers! I mean a great deal to them!

JOHNNIE: You mean nothing at all to them. You know it.

KAY GONDA: [*Looking at him almost with hatred*] I thought I knew it— an hour ago. [*Whirling upon him*] Oh, why don't you ask me for something?

JOHNNIE: What do you want me to ask you?

KAY GONDA: Why don't you ask me to get you a job in the movies, for instance?

JOHNNIE: The only thing I could ask you, you have given to me already.

KAY GONDA: [*She looks at him, laughs harshly, speaks in a new voice, strange to her, an unnaturally common voice*] Look, Johnnie, let's stop kidding each other. I'll tell you something. I've killed a man. It's dangerous, hiding a murderess. Why don't you throw me out? [*He sits looking at her silently*] No? That one won't work? Well, then, look at me. I'm the most beautiful woman you've ever seen. Don't you want to sleep with me? Why don't you? Right now. I won't struggle. [*He does not move*] Not that? But listen: do you know that there's a reward on my head? Why don't you call the police and turn me over to them? You'd be set for life.

JOHNNIE: [*Softly*] Are you as unhappy as that?

KAY GONDA: [*Walks to him, then falls on her knees at his feet*] Help me, Johnnie!

JOHNNIE: [*Bends down to her, his hands on her shoulders, asks softly:*] Why did you come here?

KAY GONDA: [*Raising her head*] Johnnie. If all of you who look at me on the screen hear the things I say and worship me for them—where do I hear them? Where can I hear them, so that I might go on? I want to see real, living, and in the hours of my own days, that glory I create as an illusion! I want it real! I want to know that there is someone, somewhere, who wants it, too! Or else what is the use of seeing it, and working, and burning oneself for an impossible vision? A spirit, too, needs fuel. It can run dry.

JOHNNIE: [*He rises, leads her to the cot, makes her sit down, stands before her*] I want to tell you only this: there are a few on earth who see you and understand. These few give life its meaning. The rest—well, the rest are what you see they are. You have a duty. To live. Just to remain on earth. To let them know you do and can exist. To fight, even a fight without hope. We can't give up the earth to all those others.

KAY GONDA: [*Looking at him, softly*] Who are you, Johnnie?

JOHNNIE: [*Astonished*] I? . . . I'm—nothing.

KAY GONDA: Where do you come from?

JOHNNIE: I've had a home and parents somewhere. I don't remember much about them . . . I don't remember much about anything that's ever happened to me. There's not a day worth remembering.

KAY GONDA: You have no friends?

JOHNNIE: No.

KAY GONDA: You have no work?

JOHNNIE: Yes . . . No, I was fired three days ago. I forgot.

KAY GONDA: Where have you lived before?

JOHNNIE: Many places. I've lost count.

KAY GONDA: Do you hate people, Johnnie?

JOHNNIE: No. I never notice them.

KAY GONDA: What do you dream of?

JOHNNIE: Nothing. Of what account are dreams?

KAY GONDA: Of what account is life?

JOHNNIE: None. But who made it so?

KAY GONDA: Those who cannot dream.

JOHNNIE: No. Those who can *only* dream.

KAY GONDA: Are you very unhappy?

JOHNNIE: No. . . . I don't think you should ask me these questions. You won't get a decent answer from me to anything.

KAY GONDA: There was a great man once who said: "I love those that know not how to live today."

JOHNNIE: [*Quietly*] I think I am a person who should never have been born. This is not a complaint. I am not afraid and I am not sorry. But I have often wanted to die. I have no desire to change the world—nor to take any part in it, as it is. I've never had the weapons which you have. I've never even found the desire to find weapons. I'd like to go, calmly and willingly.

KAY GONDA: I don't want to hear you say that.

JOHNNIE: There has always been something holding me here. Something that had to come to me before I went. I want to know one living moment of that which is mine, not theirs. Not their dismal little pleasures. One moment of ecstasy, utter and absolute, a moment that must not be survived. . . . They've never given me a life. I've always hoped I would choose my death.

KAY GONDA: Don't say that. I need you. I'm here. I'll never let you go.

JOHNNIE: [*After a pause, looking at her in a strange new way, his voice dry, flat*] You? You're a murderess who'll get caught someday and die on the gallows.

[*She looks at him, astonished. He walks to the window, stands looking out. Beyond the window it is now full daylight. The sun is about to rise. Rays of light spread like halos from behind the dark silhouettes of skyscrapers. He asks suddenly, without turning to her:*]

You killed him?

KAY GONDA: We don't have to talk about that, do we?

JOHNNIE: [*Without turning*] I knew Granton Sayers. I worked for him once, as a caddy, at a golf club in Santa Barbara. A hard kind of man.

KAY GONDA: He was a very unhappy man, Johnnie.

JOHNNIE: [*Turning to her*] Was anyone present?

KAY GONDA: Where?

JOHNNIE: When you killed him?

KAY GONDA: Do we have to discuss that?

JOHNNIE: It's something I must know. Did anyone see you kill him?

KAY GONDA: No.

JOHNNIE: Have the police got anything on you?

KAY GONDA: No. Except what I could tell them. But I will not tell it to them. Nor to you. Not now. Don't question me.

JOHNNIE: How much is the reward on your head?

KAY GONDA: [*After a pause, in a strange kind of voice*] What did you say, Johnnie?

JOHNNIE: [*Evenly*] I said, how much is the reward on your head? [*She stares at him*] Never mind. [*He walks to the door, throws it open, calls:*] Mrs. Monaghan! Come here!

KAY GONDA: What are you doing? [*He does not answer or look at her.* MRS. MONAGHAN *shuffles up the stairs and appears at the door*]

MRS. MONAGHAN: [*Angrily*] What d'ye want?

JOHNNIE: Mrs. Monaghan, listen carefully. Go downstairs to your phone. Call the police. Tell them to come here at once. Tell them that *Kay Gonda* is here. You understand? Kay Gonda. Now hurry.

MRS. MONAGHAN: [*Aghast*] Yes, sir. . . . [*Exits hurriedly*]

[JOHNNIE *closes the door, turns to* KAY GONDA. *She tries to dash for the door. The table is between them. He opens a drawer, pulls out a gun, points it at her*]

JOHNNIE: Stand still. [*She does not move. He backs to the door and locks it. She sags suddenly, still standing up*]

KAY GONDA: [*Without looking at him, in a flat, lifeless voice*] Put it away. I will not try to escape. [*He slips the gun into his pocket and stands leaning against the door. She sits down, her back turned to him*]

JOHNNIE: [*Quietly*] We have about three minutes left. I am thinking now that nothing has happened to us and nothing will happen. The world stopped a minute ago and in three minutes it will go on again. But this—this pause is ours. You're here. I look at you. I've seen your eyes—and all the truth that man has ever sought. [*Her head falls down on her arms*] There are no other men on earth right now. Just you and I. There's nothing but a world in which you live. To breathe for once that air, to move in it, to hear my own voice on waves that touch no ugliness, no pain . . . I've never known gratitude. But now, of all the words I'd like to say to you, I'll say just three: I thank you. When you leave, remember I have thanked you. Remember—no matter what may happen in this room. . . . [*She buries her head in her arms. He stands silently, his head thrown back, his eyes closed*]

[*Hurried steps are heard rising up the stairs.* JOHNNIE *and* KAY GONDA *do not move. There is a violent knock at the door.* JOHNNIE *turns, unlocks the door, and opens it. A police* CAPTAIN *enters, followed by two* POLICEMEN. KAY GONDA *rises, facing them*]

CAPTAIN: Jesus Christ! [*They stare at her, aghast*]

POLICEMAN: And I thought it was another crank calling!

CAPTAIN: Miss Gonda, I'm sure glad to see you. We've been driven crazy with . . .

KAY GONDA: Take me away from here. Anywhere you wish.

CAPTAIN: [*Making a step toward her*] Well, we have no . . .

JOHNNIE: [*In a quiet voice which is such an implacable command that all turn to him*] Stay away from her. [*The* CAPTAIN *stops.* JOHNNIE *motions to a* POLICEMAN *and points to the table*] Sit down. Take a pencil and paper. [*The* POLICEMAN *looks at the* CAPTAIN, *who nods, baffled. The* POLICEMAN *obeys*] Now write this: [*Dictates slowly, his voice precise, emotionless*] I, John Dawes, confess that on the night of May third, willfully and with premeditation, I killed Granton Sayers of Santa Barbara, California. [KAY GONDA *takes a deep breath, which is almost a gasp*] I have been absent from my home for the last three nights, as my landlady, Mrs. Sheila Monaghan, can testify. She can further testify that I was dismissed from my job at the Alhambra Hotel on May third. [KAY GONDA *starts laughing suddenly. It is the lightest, happiest laughter in the world*] I had worked for Granton

Sayers a year ago, at the Greendale Golf Club of Santa Barbara. Being jobless and broke, I went to Granton Sayers on the evening of May third, determined to extort money from him through blackmail, under threat of divulging certain information I possessed. He refused my demands even at the point of a gun. I shot him. I disposed of the gun by throwing it into the ocean on my way back from Santa Barbara. I was alone in committing this crime. No other person was or is to be implicated. [*Adds*] Have you got it all? Give it to me. [*The* POLICEMAN *hands the confession to him.* JOHNNIE *signs it*]

CAPTAIN: [*He cannot quite collect his wits*] Miss Gonda, what have you got to say about this?

KAY GONDA: [*Hysterically*] Don't ask me! Not now! Don't speak to me!

JOHNNIE: [*Hands the confession to the* CAPTAIN] You will please let Miss Gonda depart now.

CAPTAIN: Wait a minute, my boy. Not so fast. There's a lot of explaining you have to do yet. How did you get into the Sayers house? How did you leave it?

JOHNNIE: I have told you all I'm going to tell.

CAPTAIN: What time was it when you did the shooting? And what is Miss Gonda doing here?

JOHNNIE: You know all you have to know. You know enough not to implicate Miss Gonda. You have my confession.

CAPTAIN: Sure. But you'll have to prove it.

JOHNNIE: It will stand—even if I do not choose to prove it. Particularly if I am not here to prove it.

CAPTAIN: Gonna be tough, eh? Well, you'll talk at headquarters, all right. Come on, boys.

KAY GONDA: [*Stepping forward*] Wait! You must listen to me now. I have a statement to make. I . . .

JOHNNIE: [*Steps back, pulls the gun out of his pocket, covering the group*]

Stand still, all of you. [*To* KAY GONDA] Don't move. Don't say a word.

KAY GONDA: Johnnie! You don't know what you're doing! Wait, my dearest! Put that gun down.

JOHNNIE: [*Without lowering the gun, smiles at her*] I heard it. Thank you.

KAY GONDA: I'll tell you everything! You don't know! I'm safe!

JOHNNIE: I know you're safe. You will be. Step back. Don't be afraid. I won't hurt anyone. [*She obeys*] I want you all to look at me. Years from now you can tell your grandchildren about it. You are looking at something you will never see again and they will never see—a man who is perfectly happy! [*Points the gun at himself, fires, falls*]

CURTAIN

SCENE 4

*E*ntrance hall in the residence of KAY GONDA. *It is high, bare, modern in its austere simplicity. There is no furniture, no ornaments of any kind. The upper part of the hall is a long raised platform, dividing the room horizontally, and three broad continuous steps lead down from it to the foreground. Tall, square columns rise at the upper edge of the steps. Door into the rest of the house downstage in wall Left. The entire back wall is of wide glass panes, with an entrance door in the center. Beyond the house, there is a narrow path among jagged rocks, a thin strip of the high coast with a broad view of the ocean beyond and of a flaming sunset sky. The hall is dim. There is no light, save the glow of the sunset.*

At curtain rise, MICK WATTS *is sitting on the top step, leaning down toward a dignified* BUTLER *who sits on the floor below, stiff, upright, and uncomfortable holding a tray with a full highball glass on it.* MICK WATTS' *shirt collar is torn open, his tie hanging loose, his hair disheveled. He is clutching a newspaper ferociously. He is sober.*

MICK WATTS: [*Continuing a discourse that has obviously been going on for some time, speaking in an even, expressionless monotone, his manner earnest, confidential*] . . . and so the king called them all before his throne and he said: "I'm weary and sick of it. I am tired of my kingdom where not a single man is worth ruling. I am tired of my lusterless crown, for it does not reflect a single flame of glory anywhere in my land." . . . You see, he was a very foolish king. Some scream it, like he did, and squash their damn brains out against a wall. Others stagger on, like a dog chasing a shadow, knowing damn well that there is no shadow to chase, but still going on, their hearts empty and their paws bleeding. . . . So the king said to them on his deathbed—oh, this was another time; he was on his deathbed this time—he said: "It is the end, but I am still hoping. There is no end. Ever shall I go on hoping . . . ever . . . ever." [*Looks suddenly at the* BUTLER, *as if noticing him for the first time, and asks in an entirely different voice, pointing at him*:] What the hell are you doing here?

BUTLER: [*Rising*] May I observe, sir, that you have been speaking for an hour and a quarter?

MICK WATTS: Have I?

BUTLER: You have, sir. So, if I may be forgiven, I took the liberty of sitting down.

MICK WATTS: [*Surprised*] Fancy, you were here all the time!

BUTLER: Yes, sir.

MICK WATTS: Well, what did you want here in the first place?

BUTLER: [*Extending the tray*] Your whiskey, sir.

MICK WATTS: Oh! [*Reaches for the glass, but stops, jerks the crumpled newspaper at the* BUTLER, *asks*:] Have you read this?

BUTLER: Yes, sir.

MICK WATTS: [*Knocking the tray aside; it falls, breaking the glass*] Go to hell! I don't want any whiskey!

BUTLER: But you ordered it, sir.

MICK WATTS: Go to hell just the same! [*As the* BUTLER *bends to pick up the tray*] Get out of here! Never mind! Get out! I don't want to see any human snoot tonight!

BUTLER: Yes, sir. [*Exits Left*]

[MICK WATTS *straightens the paper out, looks at it, crumples it viciously again. Hears steps approaching outside and whirls about.* FREDERICA SAYERS *is seen outside, walking hurriedly toward the door; she has a newspaper in her hand.* MICK WATTS *walks to door and opens it, before she has time to ring*]

MISS SAYERS: Good evening.

[*He does not answer, lets her enter, closes the door and stands silently, looking at her. She looks around, then at him, somewhat disconcerted*]

MICK WATTS: [*Without moving*] Well?

MISS SAYERS: Is this the residence of Miss Kay Gonda?

MICK WATTS: It is.

MISS SAYERS: May I see Miss Gonda?

MICK WATTS: No.

MISS SAYERS: I am Miss Sayers. Miss Frederica Sayers.

MICK WATTS: I don't care.

MISS SAYERS: Will you please tell Miss Gonda that I am here? If she is at home.

MICK WATTS: She is not.

MISS SAYERS: When do you expect her back?

MICK WATTS: I don't expect her.

MISS SAYERS: My good man, this is getting to be preposterous!

MICK WATTS: It is. You'd better get out of here.

MISS SAYERS: Sir?!

MICK WATTS: She'll be back any minute. I know she will. And there's nothing to talk about now.

MISS SAYERS: My good man, do you realize . . .

MICK WATTS: I realize everything that you realize, and then some. And I'm telling you there's nothing to be done. Don't bother her now.

MISS SAYERS: May I ask who you are and what you're talking about?

MICK WATTS: Who I am doesn't matter. I'm talking about—[*Extends the newspaper*]—this.

MISS SAYERS: Yes, I've read it, and I must say it is utterly bewildering and . . .

MICK WATTS: Bewildering? Hell, it's monstrous! You don't know the half of it! . . . [*Catching himself, adds flatly*] I don't, either.

MISS SAYERS: Look here, I must get to the bottom of this thing. It will go too far and . . .

MICK WATTS: It has gone too far.

MISS SAYERS: Then I must . . .

[KAY GONDA *enters from the outside. She is dressed as in all the preceding scenes. She is calm, but very tired*]

MICK WATTS: So here you are! I knew you'd be back now!

KAY GONDA: [*In a quiet, even voice*] Good evening, Miss Sayers.

MISS SAYERS: Miss Gonda, this is the first sigh of relief I've breathed in two days! I never thought the time should come when I'd be so glad to see you! But you must understand . . .

KAY GONDA: [*Indifferently*] I know.

MISS SAYERS: You must understand that I could not foresee the astounding turn of events. It was most kind of you to go into hiding, but, really, you did not have to hide from me.

KAY GONDA: I was not hiding from anyone.

MISS SAYERS: But where were you?

KAY GONDA: Away. It had nothing to do with Mr. Sayers' death.

MISS SAYERS: But when you heard those preposterous rumors accusing you of his murder, you should have come to me at once! When I asked you, at the house that night, not to disclose to anyone the manner of my brother's death, I had no way of knowing what suspicions would arise. I tried my best to get in touch with you. Please believe me that I did not start those rumors.

KAY GONDA: I never thought you did.

MISS SAYERS: I wonder who started them.

KAY GONDA: I wonder.

MISS SAYERS: I do owe you an apology. I'm sure you felt it was my duty to disclose the truth at once, but you know why I had to keep silent. However, the deal is closed, and I thought it best to come to you first and tell you that I'm free to speak now.

KAY GONDA: [*Indifferently*] It was very kind of you.

MISS SAYERS: [*Turning to* MICK WATTS] Young man, you can tell that ridiculous studio of yours that Miss Gonda did not murder my brother. Tell them they can read his suicide letter in tomorrow's papers. He wrote that he had no desire to struggle any longer, since his business was ruined and since the only woman he'd ever loved had, that night, refused to marry him.

KAY GONDA: I'm sorry, Miss Sayers.

MISS SAYERS: This is not a reproach, Miss Gonda. [*To* MICK WATTS] The Santa Barbara police knew everything, but promised me silence. I had to keep my brother's suicide secret for a while, because I was negotiating a merger with . . .

MICK WATTS: . . . with United California Oil, and you didn't want them to know the desperate state of the Sayers Company. Very smart. Now you've closed the deal and gypped United California. My congratulations.

MISS SAYERS: [*Aghast, to* KAY GONDA] This peculiar gentleman knew it all?

MICK WATTS: So it seems, doesn't it?

MISS SAYERS: Then, in heaven's name, why did you allow everybody to suspect Miss Gonda?

KAY GONDA: Don't you think it best, Miss Sayers, not to discuss this any further? It's done. It's past. Let's leave it at that.

MISS SAYERS: As you wish. There is just one question I would like to ask you. It baffles me completely. I thought perhaps you may know something about it. [*Points at the newspaper*] This. That incredible story . . . that boy I've never heard of, killing himself . . . that insane confession. . . . What does it mean?

KAY GONDA: [*Evenly*] I don't know.

MICK WATTS: Huh?

KAY GONDA: I have never heard of him before.

MISS SAYERS: Then I can explain it only as the act of a crank, an abnormal mind . . .

KAY GONDA: Yes, Miss Sayers. A mind that was not normal.

MISS SAYERS: [*After a pause*] Well, if you'll excuse me, Miss Gonda, I shall wish you good night. I shall give my statement to the papers immediately and clear your name completely.

KAY GONDA: Thank you, Miss Sayers. Good night.

MISS SAYERS: [*Turning at the door*] I wish you luck with whatever it is you're doing. You have been most courteous in this unfortunate matter. Allow me to thank you.

[KAY GONDA *bows.* MISS SAYERS *exits*]

MICK WATTS: [*Ferociously*] Well?

KAY GONDA: Would you mind going home, Mick? I am very tired.

MICK WATTS: I hope you've . . .

KAY GONDA: Telephone the studio on your way. Tell them that I will sign the contract tomorrow.

MICK WATTS: I hope you've had a good time! I hope you've enjoyed it! But I'm through!

KAY GONDA: I'll see you at the studio tomorrow at nine.

MICK WATTS: I'm through! God, I wish I could quit!

KAY GONDA: You know that you will never quit, Mick.

MICK WATTS: That's the hell of it! That you know it, too! Why do I serve you like a dog and will go on serving you like a dog for the rest of my days? Why can't I resist any crazy whim of yours? Why did I have to go and spread rumors about a murder you never committed? Just because you wanted to find out something? Well, have you found it out?

KAY GONDA: Yes.

MICK WATTS: What have you found out?

KAY GONDA: How many people saw my last picture? Do you remember those figures?

MICK WATTS: Seventy-five million, six hundred thousand, three hundred and twelve.

KAY GONDA: Well, Mick, seventy-five million, six hundred thousand people hate me. They hate me in their hearts for the things they see in me, the things they have betrayed. I mean nothing to them, except a reproach. . . . But there are three hundred and twelve others—perhaps only the twelve. There are a few who want the highest possible and will take nothing less and will not live on any other terms. . . . It is with them that I am signing a contract tomorrow. We can't give up the earth to all those others.

MICK WATTS: [*Holding out the newspaper*] And what about this?

KAY GONDA: I've answered you.

MICK WATTS: But you are a murderess, Kay Gonda! You killed that boy!

KAY GONDA: No, Mick, not I alone.

MICK WATTS: But the poor fool thought that he had to save your life!

KAY GONDA: He has.

MICK WATTS: What?!

KAY GONDA: He wanted to die that I may live. He did just that.

MICK WATTS: But don't you realize what you've done?

KAY GONDA: [*Slowly, looking past him*] That, Mick, was the kindest thing I have ever done.

CURTAIN